C000279602

ABOUT THE AUTHOR

Joan Rowe was born in Merseyside during the Second World War. She describes herself as cosmopolitan, having lived in twenty-three homes across Britain and abroad. A military childhood and a much interrupted education meant a lack of early opportunity to follow a conventional route into a music career, or writing; her two passions. Through sheer persistence and tenacity Joan became a nationally recognised "Music Teacher of the Year" – a pianist, oboe and recorder player, and an examiner for the Royal Schools of Music. Joan has written extensively about music education, and has taught in schools, colleges and university. *In Search of Home*, Joan's personal memoir was published in 2006, copies of which are held in libraries where she has lived. In order to write the memoir, Joan made journeys to all but one of the homes where she had lived. It was a strange pilgrimage. Joan now lives in Edinburgh, near to her daughter, who is a professional composer.

DUTY

JOAN ROWE

Copyright © 2014 Joan Rowe

The moral right of the author has been asserted.

Apart from any fair dealing for the purposes of research or private study,
or criticism or review, as permitted under the Copyright, Designs and Patents
Act 1988, this publication may only be reproduced, stored or transmitted, in
any form or by any means, with the prior permission in writing of the
publishers, or in the case of reprographic reproduction in accordance with
the terms of licences issued by the Copyright Licensing Agency. Enquiries
concerning reproduction outside those terms should be sent to the publishers.

Matador
9 Priory Business Park
Kibworth Beauchamp
Leicestershire LE8 0RX, UK
Tel: (+44) 116 279 2299
Fax: (+44) 116 279 2277
Email: books@troubador.co.uk
Web: www.troubador.co.uk/matador

ISBN 978-1783062-362

British Library Cataloguing in Publication Data.
A catalogue record for this book is available from the British Library.

Typeset in Aldine by Troubador Publishing Ltd
Printed and bound in the UK by TJ International, Padstow, Cornwall

Matador is an imprint of Troubador Publishing Ltd

For all the lost boys

CHAPTER ONE

1894 London

Alice shrieked with exasperation, annoyed at her own impatience, and lack of foresight about the black dress she had been struggling to fit into. She fled down the stairs, tearful and almost losing her footing as she went.

'Mrs Cole! Mrs Cole! Are you there?' she cried.

'Good gracious, miss. Whatever is the matter? I thought there must be a fire or something.'

'Please, lovely Mrs Cole, do come and give me a hand. I haven't worn this dress since poor mother passed. I'm afraid I have filled out a bit since then. I can't manage the buttons. Will I be able to wear it?'

'Here, let me take a look.'

The lovely Mrs Cole sorted the buttons, she having more patience than Alice, for doing intricate things.

'The dress will suffice for a while Miss Alice, but next time we will see if the seams can be let out a little, then it will last a bit longer.'

'Thank you so much Mrs Cole. I am all fingers and thumbs this morning. My head is in a whirl, worrying about poor Frances and Alfred. Where is Alfred by the way? Has he had breakfast?'

'No, miss. I believe he is in the parlour. I suspect that he has been there all night. He was asleep on the green sofa when I arrived at six o'clock.'

'Goodness me. He must have something to eat. He won't manage the day ahead if he doesn't. I'll see if I can persuade him.'

Mrs Cole returned to her kitchen.

Satisfied that she was decently enough dressed in her mourning gown, out of respect for the captain, Alfred's deceased father, Alice made her way to the parlour.

'Alfred, Alfred dear, wake up.' She shook her brother-in-law's shoulder gently. He flinched, and roused himself at her touch.

'Have you slept here all night?' she asked him.

He nodded, rubbing his bleary eyes.

'What time is it? I must have dropped off,' he said, 'so much to read, so much to do, people to see. It's all overwhelming.'

'I know, silly, you have to take one thing at a time. Just now you need to get up and eat breakfast if you aren't too faint during the service. Then you have to change, and be ready for Mr Lawrence when he arrives with the carriage. He will help you with all the papers, won't he?'

Alfred dragged himself from the sofa, leaving behind a pile of crumpled papers.

'Don't chide me today, Alice. I shall need every bit of kind encouragement you can muster if I'm not to disgrace myself.'

'Of course, Alfred. You have all possible support and sisterly love. You must know that. After all, you and Frances have practically brought me up. Now it's my turn to look after you both.'

He kissed her cheek.

'Anyway, what do you mean? How could you possibly disgrace yourself?'

He straightened himself up, and headed towards the stairs, with Alice following him.

'There will be many important people at the funeral. I don't know half of them, and they hardly know me. I am more than a little anxious. I will be greatly relieved when it's all over. Actually, I'm dreading the lunch more than the funeral. I have to give a speech.'

'You will be absolutely fine. You have it all written down haven't you?'

He nodded, and felt in his pocket to make quite sure that the speech, over which he had agonised the night before, was still there.

'Well then,' said Alice, 'you can always read it from the paper, if you have to. No one will mind in the least. It's the words that matter. You always find the right things to say.'

Alice gave him a reassuring hug then walked him to the stairs.

'Don't be too long,' she called after him, 'Mrs Cole has muffins, your favourite!'

'I'll look in on Frances when I'm dressed,' he said, 'I don't like leaving her today, but I must.'

'Don't worry Alfred. We will look after her. Doctor Ingram says she must stay in bed because her feet are very swollen, and she needs to be quiet. I shall read to her, and Ellice might call later on.'

Alfred frowned. He wasn't too thrilled at the thought of Ellice Bell visiting his wife. She was too excitable, and too loud. Still, she was good for Alice. She needed friends of her own age.

'Dear, sweet Alice. You will make someone a wonderful wife one day. You are so organised, so sensible and kind-hearted.'

Alice chortled.

'I'm not sure if I want to be a wife,' she teased, 'I want my own life!'

Alfred thought that remark more typical of her friend, but he didn't rise to Alice's provocative, though light-heartedly delivered statement. He was too pre-occupied just then. But it was true; Alice was very sensible, practical and kind. She cared for everyone. Perhaps, Alfred thought, because Alice was still only eighteen, and not yet experienced in too many worldly matters, she was very trusting. She saw no harm in anyone. She had yet to learn how to discriminate between genuine people, and the less desirable. She treated everyone the same. Alfred hoped that Alice's kind and sympathetic nature would not encourage people in the future to take advantage of her. He felt a great responsibility towards his wife's sister.

Alfred changed hurriedly, so that he could spend a few minutes with Frances before Peter Lawrence, his friend and lawyer, was due to arrive.

'Don't let Ellice get you too excited,' he begged Frances, 'you know what she's like, full of militant spouting, and always pressing leaflets at you. Alice has promised to keep things quiet for you, my darling. I will be home as soon as I possibly can.' He tucked the sheets around her tenderly and smiled, then blew her a kiss from the doorway, as he left the bedroom.

Alice brought a napkin to put under Alfred's chin, as he had refused to sit down to eat his muffins. Time was short, he said, and he was too nervous to sit still.

'I've let Mr Lawrence into the parlour,' Mrs Cole announced. 'He came bearing flowers for Mrs Richards, which I have placed in the lounge until I go up to her. The carriage is waiting for you Mr Alfred.'

'Thank you Mrs Cole.'

She gave Alfred a sympathetic smile.

'Good luck. I will be thinking of you. We all will.' Mrs Cole sniffed discreetly into her handkerchief. It wasn't that she had felt overly fond of Captain Richards when he was alive. In fact, although he had always been polite towards her, and she had no real complaints about him, he had always seemed remote and secretive.

As a servant, of course, this was of no consequence to her personally but she had always felt very close to Alfred's mother, Rose Maud and to Alfred as she watched him grow up, largely without the presence of his father, who was frequently away at sea.

Violet Cole had been Alfred's unofficial nanny at times. She now saw him grown up, head of his own family, experiencing his father's funeral by himself. Alone, except for the hard-faced lawyer, Peter Lawrence.

4

Alfred's friend chivvied him to the door.

'Come on, old chap. We don't want to be late. That would never do, would it? The chief mourner needs to be first at the church.'

Secretly, Alfred didn't really care if they were late. In fact, if there had been a way of avoiding it, he could have cheerfully run away from it all. However, common sense reined, and he got on with it.

His companion talked constantly during the ride, much to Alfred's annoyance, but at least it did temporarily distract him from becoming overly morose. He had to keep up appearances.

'We were lucky to book the Cafe Royal for the lunch, eh? They are usually booked up for weeks ahead.' Alfred grunted a reply.

'When are we going to deal with the will, Alfred? How about one day next week, while you still have leave from the *Gazette*?' Alfred turned angrily on his friend.

'Good God Peter, my father isn't even buried yet. Do we have to discuss it right now?'

'Sorry old chap, but we do have to do it soon. There's a lot to sort out, which you don't know about. It isn't all straightforward you see, especially the foreign stuff.'

'We'll do it next week then,' Alfred conceded crossly. 'But can we please leave it alone for now?' Peter Lawrence had no idea that he had just made a casual throwaway remark which set Alfred's brain racing. They travelled the remainder of the journey in silence, his companion at last taking the hint that he was making Alfred feel worse, not better.

St. James' Church, Piccadilly, was filled to capacity with people whom Alfred was only vaguely familiar. He had been solely responsible for choosing the music and the readings, all of which his mother would have completely approved. Yet, in reality, the service seemed to progress somewhere else, way above Alfred's head. He hardly assimilated any of it. Instead, he allowed his thoughts to wander to a much happier place, as he remembered his mother.

Afterwards, the day became dull and thundery. The persistent drizzle added to the grimness of the occasion, though, deep in thought beside his father's grave, Alfred hardly noticed the dank weather. He was glad that Alice and his wife were safe at home.

The hearse moved away. The other mourners, uncertain if they should wait, had begun to disperse, murmuring amongst themselves. Alfred moved away too and beckoned his carriage. He began to focus more clearly on the job in hand. He took out his speech notes to remind himself of the opening few words. He would be all right once he got started, though it wouldn't be an easy task.

Captain George Richards had been an emotionally remote figure in his son's life. Relations between them were as cool on the day that his father had died as they were throughout his childhood, and during his adult life. Alfred had been his mother's son in every way. By contrast, Alfred's life with his mother Rose Maud had been idyllic, and he had adored her.

Suddenly, he experienced an unexpected and unusual sense of liberation. Then fleetingly, feelings of guilt, rather than sadness, that he should be feeling that way.

They were half an hour late arriving at the Cafe Royal. The driver had to negotiate his place with the other drivers.

'Make way, there, gentlemen please. I have the chief mourner here.'

Peter Lawrence made his presence felt too, and the other drivers obliged, so that Alfred could alight under the canopy.

The guests disembarked and hurried inside, leaving their coats, hats and canes with the cloakroom staff.

'Brandy sirs? To ward off the cold?' The waiters handed out trays of drinks as soon as everyone was seated. Alfred declined, knowing that the sherry would very soon follow with the soup.

'Thank you, no,' he said, 'I need to keep a clear head.' When the hors d'oeuvres were swiftly offered Alfred accepted a small portion of anchovies with toast and made his sherry last.

It wasn't until after the fish and entreé courses had finished that anyone other than the waiters spoke with him. Peter Lawrence had found Alfred rather heavy going for most of the day. He said he felt that he should mingle with the other guests. Alfred was somewhat relieved. The buzz of conversation had surrounded him, but hadn't actually included him. He didn't mind. That was, he didn't mind until the Reverend Morris, who had conducted the funeral service at St. James', loomed towards him.

'Hello again Mr Richards, how are you feeling now?'

'Well enough Reverend Morris, thank you. Better for having some warm food.'

'Yes of course,' the reverend bumbled, 'and very fine food it is too.'

Alfred felt very ungracious wishing the Reverend would go away and leave him alone. Alfred just couldn't deal with small talk. He was glad for once that Peter Lawrence had returned to interrupt them.

'Cheer up, Alfred. Dessert is on its way. There is some sort of delay in the kitchens. The waiters are in a bit of a dither.' The speeches seemed to go on and on forever, but the tables were eventually cleared. Alfred delivered his short, but efficient speech of thanks and appreciation, remembering all the people on his father's list, in order of their importance. He felt a huge sense of relief as the gentlemen were invited to take their coffee, cigars and more brandy in the more comfortable lounge.

Peter Lawrence congratulated Alfred.

'Well done, old chap. All that worrying about the speech; you were magnificent. I thought you would be all right, and you were.'

'Thank you Peter,' he replied, 'I suppose on a different occasion this is where the gentlemen retire to play card games into the small hours?'

'Yes indeed. Your father spent many hours here doing just that. I have my suspicions that he really hung on to spy on Oscar Wilde and his cronies, and all their antics.'

'I wouldn't know about any of that,' Alfred commented. He looked at his watch, hoping that the ordeal would be soon over. Any time now the commissionaire would begin to announce the carriages as they arrived to take people home. A few anxious guests had already begun to move towards the door.

'Goodbye Alfred, splendid meal, thank you, stay in touch,' said one, pressing a business card into his hand. Alfred thanked him.

'Thank you Mr Richards, goodbye.' There was another handshake and another card for his wallet, until, unusually, the commissionaire closed the lounge doors, instead of opening them, preventing guests from moving towards the vestibule and cloakrooms.

'What seems to be the trouble?' Peter Lawrence shouted.

'Why can't these people leave?'

The noise and commotion grew into a frantic crescendo as the staff tried to keep the doors closed, and the gentlemen who wanted to leave pushed from the inside. The fact that some of them were more than a little inebriated, just added to the chaos.

Alfred, now weary and upset, pushed his way through the melee towards the policeman who had just arrived. The manager was in a highly distressed and apologetic state.

'Gentlemen, please. Do return to your seats,' he pleaded emphatically, 'I am so sorry for the delay. The police are here to investigate a serious incident. I am sure it won't be much longer. Please be patient.'

More drinks were offered to the disgruntled guests, and the cacophony of voices just became louder. Alfred's head was spinning.

He approached the police officer a second time and explained about his wife, sick at home, and by now would be worried about his absence.

'Please let me make a telephone call?' he asked the officer.

'I'm sorry sir, my orders are to detain everyone here for the time being. If you give me the details I can ask that we make the call for you.'

Alfred wasn't happy about Alice and Frances receiving a call from the police. They would worry even more. However, as he had little choice, Alfred trusted the officer with the number.

'Here, when can we leave?' shouted someone.

'It's getting late!' shouted the man's friend.

It was left to an indiscreet junior servant to whisper the truth of the situation.

'There's been a murder! One of the wine waiters has been stabbed to death in the cellars.'

As the gossip grew into extreme panic, the police officer hurried the servant away from the lounge. A senior officer appeared and confirmed the incident.

'Apologies gentlemen, but we will have to speak to every one of you to confirm all movements in and out of this room.'

Alfred, near a state of total exhaustion, felt the start of a chill. He wanted nothing more than his warm bed.

Three more long hours elapsed before the police had finished their questioning and the guests could make their way home. The carriage drivers returned one by one.

'We should get a handsome tip for this time of night,' said the first driver, to the doorman.

'Good night driver,' the doorman raised his hat.

Alfred was so relieved to be on his way home. It didn't matter that the journey was another five miles to go, and in the darkness. He was soon lulled off to sleep by the motion of the carriage.

The driver eventually slowed to a halt. Alfred woke with a start.

He was instantly alert. He paid the driver.

'Thank you very much, sir, very generous of you.' The driver doffed his cap, but Alfred was already leaping up the front steps to the house. He rang the bell furiously whilst trying to locate his front door key. Mrs Cole would have gone home by now. He sensed that something was wrong. The lights were still burning. Perhaps the lights had been left on for him.

He opened the door to find Alice in a tearful and agitated state.

'Alfred, thank goodness you are home. We have been so worried. Where have you been until this hour? Frances needs the doctor at once. I can't leave her. She has a dreadful fever, and the baby is coming. It's too soon Alfred! What shall I do?'

'Alice, I am so sorry. Did you not receive a call from the police? There was a terrible incident at the Cafe Royal and we were all detained. They promised to telephone.'

Alice looked even more terrified and Alfred did his best to calm her. 'I will tell you all about it later, but first we must get Doctor Ingram here. There is no time to waste. You go up to Frances and I will be there as soon as I can.'

Alfred was deeply worried, but he knew that he had to keep his composure now, for everyone's sake. He worried that the stresses of his day had caused this apparent premature labour for Frances.

Doctor Ingram, who had been the family doctor for many years, and had only recently cared for Captain Richards, came very quickly.

He knew that he would not have been called at this time of night unless there was a very pressing reason. The nursery nurse would not be expected for another four weeks as she was engaged elsewhere.

Alice, nervous and inexperienced, was distraught.

'It's my fault!' she cried. 'I tried to keep her quiet and happy, then we worried about Alfred, and she couldn't rest.'

Doctor Ingram spoke kindly, but firmly to Alice. 'Hush, my dear, it isn't your fault. This could have happened at any time. It is a very common occurrence. Now, dry your tears. We need you to be very helpful. My driver is waiting outside. He will take you, with this note, to bring Mrs Cole here as quickly as possible.'

No thought was given to Mrs Cole's personal situation. She had a sick husband at home and a daughter who had recently given birth to her second child. Her sons had been sent to the country to live with relations. No, she was a domestic servant, and was just expected to leave everything in her household to cater for every wish of her employer. She did it gladly, especially in this instance.

The doctor's carriage returned quickly, and ignoring the usual protocol of staff using the basement entrance, Mrs Cole hurried up the front steps, unbuttoning her coat as she went. Alice followed on behind.

Mrs Cole did not need to be told what she had to do. She had encountered this situation many times before. She had assisted many women and midwives. In fact, it was rare to find a personal doctor unless it was a matter of life and death.

'Child-bed fever?' she checked with the doctor. He nodded.

'How soon can we expect the child?' she asked.

'Very soon, my dear Mrs Cole. I fear Mrs Richards will have little recall of this night... that is if she makes it through,' he whispered.

Alfred, by now distraught, and all of the day's previous happenings completely out of his mind, was despatched to sit outside the room. Alice waited anxiously beside him for a while, but then, forgetting her nervousness and lack of experience, she begged to help.

So, Alice and Mrs Cole worked as a team, forgetting all nonsense about class or status. Alice was sent in search of extra sheets and towels, and a fresh gown for Frances, while Mrs Cole refilled water bowls and jugs as required. The doctor had administered a small amount of chloroform to ease the discomfort for Frances. This relatively new miracle aid, so praised by Queen Victoria herself, often prevented mothers from participating fully during the birth process. In this case, Frances had been struggling for many hours, and was suffering a high fever.

'That's it, Miss Alice, you keep the cold compresses on her head. Talk to her. She will hear you,' Mrs Cole encouraged.

'We're all here for you Fran. It won't be long now,' Alice whispered gently to her sister.

Suddenly Frances roused from her induced twilight state and emitted a long, piercing scream, the like of which Alfred had never heard before.

The child was quickly delivered. Frances sank back into the pillows, totally exhausted. The doctor and Mrs Cole looked at each other ominously. Doctor Ingram looked at his watch. He shook his head.

The child appeared motionless, silent and slightly blue. Alice fled from the room to fetch Alfred. He couldn't believe what the doctor was saying to them.

'Mrs Cole, I doubt that this lady will have any further children.'

He turned away to tend to Frances, but not before he handed the tiny bundle over to her, 'You'd better wrap him up and put him under the bed for now.'

Mrs Cole was horrified and, unbelieving, she took the child.

'Then we'd better save this one!' she cried.

Alfred and Alice, clinging to each other, watched. Mrs Cole carefully unwrapped the bundle from the towel. She placed the tiny body on a side table, on a pile of soft clean sheets, and she began to gently massage his little chest, then his back. She opened his mouth and cleared away the mucus with her fingers. She tenderly laid him over her shoulder and began to massage again. After several agonising minutes there was the faint sound of a tiny splutter, then an audible gasp for breath. Eventually there was a little, feeble cry.

'Well done, Mrs Cole,' the doctor said matter-of-factly, 'I felt certain that we had lost him!'

She could hardly contain her rage at the doctor's attitude, and his response to her. She gave him a long, silent stare. She cleaned the baby before wrapping him in a clean sheet, and handing him to Alfred.

'Thank you, Mrs Cole, thank you,' he uttered, the tears now coursing down his cheeks. He kissed the child then handed him to Alice while he kissed his wife's forehead.

Frances drifted in and out of her fever for several more hours. Doctor Ingram left during the early hours of the morning, with the instruction to keep Frances cool, and to telephone him immediately if there was any deterioration in either Frances, or the baby.

Alice, Alfred and Violet Cole sat with Frances all night long, taking it in turns to cool her, and to watch the baby constantly.

When Frances woke and fully realised her situation, she remained worried, weak and tearful. There was a great sense of relief that at least she appeared to be recovering, if slowly, from her ordeal. The concern now was for the baby. Mrs Cole took Alfred to one side.

'Premature babies need to be fed very carefully,' she told him. 'This baby needs his mother's milk, a little and often.'

'What shall we do?' he asked.

'Mr Alfred, sir, I'm afraid Mrs Richards has very little milk to give. It is not sufficient. We need to do something very quickly.' Alice, completely uneducated in such matters asked whether milk from the kitchen would suffice.

'No, miss,' Mrs Cole said gently, 'it would be altogether too rich and would upset the baby's stomach.'

As an immediate course of action Mrs Cole had given the baby tiny sips of boiled and cooled water and sugar, until a solution could be found. She had an idea but hesitated to suggest it to Frances directly, mindful of her fragile, emotional state. There was no way but to broach the subject immediately with Alfred.

Deeply concerned, Alfred was willing and open to any course of action which would help the situation, and Frances. He could not even contemplate returning to his work at the *London Gazette*, or to sort out his father's affairs, until he was certain that everything was well at home.

Alfred explained to Frances, as gently as he could, how urgent it was that the baby received nourishment immediately.

'Mrs Cole's daughter Lily will happily send her milk for us.' He was relieved that Frances had so readily agreed, but then stunned by her further responses. Tearfully, Mrs Cole explained that Frances was quite willing to what had been suggested, so long as she didn't have to see it happening, or be involved in any way with the procedure. The matter was compounded when Frances refused to hold the child when it was not being fed.

'Oh! Fran darling,' pleaded Alice, 'he is such a tiny, sweet thing. He needs his mother's warmth and loving cuddles.'

Mrs Cole, quick and sensitive, and always ready to calm any situation to the best of her ability, ushered both Alice and Alfred out of the room, and away from Frances.

'Things will settle down. Mrs Richards has been very ill and through a very frightening ordeal. She will recover, in time, and she will want to hold the baby when she is ready. Do not fret.'

Frances remained fragile in body and in spirit, for some time. At last, when she had seemed to have a better day, Alfred took her out for a stroll in their Highgate garden, which was now beginning to show signs of spring, after a long, difficult winter. Alfred was quick to see the comparison with Frances.

'Look Frances, isn't it lovely to see the pink blossom starting to grow. The garden is coming alive again, just like you. It is lovely to see your cheeks take on a bit more colour.'

She seemed quite unmoved by the garden, and in spite of being well wrapped up in her furs, complained of a chill in the air.

Alfred was patient with Frances, convinced, as Mrs Cole had suggested, that it was just a matter of time before she would take joy in things as she used to do. He hoped that the new nurse would be of great help.

'Ah! Look, Frances, here is Miss Appleton. I expect she has come to take you up for your afternoon nap.' Alfred greeted Miss

Appleton, and raised his hat. He made a mental note that she hardly ever smiled in response.

'Come along Mrs Richards, it's time you were resting now,' Miss Appleton encouraged her, 'Take my arm.'

Alfred was not quite sure whether he would take to Miss Appleton, and neither would Alice or Mrs Cole. Still, it was early days, and he sincerely hoped that it would not only help Frances, having Miss Appleton around, but it would also relieve Mrs Cole somewhat.

Alfred was aware that a heavy burden had been placed upon Mrs Cole, and her daughter Lily. The past few months had not been easy for anyone. He felt deeply indebted to the Cole family and to Violet Cole, in particular. She was always aware of her status as a servant, but she happily accepted her place, as she had always been decently treated. Inwardly, she felt very close to Alfred, and he felt the same towards her. He continued to address her as Mrs Cole, and she addressed him as Mr Alfred. The new baby would be addressed as Master Charles and his mother as Mrs Richards, never Frances. Alice was known as Miss Alice.

Alice had lived with Frances and Alfred since her parents had both passed away. In fact, they had come to join her in the Coombe family home. The expectation was that Alice would be a companion and helper for her sister, until such time as she became married herself. In the meantime, Alice, a usually cheerful, intelligent and resourceful young woman, would continue to read books, sew fine things, and aim to be a more proficient singer and pianist, as well as involving herself in the church and charitable ventures. Although now Alfred was more than a little concerned by her friendship with Ellice Bell.

Mrs Cole had her motherly eye on the situation with Ellice Bell, but saw no harm in it up to then. She had taken Alice under her wing since the events surrounding baby Charles' birth. Alice had learned so many things about marriage and childbirth, which may have proved to be a stark awakening for her in years to come, that she too was grateful for Mrs Cole's expertise and encouragement. Mrs Cole was simply a treasure.

CHAPTER TWO

When Alfred Richards was sure that domestic life was returning to a more settled routine, he returned to work at the *London Gazette*.

'Good Morning, Mr Richards. It is good to welcome you back.'

'Thank you,' he replied to his secretary, 'it is good to be back, though I shall only be here for mornings this first week or so. I can see that things have been progressing efficiently without me,' he joked.

He had a very competent team of workers, and office staff, who kept the whole organisation running like clockwork. For that he was relieved and thankful. He had so much to consider now, but as Alice had reminded him, he must take one thing at a time, if he wasn't to feel overwhelmed by everything before him.

He could afford to look ahead and build for his entire family's future. The details of his father's will were complex, and would take some time to unravel and resolve. But it was clear that they would be more comfortably off, and Charles would have a good education.

Then there was the question of his father's former house in Kensington, where Alfred had grown up. He had dithered about the question of the house, but he could dither no longer. He had very mixed feelings about it. There were happy childhood memories of his mother, but these also became, from time to time, blurred, with less happy times when his father took to one of his rages.

It seemed to Alfred that every time he thought about the house in Kensington he could not wipe away the unhappy times there. Perhaps, on reflection, it might prove to be a good thing, cathartic even, to take over the house and completely re-furbish the place. He could think of many other uses for it. But for now that would have to wait. He would give it more thought, and he would discuss it with Frances when she felt ready.

Before anything could be properly decided, Alfred had to face the mammoth task of disposing of his father's belongings. He would have to seek the help of some of his father's friends and associates so that really important things were not lost, or inadvertently thrown away. It seemed a daunting task ahead, but he would attack it with a certain amount of relish. Even as a boy, there were things, books, papers, maps, military papers that he had never been allowed to look at. Now he could, and with the benefit of hindsight, and military advisers, he looked forward to beginning the task.

The Kensington house had been home to at least three generations of the Richards family. They would not have described themselves as upper class, but rather as middle class, and aspiring. They were, in the past, senior navy or army officers, company directors, that sort of thing, and they enjoyed a busy social life in the city.

Alfred and Frances were different. The social scene mattered little to them, beyond their immediate circle. Apart from family friends, Frances had friends connected with the church where her father had been the minister, and Alfred's acquaintances ranged from work colleagues at the *Gazette*, and in the publishing business. They both had friends in musical circles, choirs and concert-going, friends mostly cultivated through friends of Alfred's mother.

His thoughts kept wandering back to Kensington. It would be very useful to be nearer the city, Alfred thought, and the garden was bigger there, well screened by high hedges and rhododendrons. He remembered the smell of the flowers, especially the honeysuckle on warm summer evenings, as they had taken tea on the terrace. Yes, suddenly invigorated, he was sure that Frances would grow to love the place.

Alfred didn't mind going to work at the *Gazette*, though there were times when he felt a deep sense of personal frustration. The *Gazette*, long thought of as the mouthpiece of the army, the court circular and happenings in upper class circles of society, had been the same since its inception. It would never change.

He was a highly creative person, an artist of no mean talent, though quite unable to use his gifts at the *Gazette*. The possibility of following a different career path had been quite out of the question whilst his father was alive, and now he had a family to consider. Later, he decided, he would see what he could do for himself.

The morning the new machinery was to be installed in the print room at the *Gazette*, did not run as smoothly as everyone expected, not least for Alfred. The lifts and pulleys were a jumbled mass of ropes and metals, and tools lying about in every corner.

'It's like a jigsaw puzzle on a gigantic scale sir,' one worker told Alfred. 'How are we to sort it all out?'

'There will be a supervisor here shortly. Leave everything alone until he appears, will you do that?'

'Whatever you say, Mr Richards, but it's difficult to know what piece of metal or wood is important in the first instance. I don't reckon with all these parts just lying about higgledy-piggledy!'

'Thank you Mr Foreman. Please bear with us. The manufacturer will be sending his representative very shortly, and will supervise the installation.'

Just then there was an almighty crash as two workmen tried to move a piece of equipment across the floor and, because it proved too heavy for them to lift, it was quickly dropped again, landing on one of the men's feet. His screams could be heard throughout the workshop, and people came running from every corner to see what had occurred.

'Someone ring for the ambulance. Quickly! This man is badly hurt.'

'We'll need the fire brigade too, sir. Nobody can lift this thing off his feet.'

The man's screams stopped and he lost consciousness. There was blood everywhere and, unable to help, the workers stood in silence, shocked at the horrific scene before them.

The injured workman was eventually removed to hospital, his feet very badly bleeding and crushed.

'He'll be lucky to work again!' shouted a worker.

'Who's going to tell his family?'

'I said we shouldn't have this new-fangled machinery,' said the union man. No good will come of it. When it's up and working, it'll do us out of jobs anyway. I vote we down tools, and go on strike. Who's with me then? Hands up for a walk-out?'

Not all of the men were anxious to vote for strike action. They needed their wages, and it would be hard to live without them.

'Men, come back please,' pleaded Alfred, 'nothing will be solved like this. I am sorry the man was badly hurt, but you were all asked to leave the machinery alone, until supervised.'

'Are you saying it's the man's own fault then?' shouted someone.

'You were all given clear instructions.'

'Yes, we were. Mr Richards is quite correct.'

Some of the men shifted away, and made for the doors as the new supervisors were arriving. They were met by a barrage of angry, violent workers, who were more than ready to smash up the new machines.

Alfred urged the union man to call back the men who were angry and wanting to leave.

'Look gentlemen,' he begged them to return and come forward to listen to what he had to say. He climbed up onto a desk so that he could be seen by all the men, not just the few at the front.

'I can understand your anger at the man's accident, but that was not the fault of management. You did all have clear instructions. I am very sorry to hear about the man's injuries, and we will do our very best to look after him. Now we have the engineers here to help put together the new presses, and I hope that you will see this as a new and exciting venture into the future role of publishing. It is not designed to take anyone's jobs, in fact it may mean, if we do well, that we can expand our work. There could very well be more jobs for the future.'

This had been Alfred Richards first real experience of industrial relations, which had not run entirely smoothly. He did however have the great advantage of knowing the work from top to bottom.

From the outset, as a boy, he had never been afraid to get his own hands dirty on the shop floor. He had been a willing worker who had been prepared to learn every job within the business. He had worked as a general office boy, then in the warehouse and packaging, the distribution service, and then, after training in the print room, he became a skilled and careful compositor, able to work at high speed whenever he was required to do so. He quickly rose to the managerial roles, but most of all he was respected for his intelligence, his tact and great gift of diplomacy. Amiable and approachable, he knew the men.

The new situation which faced him had arisen through the march of industrial progress. It presented him with his greatest challenge so far. Whilst working to restore calm and confidence in his workforce he continued negotiations with the directors, suggesting that rather than leaving men out of work, this could be seen as an opportunity to expand operations.

To Alfred's great credit, he also took the opportunity to speak up for himself, and succeeded in persuading the directors to allow him a little artistic leeway in setting the headlines. The setting and wording of headlines had, until then, been unknown. The script was always uniform in long continuous columns. Alfred explained his ideas.

'The *Gazette* is facing more competition now from other papers, gentlemen. It is essential that we develop more striking headlines, more succinct wording, and some posters on the streets. Don't you agree that we could boost sales many times over?'

'Very well, Mr Richards,' said the chairman, 'you may have a free rein, for now. But mark you, there is to be no sensationalism. We only publish the truth, verifiable fact, do you understand?'

Alfred nodded his agreement, and delighted, he told the men the news they were waiting for.

The men returned to work, if a little grudgingly, and some were encouraged to work with the supervisors, installing the new printing presses. Alfred was relieved. He could now concentrate on matters at home.

Now that Frances was showing signs of recovery, the christening was uppermost in her mind. Emotionally, still fragile, she seemed only to be able to concentrate on one thing at a time, but she was at least being positive about the baby's big day. She became irritated and frustrated if too many demands were made of her.

Miss Appleton seemed to be a highly efficient, no-nonsense kind of child nurse. Alfred thought that might help Frances.

'She's very brusque,' Alice told him, 'Fran and I feel rather intimidated by her, but perhaps it's because she's new.'

'Yes, I expect so,' he replied sympathetically, 'but at least she is taking the bulk of the nursery work from you and Mrs Cole.'

'We are grateful for that,' said Alice, 'perhaps we shall grow to like her. We must forgive what seems like unfriendliness, for now.'

'Well, it won't be forever, will it, sweet sister?'

Alice sought some comfort from Mrs Cole. 'Alfred thinks we should grin and bear it!' she told Mrs Cole.

'I expect we shall get used to her, miss.'

'I feel more than a little left out now. Miss Appleton won't let me help with anything,' Alice complained. 'She gently ushers me from the room. Frances too, sometimes.'

'Yes, miss, I have noticed that it is she who sets the baby's timetable, chooses his clothes, and has now done away with Lily's milk. Still, the little mite seems to be thriving on the bought milk.'

'Frances hasn't objected to that, Mrs Cole, but it was very good of Lily to come to the rescue when it was vital to feed the baby.'

Mrs Cole quite happily resumed her role as housekeeper. She liked nothing better to have a house in full, clean, working order. She was a perfectionist. All the family had to do was to look after Frances, and restore her to full health and happiness.

When Miss Appleton was out walking the baby in his carriage, and Frances was having her afternoon nap, Alice took to gravitating to the kitchen, and Mrs Cole.

Resuming her servant's role, Mrs Cole welcomed Alice into her domain.

'Good afternoon, miss,' she would say, 'can I make you a cup of tea? Shall I bring it into the parlour for you?'

'I'd love a cup of tea thank you, Mrs C, but I'd rather have it here, if that's all right with you?'

'Yes, of course it is, miss. I'd better put a small cloth on your tray, and I'll wipe down the chair before you sit on it. We don't want to spoil your dress now, do we?'

Alice felt comfortable in Mrs C's company, quite the opposite to her feelings when she was around the new nurse. Mrs Cole reminded her of her own mother, who had always been a genteel, calm, but homely country parson's wife. She had in her own way helped minister to the sick and elderly in their parish. Her father, Reverend Charles Combe, had been a highly learned, respected minister. He used to write serious books, and poetry, which had so impressed Alfred's mother. That is, in fact, how the two families were brought together, at a poetry evening, organised by Alfred's mother. Alice missed them so.

Mrs Cole had become Alice's substitute mother. She could tell her anything and know that it would be a secret between the two of them.

'It seems such a long time ago since Frances and Alfred were married, yet it was only four years,' Alice reminded Mrs Cole.

'Yes, miss. I remember you as a young girl with unruly blonde ringlets, and we had trouble making your headdress stay in place. I still remember the smell of the orange blossom.'

'It was so romantic, wasn't it?'

Mrs Cole smiled as she remembered the day.

'Here miss, drink your tea before it goes cold.'

'I don't think Miss Appleton likes me,' she said, changing the subject, and becoming more serious. 'She wouldn't let me help with the baby. Frances is too nervous around her, so she won't say anything to Miss Appleton. Will you ask her Mrs C, please? I'd love to help sometimes. I could easily dress him, or take him for walks in the pram.'

Mrs Cole smiled kindly, but continued her work, rolling out the ginger biscuits. Alice told her that she would love to be a nurse one day.

'Wouldn't it be good experience for me?'

'You'd better take that up with Mr Alfred and Mrs Richards, miss. I'm sure they would have something to say about you becoming a nurse.'

'Why shouldn't I become a nurse?' Alice said petulantly.

'Well, it isn't for me to say, miss.'

Alice changed the subject, but knew she would return to it. Mrs Cole was going to be her greatest ally. She could feel it.

Miss Appleton returned from her walk with baby Charles. She made her way to the kitchen, instead of ringing the parlour bell for her tea. She was surprised to see Alice sitting there by the kitchen table, but nothing was said. Miss Appleton's raised eyebrows and dismissive expression was enough to impart to Alice that she ought to be elsewhere. Alice promptly made her way upstairs to spend a few precious moments with the baby before he was whisked away to the nursery.

Mrs Cole laid a fresh tray, and took Miss Appleton's instructions: China tea with lemon, and two shortbread biscuits.

'I will bring the tray to the parlour for you, Miss Appleton.' The nurse nodded her thanks, and returned to the parlour to await her tea, before the evening routine with the baby.

Violet Cole was the soul of discretion. She had been employed in domestic service for a very long time, almost all of her adult life. She had learned when to speak and when to be silent. She knew her place, and didn't mind it. Relations between her and Miss Appleton would remain cordial. Neither of them felt the need to converse about anything personal. Their conversations were merely concerned with the household, and its smooth running on a day-to-day basis. That didn't mean that her patience was endless. At times she felt it sorely stretched. So far, she had managed to maintain a dignified silence at times like these. One day, she felt sure that she would be forced to speak up on Alice's behalf, but how to broach the subject continued to vex her. She would ponder the problem a little longer.

Alfred continued to be patient with Frances. He made few demands of her. He recognised the huge trauma she had suffered, and he wanted nothing more than to have his old, happy Frances back again.

'You seem so much brighter today my darling,' he encouraged her. 'Let us all go to Regent Street, and Peter Robinson, or to the new Oxford Street department stores. We can choose new clothes for the christening day. Maybe you would like to choose some jewellery to mark the occasion?' His thoughtful generosity merely reflected his delight that Frances seemed to be well on the way to full health.

Frances thanked him, without expressing any desire for herself, but strangely, and quite pointedly, she requested a new robe for the baby. She did not want to use any faded family heirlooms.

As this was the first attempt by Frances to take any interest in what was going on, Alfred was reluctant to argue. Frances could have anything she wished. Apart from Alice there were no other surviving relations to offend, should they not use the family heirlooms.

So, a few days later, Alfred arranged an open carriage to be waiting for them to take all three of them on their mission to the city. The day was pleasantly warm and bright, and a casual, unknowing observer could easily have been persuaded that they were looking at an impressionist painting. A young couple, with friend, dressed in their finery, with not a care in the world. The ladies held their parasols in case the sun became too bright. Frances wore her green silk, and an elegant hat, adorned with pink roses. She appeared calmer than she had for months, and although she had little conversation, she appeared to be enjoying the ride. Alfred gave her a reassuring smile, and squeezed her hand.

Alice looked younger than her eighteen years, dressed entirely in white, with just a narrow pink ribbon circling her waist. She was excited about their trip, and couldn't help pointing things out to Frances, as though her sister was unaware of the lovely houses and gardens along their way.

'Look, Fran! Look at the magnolias. Aren't they magnificent? Smell the lilac. Oh! It's so good to have the winter over at last.'

Frances smiled and nodded in agreement.

Alfred playfully toyed with his silver-topped cane and remembered to raise his hat as they passed one of their near neighbours, and, as they trundled on towards the city, he became immersed in his own thoughts. This new feeling of being head of his family and in charge was exhilarating for him. He was though, mindful of much of his mother's advice and maxims for life. What was it that she had said most often? Alfred recalled, 'Never make instant decisions. Think of all the consequences first. Then make the decision again.' Yes, that was sound advice. That's what he would do.

The gentle, semi-rural ride from Highgate towards the city became less pleasant as the driver encountered more road traffic. Carriages of every shape and size vied for space on the roads with horse omnibuses, and the newly invented noisy motor vehicle, which resembled a horse carriage, but without the horse. These vehicles were a nuisance, and seemed to do nothing but stop and start. As the motor drivers got out of their cars to assess engine problems, they not only held up the carriage traffic, but often cursed the carriage drivers, since the horses did what horses do, and caused a troublesome mess anywhere on the road.

Alfred knew this situation would change before long. The days of carriage transport were numbered and the motor cars would increase. The horses would eventually disappear from the streets of London and all of the jobs connected with riding and looking after horses would also disappear. It was progress. They were living in very exciting times in one sense, except for the rumours of impending war across several countries.

Scientists, engineers and architects were all forging ahead with new inventions. Doctors were finding cures for illnesses, and as people flocked from the countryside and rural life to seek work and what they perceived to be a better life in the cities, new social housing was being developed as fast as builders could achieve it. *Yes*, Alfred mused, *this way of life will surely change and many new challenges will be undertaken*. For the first time he felt that he might have choices, opportunities to follow his dreams.

He didn't mind in the least taking a seat in the Peter Robinson store ladies' department, or in the other stores they visited in Bond Street and Regent Street. He was thankful and pleased that Frances seemed to be enjoying every moment of the excursion. He hoped that she wouldn't be over tired, with all the excitement.

As the ladies shopped, discussed and compared their purchases, Alfred escaped into his own world of thought. He had made a firm decision that they would move to his father's house in Kensington. Now he was considering all the consequences, good and bad, just as his mother had always urged him to do.

Alice jolted him from his reverie.

'Do look Alfred. Doesn't Fran look good in mauve?'

'Yes, it's lovely,' he said, 'it looks especially nice with the pendant. It was a good choice to buy amethysts with the silver filigree. How clever of you both.'

A long time was spent choosing the christening gown, but eventually they found just the right thing. Not too ostentatious, but plain satin, with a hint of French lace down the centre panel. Everyone was pleased.

The shopping expedition was over, and deemed highly successful. Alfred took his ladies for lunch at Fortnum and Mason's, a rare and extravagant treat. With the afternoon and the best of the sunshine disappearing it was time to journey home to Highgate. There was a slight chill in the air, and the homeward driver travelled a different and quicker route. This time they went by the heath, where families were still playing cricket, or just walking and enjoying the fresh air.

CHAPTER THREE

The day of the christening arrived, and everyone was in a high state of excitement and anticipation. There would be up to thirty guests for refreshments after the ceremony at Highgate Church.

'What will we do about the chairs, Mr Alfred?' Mrs Cole was more than a little anxious about seating the guests, and she was sure they did not have enough china.

'Don't worry, Mrs C,' he reassured her. He was slightly amused at this usually very competent and capable woman suddenly becoming agitated and worried about chairs. After all she had been arranging dinner parties and other functions in the household for many years.

'I must get it right for you. It's a very special day.'

'We will use the parlour,' Alfred explained. 'We can gather up all the small tables in the house and deck them out in white damask. People will sit in small groups using the sofas and small chairs. The gentlemen won't mind standing. It won't be a lengthy affair. You mustn't worry about a thing. Alice will help you, and there's Miss Appleton.'

Mrs Cole frowned at this, but added, 'And Lily will help with the drinks, sir, if that is all right?' Overwhelmed by the task in hand she had addressed Alfred as "sir", something she never usually did.

'Yes of course, Mrs C, everyone will help.'

He had noticed her fluster, but did not make any further reference to it. To him it was of no consequence. He was amused.

Alfred's even temper and generally optimistic nature had stood him in very good stead up to now. He had a great capacity to be happy and to find the best in people, but he was shrewd enough to know when people might be trying to manipulate him. At home he was able to completely close off his mind to the worries of his working day.

He was appreciative of those around him, whatever their strengths or weaknesses might be.

Alice thought that she might test Alfred's patience and kind nature before much longer. She desperately wanted to talk over her problems with him, but it would have to wait. She had to get through the christening as amicably as she could manage with Miss Appleton. She knew that Alfred had mounting problems of his own and she didn't want to add to them. No, Alice thought it better to bide her time. Her problems could wait. For now she would grit her teeth, and try hard not to upset Miss Appleton any further.

The sun streamed through the windows into the parlour, lighting up what was usually a modest room of rather subdued tones. The dark green walls and lighter damask of the chairs provided a perfect foil for the masses of white flowers which Alice had gathered from the garden. The white damask and silk cloths covering the odd assortment of small tables had lifted the entire ambience of the room.

'It looks really splendid, Miss Alice, you have done so well to fill all the vases.' They awaited Frances and her approval of the lovely sight.

'Mrs Richards should be very pleased with it all.'

'Yes, Mrs Cole, and you and Lily have helped as well. I hope that Frances doesn't feel that we have taken over.'

Frances was taking her time dressing, and laying out the new christening robes that she had chosen for the baby. She caressed the little bonnet and straightened out the lace panel on the gown which she would dress him in after their light lunch.

Life had seemed very unreal to Frances, until now. She remembered the pain and the fear, but not actually the moment of birth. Being so terribly ill afterwards had robbed her of the immediate bonding process with the baby, and even afterwards, when she had almost recovered, she felt that the child did not belong to her.

Someone else had fed him, bathed and dressed him, and put him in his crib, to sleep. All responsibility had been removed from her, for the kindest of reasons. *Well, not today*, she thought. Today she would dress the baby herself. She was his mother.

Frances was determined that today of all days she would try her very best to sparkle and enjoy the day.

Alice bounded up the stairs to find Frances.

'There you are! Fran, do come and look at the parlour. It looks magnificent. Alfred is arranging the christening gifts in the hall. I've never seen so much silver. The gifts have been arriving all morning!'

There were silver goblets, a child's set of cutlery, rattles and teething rings, inscribed plates and a superb silver ship from Doctor Ingram. The card which came with the silver ship was very beautifully inscribed, *"For Charles George Richards on his christening day, and also in remembrance of his grandfather, Captain George Richards."*

Mrs Cole reminded Alfred and Frances that it was usual for the christening gifts to be displayed by the cake. So everything was removed from the hall and re-arranged by the christening cake in an alcove of the parlour. Everyone agreed that the whole arrangement was preferable to a much more formal use of the dining room.

Alfred took Mrs Cole to one side.

'Thank you so much, dear Mrs C, you have been marvellous, yet again.' Then, to her great surprise, he whispered in her ear, 'When we move to the big house we will never have this problem again.' His blue eyes twinkled and he put his finger to his lips.

Mrs Cole gasped. 'Not a word to anyone just yet, you understand?' The news was to be a special surprise for Frances. He would tell her after all the guests had gone home.

Violet Cole was stunned. She felt uneasy about her position. She would have plenty of questions for her employer later. She strived to regain her composure, gave the parlour a final dusting and check over before she returned to the kitchen.

She was unprepared for the first moment of discord which occurred when Miss Appleton surveyed the parlour. She stood in the doorway, straight-backed and haughty. Her head spun round in short jerks, rather like an ostrich, and then she sneezed violently.

'Who put all these flowers in here?' she bellowed. 'Mrs Cole, where are you?'

Miss Appleton made her way to the kitchen.

'There you are!' she said accusingly, 'Mrs Cole, why did you place so many flowers in the parlour? There are far too many. I am already affected by them. You will have all the guests sneezing. Get rid of some of them, please.'

Alice had heard the commotion.

'Actually Miss Appleton,' Alice retorted angrily, 'I put the flowers there and we all like them. Alfred, Frances, Mrs Cole; all of us.'

Miss Appleton was livid, though she knew that she had over stepped the mark by chastising Mrs Cole. She drew herself in, and became even taller, her thin neck appearing even more ostrich-like. Her face reddened as she stalked out of the parlour and headed up to the nursery.

Although Alice was annoyed that the incident should have occurred on today of all days, she was actually quite glad to have had her first real confrontation with the nursery nurse. It showed everyone that she was not prepared to be treated like a child, or to be ordered about. She decided then and there that she would continue to speak up for herself if it proved to be necessary.

Frances, of course, was unaware of this incident. She was protected, as usual, from anything unpleasant.

Mrs Cole had prepared a light lunch of cold meats, cheese and newly baked bread. On this occasion the family were more than happy to eat in the kitchen.

'It's like a picnic,' enthused Alice, 'what fun!' She was trying to deflect the unpleasantness with Miss Appleton, for the sake of Frances.

Alfred joined in the gaiety.

'Yes, we've had altogether too much sadness and stress this year. Poor Fran has hardly seen the outside world. It is good for her to have something happy and joyous to experience at last.'

Miss Appleton had disappeared to the nursery with her lunch. There was no way after the unsavoury happenings that morning over the flowers that she wanted to partake her lunch with the family.

Frances and Alice busied themselves dressing. Frances wore her new mauve dress and amethyst jewellery. She asked Alice if it seemed out of place and too ostentatious, since technically they should have been in mourning for a few more months.

'Don't be silly. Of course not. It's just perfect and you look really beautiful,' Alice assured her, 'the amethysts match your eyes.' Frances seemed satisfied.

'I don't think I will wear my cream lace after all,' Alice decided, 'I will wear my blue dress. That way I will not overshadow the baby's christening gown.'

Alice would be the chief godmother, and Miss Ellen Bell would be the second sponsor. Doctor Ingram and Mr Peter Lawrence would be the baby's two male godparents. Each of them saw it as a great honour to be asked, and they would carry out their duties with diligence and love. Mrs Cole, however, regarded both Mr Peter Lawrence and Doctor Ingram with much disdain. Still, Frances seemed happy with the arrangement. She was always guided by Alfred, and trusted him in everything.

The grandfather clock ticked away in the hall and Mrs Cole gave it yet another unnecessary polish. She checked for the umpteenth time that all was in order for the expected guests. Satisfied, she allowed herself a few minutes to remove her apron, and tidy her fine, wayward hair. As it was a special occasion she put a dab of powder and a touch of discreet lipstick on her pale face.

'Oh! Mrs Cole, you look very pretty,' Alice complimented her. Mrs C gave a little girlish giggle, and blushed.

'I'm just going to the nursery to fetch baby Charles for Mrs Richards to dress,' Alice said, 'then I think we will all be ready for the guests arriving.'

'Doctor Ingram is here already, miss. He arrived with Mr Lawrence and Miss Bell. I've put them in the parlour.'

'Thank you, Mrs C, I'll be down shortly.'

Alice headed towards the nursery, and as she approached the door she trod softly, as she was not quite sure what she was going to encounter. The door was slightly ajar and Alice peered in. She heard Miss Appleton singing softly to the baby. Alice smiled to herself. Obviously the nurse was not too upset by their earlier altercation. Alice could not have been more mistaken. She was shocked beyond belief.

Miss Appleton had taken it upon herself to dress the baby in his christening finery, although she had been expressly told that Frances wanted to do it herself. But the most alarming sight was the nurse holding the baby close in her arms, rocking back and forth, and kissing him repeatedly. She sang, *'Kiss your Mamma, Kiss me do, Kiss your Mamma, I love you.'*

Alice was rooted to the spot, unable to move or speak.

Miss Appleton stopped singing, but was completely unaware of Alice standing in the doorway. She seemed to be in a strange twilight world of her own as she whispered to the unknowing baby.

'We'll show them. We'll show them all. They can have their party and then we will go away. Just you and me.' She kissed the baby again and continued rocking him back and forth. She was still humming, and had a faraway look on her face.

Alice realised that something was very wrong. She instinctively knew that she could not handle the situation herself. She tiptoed away from the door, and then ran downstairs as fast as she could.

'Doctor Ingram, Doctor Ingram! Please come. There is something very wrong with Miss Appleton.'

'Why child, get your breath. Calm down, take a deep breath and tell me what has happened.'

'It's Miss Appleton. She's behaving very oddly. She has dressed the baby, and Frances was to do that, but there's something else. Come and see for yourself. Come! Hurry!'

Doctor Ingram excused himself from the parlour and the pair proceeded upstairs, encountering Alfred coming in the opposite direction

'Hello you two,' he greeted them. 'I'm off to meet the guests now. Is the baby ready for Frances?'

'Ah, Alfred. Please come with us. We have a problem. There is something very wrong with Miss Appleton.' Alice recounted what she had seen.

They reached the nursery, but instead of waiting timidly as she had before, Alice pushed the door, reassured by the support of Alfred and the doctor.

'Where is she?' Alfred searched around the nursery. 'She isn't here. Neither is the baby. Where can she have gone in so short a time?'

All three of them were in a state of panic.

'You search this floor Alice,' suggested Alfred, 'and take the doctor with you. I will go down the back staircase. She can't have gone through the front door. Somebody would have seen her.'

Mrs Cole intercepted Alfred as he reached the downstairs conservatory.

'The pram is gone, Mrs Cole. Did you see Miss Appleton?'

'Yes, Mr Alfred. What on earth is going on? Miss Appleton fair ran me down; she was in a great hurry taking the baby out in the pram. I shouted after her, but she ignored me.'

'Which way did she go?' he asked.

'She took the back path, out of the garden, and down the lane towards the heath. I don't understand why she was out at all.'

'I'm sorry Mrs C. We seem to have a crisis, and I will have to call on you to keep everyone calm until I return. Alice and Doctor Ingram are searching the upper floors. Could you find them please and ask Doctor Ingram to telephone for an ambulance. I will explain everything later. I must run after Miss Appleton.' Alice and the doctor found Mrs Cole in a distressed state.

'Mr Alfred has run after her,' she cried, 'he asked that the doctor telephone for an ambulance. Clearly, Miss Appleton has had some kind of nervous episode and isn't in her right mind, poor thing.'

Mrs Cole remembered how strange Miss Appleton seemed that very morning, and what a great fuss she had made over the flowers.

'Perhaps we shouldn't have been cross with her,' said Alice.

'Never mind that now, ladies, I think you should go and look after Frances and the guests. Someone will have to ask the vicar if he can delay the service for a while. I'll see if Mr Lawrence will take a stroll to the church. I need to be here for when the baby is returned. I hope he has not come to any harm.'

'Surely not?' said a shocked Alice, 'I thought Miss Appleton was rather strange, but she wouldn't hurt the baby, would she?'

'Let's hope not,' comforted Mrs Cole.

The parlour was full of excited guests who were all sipping lemonade which had been hurriedly found by Mrs Cole and Lily. It was an attempt to divert their attention from the crisis at hand. As yet nobody was any the wiser, though Frances was by now feeling anxious. *It must be time to fetch the baby down*, she thought.

Alice seated her sister next to Miss Bell, who chattered

constantly and would occupy Frances for a little while.

'Ellice, please will you come and help?' Alice caught the arm of her best friend, Miss Bell's lively and eccentric niece.

'What is it? Don't ask me to the church will you? I just came to bring Aunt Bell, and a gift for the baby.' She handed Alice the small wooden box, containing a silver pen and pencil set for when the baby was older.

'Perhaps he'll be a writer, eh?'

'Well he won't be anything at all if we don't hurry and find him. The nurse has taken a nervous turn and run off with him in the pram! Alfred has gone after her. We should go too.'

'Good gracious Alice, let's go!' Ellice shouted.

The two girls ran after Alfred, through the garden and along the lane leading to the heath.

'There's Alfred. Look. I've never seen him run like that,' Ellice remarked.

'Poor Alfred,' her friend said, breathlessly, 'I didn't know that I could run this fast either.'

They caught up with Alfred.

'I'm so glad to see you both.' He was very flustered.

'Look, she's over there!' Alice cried, 'She's heading for the lake, Alfred!'

Alfred's heart was thumping, but he gained pace on the runaway Nurse Appleton as she stopped to lift the baby from the pram. She wrapped him carefully in his blanket, and cuddled him close to her. She seemed totally unaware of anything or anyone nearby. She left the pram and walked slowly towards the water.

Alfred caught up with Miss Appleton, and trod gently beside her.

'There you are,' he said very quietly. 'Did you decide to come out for a little walk before the christening?' He touched her on the arm and went to take the baby from her. She screamed and tightened her grip on the baby.

'You're not having him! He's mine! Go away! Leave us alone!'

Alice and her friend Ellice had reached the awful scene. Alice looked completely stunned. She didn't know what to say. Ellice comforted her.

'Leave it to Alfred, he's brilliant. It's best if we just stand back a little. Alfred knows we are here.'

Alfred too was shocked, but realising the seriousness of the situation he remained outwardly calm, and rational, just as he had done in the threatened strike at the *Gazette*. He had managed to quell the men's anger, but this was a completely different situation.

He placed his arm on Miss Appleton's shoulder, and she recoiled slightly. He spoke gently to her.

'Now then Miss Appleton, I expect you are overwhelmed by all the excitement. Frances is waiting for the baby. Do let Alice take him.'

She handed the baby over to Alice without any further argument or irrational behaviour. She pulled her jacket revers close up to her neck and held them there as though she was sheltering from a storm. Her body stiffened and her eyes took on a glassy stare.

Miss Appleton was in a world of her own. She looked towards the lake and it took Alfred several minutes to move her from her transfixed state.

He indicated to the girls that they should find the pram and go ahead of him, back to the house. He would follow on behind at a slower pace, and trust that Doctor Ingram had done as he was asked to do and have an ambulance, or at least a carriage waiting to take Miss Appleton to the hospital.

Alice was tearful, and by now the baby was fractious.

'What am I going to tell Frances?' she asked her friend.

'Don't worry,' Ellice comforted her, 'the chances are that Frances has been chatting away with all the guests, and she will not have noticed that things are just a little later than planned.'

'I fear we are much later than planned. I wonder what Alfred will want to do?'

Ellice did her best to reassure Alice that Alfred would want everything to proceed as planned, if at all possible.

'I know that Mr Lawrence was sent off to the vicarage to ask the vicar to delay things. There's just the small matter of getting Miss Appleton to hospital.'

The two girls arrived back at the house, and made their way quietly through Mrs Cole's kitchen, and hurried upstairs to the nursery, before any of the guests had noticed that they were missing.

Alice couldn't stop thinking of the distressed state they had found Miss Appleton in, near to the lake by the heath.

'Do you think she was planning to drown herself, and the baby?' sobbed Alice.

'Who knows what a tortured mind she had? Poor woman. What is important now is to get her to hospital, where she will receive the care she badly needs. We must be grateful that no harm came to the baby, or to herself. Alfred will be feeling pretty wretched, but we must do as he asks, for everyone's sake.'

Doctor Ingram was waiting with a carriage. He volunteered to accompany Miss Appleton to the hospital himself. He would forgo his place at the christening, and advised Alfred to go ahead as planned.

'I would keep quiet about all of this, for now,' the doctor advised Alfred, 'let Frances have her day. I will return as soon as I possibly can.'

Alice and her friend tidied themselves and the baby, who had not come to any harm, though the dress was a little crumpled.

'Let me have the dress, quickly,' Mrs Cole asked, 'I'll give it a quick press. The iron is still warm. Then you can call Mrs Richards and she can put the baby's dress back on again.'

'Frances will have to be told what has happened, but we will try to keep it from her till after the service,' Alice said, now that she had settled herself, and to some extent overcome the shock of what had happened that afternoon.

Alfred had a very quick brush and tidy up himself, and by the time he had found Frances in the parlour things appeared to be back to normal, if a little later than planned.

Lily Cole had been working quietly in the kitchen, cooking, cleaning and making sure that everything was spick and span, no detail left to chance. Well trained by her mother, Lily had been specially employed for the day, leaving her own two children with a neighbour. Lily's husband was a soldier in South Africa and might be away for some time. So, as money was short, Lily was happy to take work wherever she could find it. She liked being in the Richards' household because she was treated well. The Richards family were not at all pompous or condescending, as other employers often were. She had heard some dreadful stories from her friends, and counted herself very lucky.

Alice and Mrs Cole explained the situation to Lily and she knew instinctively what she had to do.

'Don't worry, miss,' Lily said, 'the food is all ready now. My ma will see to that. I will change into a clean dress and apron, and I will be on hand in the parlour for anything you need, including the baby.'

'What a good person you are, Lily, and you too, Mrs Cole, I don't know how we would manage without you both.'

Frances was looking tired. Alfred was looking constantly in her direction just to satisfy himself that she wasn't too overwhelmed by all the excitement. Alice noticed that her sister was wilting a little, so she took the baby.

'Let's show him to Miss Bell. Look, Fran, doesn't Miss Bell look pretty?'

Frances admired Miss Bell's lace hat and gloves and hoped that the baby wouldn't dribble on her lovely clothes. Miss Bell was thrilled to hold the baby. She had known Frances and Alice since they were both born, and was a friend to both Alfred's and the girls' parents. She had taught both girls to play the piano, and to sing. Now though, with her failing eyesight and arthritic fingers she doubted that she would live long enough to teach the new addition to the family. Still, she was very pleased and honoured to be invited to the christening. She would travel the short coach journey to the church, with the family.

'I do wish I could have played the organ for you,' said Miss Bell wistfully, 'but, no matter, I will sing loudly and most joyfully to make up for it!'

Alice cheered up.

'I'm sure you will, Miss Bell. You will put us all to shame.' It wasn't until Alice handed the baby over to Lily, to be fed, that Frances realised Miss Appleton was not there. *And why*, she wondered, *had Doctor Ingram disappeared?*

'He will join us at the church my dear,' said Alfred, 'Miss Appleton is not too well and he has to attend to her just now.' Frances accepted that explanation and was secretly relieved not to have Miss Appleton around, though, she mused whether it was an unchristian thing to have in her innermost thoughts!

Doctor Ingram returned before the party set off for the church. Peter Lawrence had, for once, done exactly as Alfred had requested, and the vicar complied with their request for a later christening.

Just when Alfred and Alice were breathing a sigh of relief, Peter Lawrence reverted to type and in his usual tactless, brusque manner managed to upset things again.

'So, you'll be looking for a new nanny, post-haste then, Frances?'

No one had told Peter Lawrence that Frances was unaware of the situation. Miss Bell, looking very confused, sniffed into her handkerchief.

Alice led Peter Lawrence away from the group, and explained how they were attempting to keep what had occurred from Frances until after the ceremony. He apologised profusely, for his clumsiness. He was relieved to see the doctor and Alfred again.

'Help me out here, Doctor Ingram. What's a chap to do if he isn't properly informed?' He apologised again, to Alfred.

Uncharacteristically, Alfred raised his voice, the stress of the day now taking its toll on him.

'How could you be so thoughtless, Peter? If you only knew how careful we have to be with Frances. Today of all days.'

Alfred stormed out of the parlour to try and regain his composure. He returned almost immediately, apologising for his own outburst.

'No, no,' Peter Lawrence assured him. 'It was my fault entirely. How can I make amends?'

'Well,' said Alfred, 'perhaps you would like to organise the two carriages. I think we are all ready now.'

Peter Lawrence travelled in the first carriage with Doctor Ingram so that they could alert the vicar that the family and Miss Bell were close behind. There would be a dozen or more friends waiting for them at the church, all of whom would return afterwards.

Seated comfortably in the second carriage, Alfred and Alice decided to explain as gently as they could to Frances and Miss Bell that Miss Appleton had suffered a "nervous episode".

'She needs to be in hospital for a while, Fran. It's a pity that she will miss the christening, isn't it? But don't you worry. Ellice has swallowed her socialist pride, and has agreed to be at the church, to help with Charles.'

Alice stroked Fran's cheek, and moved a stray curl from her face, tucking it beneath the lace of her hat.

Frances seemed quite unworried. Alice wondered if in a strange way Frances was actually relieved. Not that she would have wished any harm to come to Miss Appleton, but relieved to be free of her bullying manner.

The vicar beamed when he saw Frances holding the baby.

'How beautiful!' he said, 'Your parents would have been so proud. We all think of them today.'

Everyone nodded in agreement, and the ceremony proceeded without any mishaps. The congregation was a mixture of old friends and family, church friends and close colleagues. Except for Ellice, everyone sang heartily, especially Miss Bell, and the godparents exuded much pride as Charles George Richards was christened.

The tea party was a huge success, due in no small part to Mrs Cole and Lily. Between them they ensured that no guest had an empty cup, and the tiny cakes and almond biscuits kept appearing as if by magic. No one would have guessed the trauma which had occurred earlier in the day.

'Goodness, how did you manage all this baking?' Alice congratulated Mrs Cole, 'It's all really delicious.'

'Thank you, miss. I'm pleased to see Mrs Richards smiling.'

'So am I,' Alice replied.

Alfred, deep in conversation with Doctor Ingram and his brother Frederick, with Peter Lawrence listening in, was explaining his decision to move to his father's old house, in Kensington.

'I was planning to announce it today,' he told them, 'but in view of the upsetting morning we have had I can't give Frances anything else to worry about today. I will wait until things are quieter, and we are alone again.'

Peter Lawrence cast a glance towards Doctor Ingram, and raised his eyebrows.

'I understand your concern,' Peter Lawrence agreed, 'but listen Alfred, old chap, isn't it about time that you stopped treating Frances like a child? Stop wrapping her in cotton wool? Surely the longer you go on cosseting her, the longer she will go on behaving like a helpless child?'

Doctor Ingram frowned, and felt compelled to add a few words of his own. Alfred resented them both.

'Frances is an intelligent and sensitive woman. She needs to feel a sense of purpose in her life. However, Peter, you must realise that Frances has had a few very difficult years. She lost both her parents, quite close together, she has looked after Alice when she was still young herself, and then the trauma of childbirth. She is still recovering from that you know. She might have died. Praise God that she, and the baby, are now well.' Alfred was impatient with his friends.

'What you two don't realise is that I am also responsible for Alice. I expect that one day she will meet some nice young man and marry, and have a home of her own. Charles will need a good education, a career, and Frances will love re-designing the house.'

Alfred calmed down.

'Let's just enjoy what's left of the day, shall we? No more cross words between friends. I can't take any more arguments.'

'Quite right,' the doctor agreed.

Sensitivity was never one of Peter Lawrence's attributes. He was much like Alfred's father. Perhaps that's why they got on so well together and the captain had trusted Peter Lawrence with all of his affairs.

The Highgate house had been Alice and Frances's childhood home, and Alfred had willingly moved there when he married Frances. It had been thought an expedient move at that time, so that they could all look after their ageing and ailing parents. By contrast the Kensington house was where Alfred had grown up, but after his mother Rose Maud had died it didn't feel like home any longer.

By the time Rose Maud had passed away the captain had retired from the navy, but he still spent a great deal of time away, or abroad, at meetings, or conferences. Alfred was never told exactly where his father was, or the nature of his work, or travels. He had decided not to live in the house by himself, with just the memories of his mother. So, marriage to Frances gave him a new home, and a happier existence. But now, as fate had dealt him a very different hand, he was looking forward to returning to the old house.

The house had been locked up since the captain had died. All the furniture had been covered in dust sheets, and pictures taken down and stacked in the corner of one room. Curtains were kept closed after the funeral, to keep the sun off the rooms, but also to discourage the peering eyes of curious passers-by.

Unlived in, and unloved, the house was cold and characterless, but that would change. Alfred was certain of it.

The guests were drifting away. Only Peter Lawrence, Doctor Ingram and his brother Frederick, editor of the *Illustrated London News* were still there admiring the sketches in the parlour, and hallway.

'Astounding!' declared Frederick. 'I find it quite fascinating that here, look, you and your mother have drawn the same view, but each has its own completely different character.'

'These are really professional, Alfred, and Rose was very talented too,' Peter Lawrence added. 'Do you ever sell your pictures?'

Alfred shook his head and smiled, wistfully.

'I have little time now to develop my work, much as I would like to do so. It is my passion. Father was right though; I would need to sell a great number of drawings in order to make a living. It doesn't matter how talented one might be, I'm afraid to say it is just something wonderful to do when one has the time to devote to it.'

Alfred denied that he was imaginative in his work. He said that he enjoyed drawing real people in real situations.

'I draw what I see,' he said.

Frederick listened carefully, and was interested in Alfred's description of himself and his abilities, though he didn't agree.

'I wonder if you would have the time and the inclination to do something for us, for *The News*?'

Alfred was taken aback by his suggestion. The man had some nerve asking a senior member of staff of a rival publication to work for him.

'It would just be a one-off, a freelance assignment. What do you think? Would you like to have a go?'

'What did you have in mind?' he asked.

'Recording history as it happens, that is our position. We're planning to run a series about men at work on the new railways.

45

We want pictures of them working on the trains, the tracks, and in the countryside. Did you know that Mr Brunel is pleasing the politicians? He aims to blend the railways with the landscape, bushes hiding the lines, embankments planted with trees and bushes, that sort of thing.'

Realising that the cake was to be cut, before everyone went home, the three men returned to the parlour. Alfred gave a very short speech, thanking people for their lovely gifts and their kind support. He gave a touching appreciation of his wife, and Alice. Then, much to her total embarrassment and astonishment, Alfred brought Mrs Cole and Lily into the parlour to publicly thank them both.

'This wonderful lady, Mrs Cole,' he gestured towards her, beaming, 'has been a tower of strength to our family for as long as I can remember. She has not only performed her duties to the highest standards and beyond, but has become a most valued and treasured friend. My wife, Frances, Alice and I are indebted to her.' There was a polite ripple of applause and agreement.

Alice stepped forward and presented Mrs C with a bouquet of flowers, and there was a smaller posy for Lily.

Mrs C was speechless, and shed a few tears, not usual for her. Even more unusual was the tiny bow she made in thanks. Lily's cheeks became more than a little red as she gave a little curtsey.

The guests dispersed and went their separate ways, except for Doctor Ingram and his brother Frederick, who lingered by the display of christening gifts. Frances thanked them both, and showed her delight at the little silver ship. The doctor remarked pointedly, 'Perhaps Charles will grow up to become a naval officer, following in his grandfather's footsteps?'

Frederick changed the subject. He was more astute than his brother. He knew that Alfred would not have those sort of expectations for Charles. In fact, Alfred would do everything he could to dissuade his son from a military career.

Frederick inspected Alfred's drawings again, and asked if they

46

could meet up soon, when they were unlikely to have interruptions. He cast an eye in his brother's direction as he spoke.

The doctor returned to the subject of Isambard Kingdom Brunel, though Frederick could see that Alfred was now completely exhausted with the day's happenings, and was finding it difficult to continue with polite conversation.

'The bridges are far too costly, and the viaducts. Ridiculous designs. They look like Renaissance balustrades, and the stations are like castles. Have you seen St. Pancras? It's like a gothic palace.'

Frederick chided him for being so old-fashioned and lacking in foresight.

'Seriously,' Frederick turned to Alfred, 'there are some real architectural marvels, especially the Forth Bridge in Scotland. Very striking. We are really keen to have some pictures of that now it is finished. How about it?'

Alfred said he would give it some thought, and he diplomatically ushered the gentlemen to the door.

CHAPTER FOUR

Violet Cole and Lily, loaded up with flowers and party left overs, struggled to clamber from the omnibus without dropping everything. They were both exhausted, in the way that felt good after a satisfying day's work, when you knew that you had done your very best, and been appreciated for it. They were longing for a cup of tea from their own teapot. They would try to put the shocking events surrounding Miss Appleton out of their minds. Lily was beginning to ponder the future.

'Ma, what will happen to the baby now? They'll need another nurse. Won't they?'

'Don't you go getting ideas my girl. You've got enough on your plate.'

'I wasn't thinking anything, Ma. But I could fill in, you know, till they get sorted.'

'You're not a qualified nurse, Lil. I'm sure Doctor Ingram will advise them what to do.'

Lily wasn't impressed. It was through Doctor Ingram that Miss Appleton had been engaged in the first place. Lily didn't like Doctor Ingram. She didn't quite know why, and she couldn't explain it. There was just something about his pompous manner, and the fact that he never seemed to look people in the eye when he was speaking with them. In company, he would scan the assembly and look over people's heads, making a mental note of who was there, and who was who. He reminded Lily of the much older, stuffy and pompous doctor who had reluctantly attended her father, Jim, when he had suffered his terrible accident. The doctor was more used to attending upper class patients, dispensing potions and pills along with sycophantic reassurances to ladies suffering the vapours!

That doctor had been reluctant to touch Jim Cole's badly crushed and bleeding leg, damaged in the collision between two racing carriages and his own timber cart. Her father had been to collect new timber for his workshop. His cart was fully loaded and he was moving carefully and steadily along Kentish Road, when the two carriage drivers decided to race each other, either side of Jim's cart. One of the carriages veered out of control, crashing into the cart and overturning it. The timber spilled onto the road into the path of the second carriage. The collision caused the genteel carriage passengers great shock, but only minor injuries, unlike the badly injured Jim.

The doctor was brought quickly, but he spent more time with the carriage passengers than with her father. Lily shivered as she remembered the accident. It had blighted their lives ever since. Her two elder brothers had to be sent to relatives in Kent, to work on a farm, while Lily was kept at home in order to look after her father.

At first, the brothers, James and Frank were not happy to be sent away. They had to work for their keep on the farm, and Uncle Joseph was harsh with them if they fell short of his expectations.

On the other hand, he would give praise when their efforts warranted it. After a while, they stopped asking to go home. They both agreed that Aunt Flo couldn't bake as well as their mother. James remained on the farm and made occasional trips home to bring fruit and some fresh vegetables from the farm.

'I'm not stopping here,' Frank vowed, 'as soon as I can I'm going to enlist in the army, and escape this boring country life.' That is exactly what Frank did. Lily's husband Eddie, driven crazy by domestic life with his in-laws, Lily and the children, joined the same regiment. *At least*, Lily thought, *if they're in South Africa together, they will be able to look out for each other.*

Violet and Lily reached the terrace, exhausted, but glad to be home at last. It had been a long and eventful day.

The front door was ajar, which surprised Lily. She pushed the door open and shouted to her father.

'Hello Pa, we're home! What are you doing with the door wide open? Who left it like that?'

Lily took her mother's coat and hat from her, and hung them up with her own things.

'I can't wait to put my feet up, Lil,' her mother said, 'I'll be in the room... see how Jim's doing.'

'All right Ma, I'll put the kettle on.'

When she reached the kitchen Lily was shocked to find an army kit bag propped against the wall beside a pair of dirty boots. There was no one there. She shouted upstairs.

'Is anyone there? Eddie, Frank?'

There was no answer.

'Ma, come quick! Come and see!'

Her mother came running.

'Look. It must be Frank back from Africa, or could it be Eddie? Surely not Eddie. He hasn't been away long enough to have got leave.'

'Well, your Pa's out cold. He stinks of alcohol. Somebody's plied him with more than just ale from the corner.'

'Well, where is he then, whoever it is?'

'Probably gone to fetch more booze.'

'I hope it's not that good for nothing husband of yours,' said Violet Cole. 'He did us all a favour when he enlisted.'

'Don't say that, Ma. He's not all bad.'

'He hasn't even seen his second child yet, and not a penny sent for his family either.'

'Oh, the kids!' cried Lily. 'I've got to fetch them from Jenny. She'll wonder where I've been. It's much longer than we expected what with all that carry on at the Richards' house.'

Lily grabbed her coat from the hall and ran as fast as she could to her friend's house at the end of the terrace. She passed by a soldier in uniform, who she didn't recognise. These days it was nothing out of the ordinary to see soldiers coming and going at all hours of the day or night. But it wasn't her brother Frank, or her husband, Eddie. The soldier gave her a shifty, sideways grin. She kept running.

Lily reached her friend's house and walked straight in.

'You've been a long time, Lil,' her friend said.

'Jenny, I'm really sorry. It's been such a day. When I've got time I'll tell you all about it.'

'They've been as good as gold, Lil. Jimmy's played all day and had a little sleep. The baby's fine. He's asleep now and he's been fed.'

'Thanks ever so, Jen,' said Lily, thrusting some money into her hand. 'I'm giving you double for being such a help all this time.'

'Are you sure, Lil? I hope they paid you well.'

Lily nodded. She gathered up the children and made her way home as fast as she could. She was anxious to get the children into their beds. Then she could try to relax a bit. *What a traumatic day,* she reflected. She had never encountered a situation like Miss Appleton's before. *Fancy a woman of her social standing and education finding herself in such a mental state.* Lily wondered if they would ever get to know the truth of the matter. Certainly baby Charles seemed to have had a narrow escape from what might have had a tragic outcome. She hugged her own children close to her. She took them straight upstairs and tucked them in to their beds. They didn't stir. She guessed that Jenny would have tired them out.

In the room Lily's mother was trying in vain to rouse her inebriated husband, who was lying awkwardly in his chair. His bad leg was lying over the side of his chair, so she straightened him out and covered him with her shawl.

'No good, Lil. We'll just have to leave him there to sleep it off.'

'He'll be all right, missus,' said the unkempt soldier who Lily recognised, having passed him in the street. He had crept back into the house while Lily was out. He had hidden himself on the window seat, partly obscured by the curtain. He had a nervous eye on the passers-by outside, but now an even more nervous, shifty eye on Lily Cole.

'That's your kit bag in our kitchen, isn't it?' Lily yelled, 'And your dirty boots. Who are you? What do you want with us?'

'Old yer 'orses,' the soldier sneered, 'you'll want to 'ear what I've come to tell you.'

'Look at the state of my husband,' Mrs Cole joined in, 'he likes his ale but he's never been like this before. What have you given him?'

'The finest malt, missus. 'E's enjoyed every drop. We've 'ad a good time 'im and me, talking about our families.'

Mrs Cole ushered them both out of the room and into the kitchen, away from Jim. The soldier put his arm round Lily's shoulder and she immediately pushed him away.

'You reek of booze, you disgusting man. Get away from me.' The soldier lurched towards the kitchen, laughing.

'The kit bag's mine all right, miss, but the boots belong to your 'usband Eddie. He copped it in Africa. Sorry to bring you the bad news.'

The two women were stunned. After the day they had both experienced, this was the cruellest blow. Lily fell into her mother's arms, shocked and dazed.

Violet Cole, being possessed of a good deal more instinct and intelligence than the soldier in front of them, listened intently to what he had to say, with more than a touch of scepticism.

The soldier said that he had travelled up from Dover when his ship had docked. Embarkation leave, he said, before he would be sent off somewhere else abroad.

'I brought you the boots. You'll be able to sell 'em down Camden,' he said. 'Of course I've 'ad to pay the train fare to London, and a cab up 'ere.'

Mrs Cole comforted her daughter, but kept her thoughts to herself, just for the moment.

'You go and sit with Jim, Lily, I'll be there in a minute.' She was not taken in by the soldier's lies, but had to act quickly for the sake of the children asleep upstairs. She rummaged in her purse and found some money.

'It's all I've got,' she lied, 'I want you to go now and leave us in peace. We've got a lot to think about.'

She picked up the soldier's kit bag and thrust it at him, not giving him time to protest, or come up with any other story that he thought he could get away with. She steered the soldier to the front door and then bolted it securely behind him. Lily reappeared in the kitchen.

'Dry your eyes, Lil. These aren't Eddie's boots. They're too small. The man's a liar!'

'How do you know that, Ma?'

'Trust me, I do know, Lil. The troop ships don't use Dover. It's Southampton, if I remember right, or some go from Tilbury, but not Dover.' She was quite adamant.

'Look, Lil, don't say anything to your Pa about this, not yet anyway. I've got the day off tomorrow. We'll go to the Army Office. They'll tell us what's happened. Usually when soldiers die, someone sends a telegram.'

Violet Cole had observed and learned much during her long working life with the Richards family, especially when the captain was home from his naval exploits. Servants overheard conversations, business dealings, travel plans, arguments, disappointments, and the joys of family life. Servants were party to everything. However, the captain and his family had only a modest household, herself, and a scullery maid. The captain described it as a "tight ship". He did not have his own carriage. He hired one as and when he needed one, since he was away for much of the time.

Implicit in Mrs Cole's job was the recognition that a valued servant kept everything they saw and heard entirely to themselves.

She was such a servant. Working class she might be, but she was an intelligent, astute woman, who had absorbed ways of living which her near neighbours might describe as la-di-dah!

She was a woman of many skills, decent and trustworthy. She had intuition, and a good grasp of proper speech and vocabulary.

In spite of her working class accent, she had, through the example of her employers, learned how to address people, and how to enunciate her words clearly. This had stood her in good stead up to now, and it would certainly stand her in good stead the following day.

After a restless night, both Mrs Cole and Lily were awake early as usual, and dressed in their Sunday clothes, despite it not being Sunday. They wore hats and gloves and carried a small handbag each, instead of their usual shopping baskets. They looked every inch a picture of middle-class respectability.

They reached the Army Office. A young soldier held the door open for them and directed them to the waiting area.

Several young men, hoping to enlist, were also waiting there. Some looked nervous, and unsure of themselves. Others, eager, chatting and joking with their friends.

'A bob a day and all found,' said one. 'I can't get that here. I can't wait to go.'

The clerk called the young men in one at a time. They left through a different door, so Lily and her mother didn't see them again.

At last the two anxious women were shown to seats in the Enquiry Office. The officer in charge stood to greet them, and even touched his cap.

'How can I help you ladies?' the officer asked.

Tearfully, Lily indicated that her mother would speak for her. The officer sat down again, and Mrs Cole gave her daughter a handkerchief, along with one of her impatient frowns.

'Good morning, officer,' Mrs Cole began calmly. She continued to relate the story of the soldier who had inveigled his way into their house the previous day. She told how he had plied her disabled husband with strong liquor, and how she had discovered later he had stolen money from a jug which was kept on the top shelf of the kitchen dresser.

The officer listened intently, without comment. When she related the soldier's version of Eddie Cole's death in Africa the officer stopped her and requested the clerk to come to the office and write everything down.

Mrs Cole was asked to repeat everything again, for the clerk. Lily looked frantic, and worried throughout the proceedings. She began to think that her mother's suspicions about the soldier might be correct.

The officer excused himself temporarily from the room, leaving the ladies with the writer clerk. The report writing finished and they were shown back into the waiting room where they sat for almost an hour. Eventually they were invited back into the private office.

This time the officer was not smiling. He was courteous, but serious.

'Mrs Cole, Miss...'

'Mrs Wilson,' Lily corrected him. 'My husband is Private Edward Wilson, sir.'

'My apologies, ladies. I'm afraid your evidence has uncovered a very serious situation.'

'Evidence!' cried Lily.

The officer assured them both that Eddie Wilson had not been killed in South Africa. In fact, he had never reached South Africa.

'It would seem,' said the officer, sternly, 'that Private Wilson and another soldier had completed the enlistment procedure, and the initial training with his regiment, but had failed to turn up at Southampton when they had been issued travel documents to do so.'

Lily was very confused, and lost for words. She did not

understand the implications, but her mother did.

'He absconded?' Mrs Cole questioned the officer.

'There is no other explanation that we can find, so far,' the officer told them. 'It is a very serious situation. The top and bottom of it is that Private Wilson and his fellow soldier appear to be guilty of desertion, at the very least.'

'What does that mean, sir?' Lily asked.

'Well, to begin with we will approach the police to find out if there is some explanation why Private Wilson seems to have vanished. The hospitals will be checked. All attempts to find him will be made, but if he has, in fact, deserted, he will most likely be sent to prison.'

The officer continued, 'If you take my advice, young lady, you will go home and try to carry on your life as normal. For now, try to put it out of your mind, and keep it from your neighbours and friends. We will contact you when we have any news. We would like you to do the same. Should you encounter either man again, you must let us know immediately.'

The officer's manner softened. He seemed genuinely sympathetic towards them both.

'Rest assured,' he told them, 'we will track them down, and you will be informed as soon as we have them in custody. At the very least it will mean a court martial.'

Mrs Cole thanked the officer in as dignified a manner as she could muster. She took the sobbing Lily by the arm, and they made their way home to Jim. They were still stunned and trying to come to terms with news of Eddie's possible desertion. They debated if they should tell Jim, or keep it to themselves.

'We have to tell him, Ma. Suppose Eddie comes back to hand himself in? What if that creepy man comes with him?'

'Well, my girl, it would certainly be the honourable thing to do, but then duty and honour seems to have eluded him up to now, doesn't it?'

They returned home to Jim, who was none the wiser, though

he did wonder why they were wearing their best Sunday clothes.

Clearly recovered from the previous day's drunken stupor, Jim was happily working away at a child's chair. He could still carve intricate designs and make beautiful small furniture, even if his legs couldn't take him very far from his work shed. As long as he had his tools close by, and a supply of decent wood, he could make anything he set his mind to. Jim's recollection of the previous day was rather vague. As far as he could remember, a soldier friend of Eddie's had called to pay his respects to his family. There had been no mention of Eddie dying, or that either of them were bound for a troopship. Whether the soldier and Eddie had hatched the plan together had yet to be discovered.

It was clear that the soldier knew the layout of the house, that the door would be unlocked, and the whereabouts of the cash in the jug on the dresser. Fortunately, he hadn't known about Jim's carefully constructed secret compartment at the back of the dresser drawers.

Jim looked up from his carving. 'Hello, where have you two been in your Sunday clothes on a Monday? Why haven't you gone to work? Where are the children?'

'We had to go out, Pa. I've left the kids next door. I'll fetch them now, and then I'll make us a drink.'

Violet Cole went to change her clothes before she sat down with Jim. She had not only to relate the happenings with the soldier, but also about the terrible happening the day before, at the Richards' house.

Jim made no comment about the Richards' episode. He was too upset about matters closer to home. He felt deeply ashamed, and he was very apologetic to his wife, for allowing himself to be so hoodwinked by the soldier, and for accepting strong liquor that he wasn't used to drinking. Violet Cole pursed her lips in disapproval, but then, more concerned with the seriousness of Eddie's actions, she spoke softly to Jim.

'You were not to know. You are a trusting soul, Jim. Now, we have a duty to Lil and the children. We must keep this to ourselves. God only knows what will happen if it becomes public. My worry is Mr Richards. I don't know how he will take it. I need to keep working. Anyway, I'm up early tomorrow. Mr Richards only gave me one day off, and we still have problems without a proper nanny.' Jim listened and nodded sympathetically. He gave her hand a gentle squeeze.

Mrs Cole tossed and turned all night, hardly sleeping. In a way she was glad to get up and go to work.

She could cope. She was a resourceful woman, capable of working on many levels at once. Her thoughts turned to the day ahead. Lily would look after Jim, and the duly repentant Jim would speak calmly with Lily. He would enjoy playing with little Jimmy at the table, having made the boy a set of building bricks from spare off-cuts. The cubes were smoothed and polished two or three times, as though they were some precious piece of fine furniture. That was how Jim coped. He couldn't make the world right, or people right, but he could make his work right, beautiful and fine. He made things which people would value and treasure forever.

'Keep the door locked!' Mrs Cole shouted before she left for work. 'Don't let anyone in. Promise?'

'OK Ma,' Lily answered.

Mrs Cole reached the Richards' house early, and immediately resumed her role as housekeeper for the family. For now, her attention had to be totally focussed on the smooth running of another family's home. In a strange way, the mantle she had assumed so readily for many years felt completely natural. Inwardly, she regarded the Richards family as her own, though she would never voice her feelings, even to Lily. It was understood, but unsaid, by both families.

She let herself in through the back kitchen door. She expected the family would still be upstairs, not yet awake. She began to prepare the breakfast, and the table in the dining room.

Everything was neat, clean and tidy as she cast her eyes over all the rooms on the ground floor. Except for the display of the christening gifts, no one would have guessed the trauma, the panic, and then the excitement which had filled the house two days before. Calm appeared to have been restored to the house. Mrs Cole hoped that calm would have been restored to the family too. Alice was sure to enlighten her.

'Good Morning, Mrs C.' Alice bounded into the dining room and gave her a friendly hug. 'I thought I smelled breakfast. I'm so pleased to see you, though you fully deserved your day off. Did you have a restful day?'

Mrs C stopped what she was doing, and before she could find a satisfactory answer her eyes filled with tears.

'Oh! Mrs C, what is it? I didn't mean to upset you. I'm so sorry. Are you unwell?' Alice asked.

'I'm quite well, thank you, miss.' She hurriedly wiped her eyes, and turned to get on with her work. 'It's all the excitement catching up with me. I'm a little tired, that's all.'

Alice was wise enough not to pursue matters just then, but she would speak with Alfred. He would wheedle out of her whatever had caused the tears.

By the time the family had breakfasted and Alice had regained her brightness, and Mrs C was more composed, things moved on smoothly. Alfred listened while Alice described Mrs C's tearful moment.

'I expect she, like us, has been greatly shocked and not a little overwhelmed by what happened to Miss Appleton, and to the baby. Then there was the christening. Mrs C isn't getting any younger you know. We all take her for granted.'

Alice agreed, and promised to be less demanding.

'After all, Alfred, I'm almost nineteen. I can't live an idle life forever. Some women are married at my age.'

'Is that what you want, Alice?' he queried.

'Not yet, silly. But one day I might, and only if I can find someone as kind and handsome as you, Alfred.'

He smiled as he watched Alice run up the stairs. She looked more like a schoolgirl than a grown woman. He knew that Alice would leave them one day. It was only right and natural that she would, though Frances would miss her sister greatly when that time came. He would miss her too.

The sisters had lived a very sheltered and cosseted life in their father's vicarage. They were largely unaware of world affairs, or even happenings outside of their immediate family and church circles.

Alfred reflected that if they had been members of the upper classes Alice would have been deliberately introduced to eligible young men, and a wider social circle. Alfred and Frances didn't regard themselves to be in that social league at all, nor did they aspire to be so. Still, Alfred was concerned that by keeping her so close, they might be limiting Alice's options in life.

He needn't have worried. Alice was already beginning to ponder her future, and was developing ideas of her own. She too was concerned that whatever she decided to do with her life, might be upsetting if she were to leave her sister to cope without her.

It seemed even more pressing now that they make some sort of decision about the captain's house in Kensington. Alfred knew that Frances was not very strong, emotionally, and whilst he was never given to making rash decisions, he realised that any new changes would add pressure to Frances. He wanted to have things clear in his own mind before he returned to his work at the *Gazette*. He had three weeks remaining of his leave.

'I shall take Frances away for a short holiday. What do you think, Mrs C?'

Alfred had gravitated to the kitchen with a dual purpose.

'Should we take the baby, or leave him with Alice and the new nurse?'

'New nurse, Mr Alfred?'

'Yes. I'm afraid poor Miss Appleton is unlikely to recover very quickly, if at all. It seems that her fiancé, who had been a soldier in

South Africa, had been killed. She was so deeply shocked and had no family to support her in her great distress that it turned her mind. She suffered delusions, and somehow she thought that he would be returning to her and to her baby.'

'So, whilst she was here with Master Charles she imagined that he was her own baby?'

'Yes, Mrs C. The doctors feel that when the truth of the situation dawned on her, she couldn't accept it, and that is when she ran off with baby Charles. Thank God that we realised in time, and managed to apprehend her before anything drastic happened.'

'How very sad,' Mrs Cole said.

'Yes it is,' nodded Alfred, 'but I hope that now you will be as pleased as we are that Miss Bell's niece, Ellice, has agreed to come and help us for a while.'

'Won't she find it all rather mundane after her busy hospital work?'

'I hope not, Mrs C. I understand the young lady has many other interests. She will be good for Alice. Someone nearer to her own age.'

'Yes, of course. That will be a good idea.'

Mrs C said that she would look forward to meeting Ellice Bell later that evening. Her spirits now raised a little, Mrs C returned to her work with renewed vigour.

It was agreed that Alice, the new nurse, Mrs Cole and Lily would between them take care of the baby so that Alfred and Frances could enjoy a short holiday by themselves. They would aim to take the train from London, and follow Queen Victoria's favourite route to Scotland, though not as far as Balmoral Castle.

The July weather was expected to be kind to them. They would travel on the Scotch Express to Edinburgh and stay in a hotel near to the station overnight, and the following morning they would take the horse omnibus to Queensferry.

At Queensferry they would stay at the old Hawes Inn, much

loved by Robert Louis Stevenson, but the main attraction was to give Alfred the opportunity, suggested by Frederick Ingram, to make sketches of the newly built Forth Bridge.

Alfred felt that his drawing skills might be a bit rusty since it was a while since he sat down to seriously concentrate on it. Still, there was only one way to find out. He would do his best to capture the Forth Bridge in different lights, and from every angle. Perhaps, if Frederick thought the work was worthy, he just might leave the *Gazette* to join the *Illustrated London News*. The thought appealed to him greatly. If it didn't work out then he would try something else. He had more or less decided that he had become bored with the *Gazette*. It wasn't that he disliked the work, and he enjoyed the camaraderie with the workers, it was just that he felt himself to be out of step with the style of the paper. He knew that it didn't reflect the world of ordinary working class people. Its social remit was geared to the establishment and the upper classes, and royalty, of course.

Frederick Ingram had been right about one thing. The *Illustrated London News* was aiming to show real people in real social and work situations. There was little text in the paper, so people who were not so literate could still be informed and more connected to a range of views. The more Alfred thought about it, the more he convinced himself that it was the best idea.

Frances dithered over her packing, and called Alice to help.

'Fran, you're only going to be away for a few days. You have enough clothes here for a world cruise.' Frances sat down on her bed and let Alice take over.

'Look Fran, one warm black coat, and a lighter one in case you find some sunshine. You sort your underclothes and I'll pack your dresses and shawls. I always think that shawls are a really good thing, one fine silk, for balmy evenings, and a warm wool one for chilly days and nights. What do you think? We must have got enough now, except for shoes?'

Frances was happy with Alice's packing, though Alice couldn't fathom why Frances felt the need to take a pair of winter boots and three extra pairs of shoes.

Alfred was amused to see Frances becoming excited for the first time in ages. She asked him how long the journey would take.

'Well, my darling, if the timetables are to be believed, the journey from King's Cross to Edinburgh should take between eight and nine hours. It depends on whether the train would need a change of engine en route, and on the length of time needed for the water tanks to be replenished.' He didn't want to admit to Frances that, although he was looking forward to the break, he was rather apprehensive about the journey. He had heard stories of the east and west coast train drivers trying to race each other, trying to cut journey times for the passengers.

Excitement and anticipation took over from the anxiety as they boarded the Scotch Express and the train left the station on time. Frances said that were it not for the noise and the smell from the engine they could have imagined themselves in a very luxurious horse carriage.

'Look, Fran, Royal Blue velvet at the windows, and edged with gold trim. Even the tiny brass lamps match. It's like a grand parlour. I'm glad we could afford to travel First Class.'

Once the train had emerged from the station they settled into a steady speed through less interesting countryside. Frances having been awake very early that morning fell asleep, so Alfred didn't disturb her. He calmed his own anxiety about the train, and as Frances slept he gently placed one of the blue cushions behind her head. He allowed his mind to wander over the possibilities of their trip. He would have to spend time sketching, and he hoped Frances would not become bored. He would have to find something for her to do.

He took out his pencil box and pad. He drew Frances as she slept. She was an easy subject. Her pale golden curls mostly hidden by her tiny hat, which he expected would fall off as she slept.

He drew the countryside as the train picked up speed. He made quick, darting sketches, just to give himself a general idea. He was fascinated by the changing light as the day wore on, and the changing vegetation and landscape as the train travelled further northwards. By the time they reached York, the sky had become much greyer, and there was a distinct chill in the air.

Frances felt refreshed by her much needed long sleep. Alfred had half-filled one of his sketch books. He had become so enthusiastic that he had to be persuaded to leave the pencils and pad behind when they went for lunch in the dining car.

'We'd like to have the steamed salmon and vegetables,' he told the waiter, 'and then we'll try the lemon soufflé, please.'

'Very well, sir, madam. Will you take any wine?'

'No, thank you,' Alfred shook his head as he automatically spoke for them both. Frances hardly ever drank, but certainly not on a long train journey when they needed to stay alert.

'We will just have some iced water, thank you, waiter.'

After their very pleasant lunch they returned to their private compartment. Frances immediately began to feel nauseous. The train had halted for a water station at York, and the train windows had been opened temporarily to let some air in, but also the smells from the station and the train engine. Frances felt very uneasy until they were safely back in their seats, and with the near windows closed.

'Frances, dear, wouldn't you be better to sit up instead of lying down,' Alfred coaxed her. He rang for the steward and asked for some more cold water for Frances. 'Sip it slowly, Fran. You will soon feel better. We're nearly half way there now.' He fussed around her with magazines, and she dutifully flicked the pages without wanting to read anything.

There is certainly a knack to looking after oneself on a moving train, Alfred thought. Walking the length of the train whilst it was in motion required a great sense of balance and you needed to adopt a really steady pace. Eating was quite difficult too, not just managing the cutlery and drinks, but the stomach too had to adjust to many new sensations.

Towards dusk the train was passing through Northumberland. The scattered trees of more southern parts gave way to taller, slender forests and firs, reminiscent of Norway. It seemed as though all the densely planted trees were struggling with each other to find the light. The fields of yellow rape had gone, and instead there were vast expanses of bracken, broom and heather. They were now much nearer the coast.

At Dunbar the air was markedly colder, and Alfred was glad that Frances was unaware of how close the train was to the steep edge of the coastline. If the train were to accidentally keel over there would surely be a very long, and very dangerous drop over the rocky cliffs, into the sea below. Alfred prayed.

Eventually the train pulled into Edinburgh's Waverley station. Frances began to take more interest as her boredom was now relieved. They were both glad to be at journey's end. They were a short walk from the station to their overnight hotel. It felt good to be on terra firma, Alfred remarked, and free of the smells of the train.

The strong, unfamiliar gust of wind which met them at the top of the station slope, took them by surprise and in spite of feeling exhausted, they managed somehow to quicken their steps.

Greeting them at the hotel, the doorman, dressed in full Scottish regalia, and accompanied by a bagpiper in green tartan, thrilled them both.

'What a wonderful welcome!' Alfred remarked loudly. Frances smiled broadly and acknowledged both the piper and the doorman.

'Good evening, madam; sir. Have ye come far?' The doorman spoke with a very pronounced Scottish accent. They would have to listen very carefully, so they would catch every word.

'From London,' Alfred told him.

'Aye, a long way indeed sir,' the man replied. He took their bags and handed them to a young steward who accompanied them to their small, but quite adequate room. After all, it was only an overnight stay. Frances was so tired that she declined supper and prepared to go to bed. Alfred had a tray brought to the room, though he, too, had little appetite. His reluctance to eat was less through exhaustion, but more from excitement and anticipation.

He would sleep less well than Frances that night.

Once Frances was asleep, Alfred found his way down to the reception desk to ask about transport to Queensferry.

'Private carriages will be few and far between in the morning, sir. New Town bankers and merchants, you see. It's not like London where you have carriages on every corner. I can reserve you seats on the horse bus, sir.'

Alfred agreed. 'Yes, thank you, the horse bus will be fine.'

'The journey takes about an hour, sir, depending on how many stops the driver has to make. The bus will stop right outside the Hawes Inn. The Inn staff will meet the bus and help you with your bags.'

'Thank you,' said Alfred, 'I am very much obliged to you. That sounds just perfect.'

Frances slept soundly. Alfred mostly tossed and turned through the night. He was glad when he heard movement in the hotel corridor and then smelled the breakfast from the kitchens below. Then, he was fully awake.

Breakfast proved to be adequate, though unremarkable. With half an hour to spare until the horse bus arrived, they decided to have a short, leisurely stroll along the famous Princes Street towards the gardens, and the huge monument to Sir Walter Scott.

Alfred sketched as they walked. He didn't want to miss a single thing of interest.

Frances was more impressed by Jenner's shop frontage on the opposite side of the road.

'That's Edinburgh's flagship store,' Alfred told her. 'It's like a Scottish Harrods. Even Queen Victoria shops here.'

There was a sparkle in Fran's eyes.

'Well, maybe on our return, my darling. We'll make time then, shall we?'

Frances nodded in girlish anticipation.

The weather seemed a touch milder, but nevertheless Alfred insisted that Frances wore her warmest coat, hat and scarf. They sat in the centre of the bus, much to the disappointment of Frances.

She wanted to see everything from the front view, but Alfred had been warned by the hotel staff to claim the centre seats. They were deemed safer, especially if the driver made speed going round corners, and besides that, it wasn't a good idea to sit right behind the horses.

Once the driver had passed through the elegant Princes Street he gathered a speed which Alfred thought bordered on the reckless. They hurried through Haymarket, a noisy hotchpotch of cobbled streets, and inns on every corner; noisy even at this hour of the day. They saw dozens of people scurrying off to work, and others setting up stalls, or a makeshift pitch where they could sell their wares to passers-by. This was a less salubrious part of town. The driver could have chosen a more scenic route to Queensferry, but it would have lengthened the journey, and this was really a workmen's bus, not a tourist vehicle. Many passengers would board the bus along the Corstorphine Road, in order to get to their places of work. Farm people, carpenters, clerks, even women carrying baskets of fresh-baked loaves to sell at Dalmeny market or Queensferry, by the harbour. Some were bound for Dunfermline, but had business in South Queensferry, before making the crossing to the other side of the river.

A mile or so out of the city and they were admiring the larger villas. Wealthier people, business people mostly, didn't care for the smells of the city, or the smoke, so they built their houses where there was clearer air, and some greenery. Here they cultivated beautiful gardens, along with friends of their own social circle, where they held parties and even dances. Further along the Corstorphine Road was the original village, the driver told them.

'Aye, it goes back to medieval times. There's a very ancient church, and a dovecot. That was there for the castle, and the laird had pigeons reared there, for his table! The castle's not there now.'

They could just catch a tiny glimpse between the stone cottages of the village green, and the huge sycamore tree.

'It looks very pretty,' Alfred said, to anyone who wanted to listen. 'What a pity we haven't time to explore there.'

'Oh,' said a fellow traveller, 'you don't want to be off exploring there now. It's all pig farms and potato fields.'

It was a new experience for Alfred and Frances. They were used to taking private carriages into London from Highgate. They were not accustomed to hearing the conversations of what Alfred termed, "ordinary people". He found it exciting and stimulating. It would have been rude to take out his sketchbook. He would have to rely on his memory in order to catch every detail of their faces.

Clearly, many of the passengers knew each other, as they made this journey every day to work, the market, or to family. It was a new experience too for both of them to smell the working clothes of fishermen and women, cobblers, and even the highly polished boots of the smarter clerks. Frances thought the nicest smell of all emanated from a covered basket of newly baked bread and scones, held closely by a woman on her way to the quayside.

The baker woman was accompanied by a small, pale-faced boy, who was constantly sniffing. Frances could only guess his age at about four or five. He was so small and thin.

As they neared the River Forth, and South Queensferry, the air was quite cool. Frances clutched her scarf to her neck, and she thanked Alfred for insisting that she wear her long coat.

'Aye, it's the breeze from the river now, ma'am,' said one of the passengers, 'best to keep wrapped up if you aren't accustomed to it.'

A couple chuntered something about "nesh southerners", but on the whole the banter was good-natured, and helped the journey pass more quickly and pleasantly.

They arrived at the Hawes Inn, not far from the pier, where the ferry was waiting to take people across the river to North

Queensferry. There was a scramble as passengers rushed to get off, so Alfred and Frances waited until the rush was over.

Frances misjudged the last step down, and as she fell rather awkwardly into Alfred's arms, she caught the hem of her coat, causing it to tear.

'Never mind, Fran. It will soon mend, I'm sure. Are you all right my dear, you aren't used to this kind of travelling, are you?'

She gave him a brave smile, and hobbled towards the door of the inn. The other passengers soon dispersed to their various destinations. A couple of the young clerks, with their highly polished shoes, made their way to the inn and lost no time in ordering drinks for themselves. Alfred and Frances were welcomed by the landlord, Dougal, and his kindly wife, Janet, who took their bags.

'Follow me sir, madam, watch your heads on the low ceiling, and the stairs are a wee bit narrow.'

Janet followed on behind.

'Take your time, ma'am,' Janet urged them. 'No need to rush here.'

'We don't want any more mishaps, do we?' added Alfred. Frances felt embarrassed as Alfred described her awkward moment alighting from the bus. Frances assured everyone that she was all right, just a little worried about her coat.

'Don't worry about that, ma'am. Let me help you off with the coat, let me see.'

Janet took the coat from Frances to examine the tear, at the same time admiring and stroking the beautiful soft cashmere.

Janet explained that there was a brilliant tailor in the village. Mr Alexander Weir. She announced his name as though he were some great dignitary.

'Mr Weir will have this as good as new in no time. Shall I take it for you?' she asked.

Frances looked to Alfred.

'Well, you can't wear it like that, can you my darling?' Frances agreed. So she entrusted her coat to Janet, and the brilliant Mr

Weir who, they were told, also made and repaired clothes for the officers on the navy ships.

'I'd like to wager that Mr Weir will have it back to you within the hour,' Janet assured them.

Frances was amazed. In London it would have taken many days to have such a job done.

After they had rested and had a small lunch in their room, the pair decided to explore the town and its river environment.

As Frances was deciding which shawl would be the warmest for a walk by the river, Alfred was examining the room.

'Isn't it fascinating Fran, to think we are here in the favourite room of Robert Louis Stevenson, surrounded by pictures of the great writer, and all the places he has visited?'

He was fascinated by its quaintness, and all of its obvious historic connections from centuries past. Frances was more interested in the heavy oak furniture, beautifully made, she thought, but dark. She examined the bed linen and was very impressed that it had all been hand sewn and embroidered. All scrupulously clean. So, the Hawes Inn had passed her test. She could relax.

'Come and look through the tiny window, Fran. See how the garden is full of straight rows of vegetables. What a colourful sight.' It was a practical use of the land, and it obviously meant the kitchen would never be short of food.

'I can't wait for dinner,' Alfred said with glee, 'Let's go for a gentle stroll around the place. Nothing too energetic.' Frances remarked that there were no flowers growing on the outside window boxes, just a few seedlings of tomato plants.

'I guess,' said Alfred, 'the winds will be harsh here for much of the time. They will have to make the best use of the good weather and the sunshine, to grow anything. There seems to be little of a frivolous nature. Everything has a purpose.'

Janet, the innkeeper's jolly wife, met the couple as they ventured out.

'A bit different to London isn't it, my dears?'

'It certainly is, Janet,' said Alfred, raising his hat to her as he would do in London. She was amused and a little flattered.

'That is why we are here,' he explained, 'to find out more about the place, the bridge, and the way people manage to live their lives here. Suddenly, it seems to us, that this tiny town, because of the bridge, has become the focus of the world's engineers as well as tourists, and business people.'

'Aye, we haven't stopped working since the bridge opened,' Janet told them, 'it will make a big difference to everyone here; let's hope it's for the good.'

That the shrewd Frederick Ingram thought the Forth Bridge worthy of inclusion in the *Illustrated London News* had excited and impressed Alfred. He was eager to start working on his sketches.

'I want to draw everything,' he told Frances, 'I'm going to start with the Inn, then the horse bus when it arrives from Edinburgh; the people and then the bridge and the river.' Frances didn't mind that Alfred would become absorbed in his drawings. She would observe things in her own way. She would probably discover more about the people than Alfred would. It would leave a lasting and unexpected impression on her memory.

Alfred wanted to capture everything he saw. His fingers were deft and accurate using the ink pen. He took things more slowly with the pencil. If his pictures were to be used in the *News* Alfred thought he should concentrate on the ink drawings.

They were persuaded to try a lunch of haggis, neeps and tatties. Frances enjoyed the vegetables, but was very unsure about the haggis, until she was assured that it was a favourite of Queen Victoria. Still, she preferred to see all of her food on the plate as individual portions, and not mixed up. You could not tell what it might contain. She decided to reserve her judgement publicly, for fear of offending the kindly Janet.

The Inn was quiet, almost deserted after lunch. The young clerks had disappeared to the loft offices at Port Edgar, the business end of town.

The beautifully repaired coat was returned within the hour, just as Janet had predicted. Alfred gathered up his drawing equipment and off they strode.

'Look, Fran, how very close to the bridge we are. It's enormous. I guess the trains will make quite a noise going across.'

They had yet to discover how the trains would disturb their sleep.

Alfred sketched away. Every angle of the bridge was covered. Close up drawings, then from a distance, Hawes Pier and its ferry terminus, and of course the different aspects and traffic on the river. Further along there were naval boats on the opposite side of the river. They found a working boat yard, rope makers and engineers' workshops. Closest to the quayside were the fishing boats, and the women working on the fish barrels, which fascinated Frances the most. The new smells from the soap factory and the whisky distillery took some getting used to.

Frances was amazed at the speed at which the women gutted and cleaned the fish. It was done with a sharp knife, in seconds.

'It has to be quick, missus,' one of the women told her, 'we're on piece work.' Frances had to ask Alfred what that meant.

'It means that they get paid for the number of barrels of fish they can fillet and salt in a day.'

'Aye sir, missus. We can process 6,000 barrels in one good season, but it's back-breaking work.'

Frances held her hands to her face, not because of the awful, strong smell, but at the shock she felt when she saw close up the red, raw-looking hands of the women. Of course, they would have to work in all weathers, which would account for their red, sometimes brown, weather worn faces, making young women look much older than their years. She was surprised to see a few of the women with very young children around them. This was surely no place for children to be playing. It was wet, slimy and dirty. One slip and it would be easy to tumble over the harbour wall and into the water.

Incredibly, just as Frances was having those thoughts there was a scream, as two small boys who had been chasing each other along the quayside and passed the fish women, slipped and fell into the river.

The women downed tools and ran to where the boys were in the water. Two men, obviously used to this dangerous occurrence, didn't offer to jump in, but fetched long poles.

'Grab the poles, you silly blighters!' shouted one of the men, 'Swim to the side. Grab hold and we'll pull you in.' Everyone assumed that the boys could swim, even though they could not have been more than five or six years old. The first boy managed the short swim to the edge and successfully grabbed the pole, and was pulled safely in. He had lost his shoes in the water so his mother hit him round the head, and dragged him away to dry off. The second boy, who was smaller, wasn't able to grab the pole. His hands were too small. He went under the water a few times, struggling to get his breath. He swallowed a great deal of water before one of the men did jump in to rescue him.

'He's unconscious,' the man said, 'someone run to the loft! Quick, see if there's a nurse there. We'll try to pump him out.' The men made great efforts to revive the boy, but to no avail. The boy was wrapped in someone's jacket, and carried to the loft offices, a short distance away.

'Find his mother,' one of the men said.

'She works in the soap factory,' said another. 'There's no father. He died on the bridge.'

The fish women watched the boy's body being carried away. They carried on working, in silence. There would be no singing today.

Frances and Alfred were horrified by their witnessing the incident, and by the very matter-of-fact way it was dealt with. They were both deeply distressed to learn that many of the fish women were widows. They had no alternative but to work. Their husbands, who had been full of hope and enthusiasm when

73

working on the bridge, had been claimed by it, one way or another. Some had fallen to their deaths through lack of safety measures, others fell through sheer carelessness, or bravado.

It was rumoured that some of the workers were suffering hangovers from too much ale the night before. Then there were those who fell during atrocious storms, their bodies swept away, never to be found. Others were overcome by toxic fumes from the lead paint.

Alfred and Frances were deeply distressed by the events of that afternoon. Their much longed for pleasant break, and the opportunity for Alfred to work at his sketching had been sorely blighted. It had, though, brought home vividly to them both the realities of living in such a place, together with the sometimes inevitable disasters which could happen on such giant engineering projects.

Alfred spent time talking with the men and Frances sympathised with some of the womenfolk on the quayside.

'It seems that this mighty bridge, this magnificent feat of engineering has brought both good and bad things to your town.' Alfred was talking to the police officer who had been brought to verify the facts of the boys' accident.

'Yes indeed it has, sir,' the policeman said. 'Many young women came here to dutifully join their husbands in what they thought would be a better life. Now, a lot of them are widows with small children. Once the bridge was finished some of the less keen men just disappeared, deserting their families.'

Alfred couldn't sleep that night. Frances, too upset to even eat or socialise, went to bed early, leaving Alfred talking long into the night with the Inn's landlord, and some of the locals, who regaled him with many more tales of the "briggers".

'Aye, the ones who stayed have had trouble finding work once the bridge was done, and some turned to drink,' the landlord explained.

'Some of the younger women, without children, have been

hoping to attract some of the men from the navy ships. You should see them on a Saturday night, getting themselves up in their flighty clothes and make-up.' The landlord obviously didn't approve.

'Thank goodness, the men prefer to frequent the bars on the other side if they can,' the landlord continued, 'I don't want any kind of trouble here. We want a quiet life now.'

Even the pretty Hawes Inn had suffered a change in fortune once Edward, Prince of Wales had officially opened the bridge, and driven home the last remaining rivet.

'Well landlord Dougal, thank you for your hospitality. It has been a dreadfully upsetting day, but the accident apart, I have found the history of this place fascinating, to say the very least. I hope we shall have a happier day tomorrow.'

Alfred took his leave and bade everyone good night.

The events of the day churned over and over in Alfred's brain, preventing him from sleep. By the time he drifted off it was time to get up again.

The next day Frances said she couldn't bear to be near the quayside where the little boy had been drowned, so they decided to hire a pony and trap, so that they could explore the villages around South Queensferry. Alfred wanted to find the stately home called Hopetoun House.

They could only view Hopetoun House from a distance. The iron gates to the long drive were firmly locked to visitors and sightseers. Alfred sketched the house. He thought the grandness of it sat incongruously beside the small fishing town by the Forth.

The display of wealth and position, beside the working poor, together with the present quite harsh, windy weather, had not gone unnoticed by Frances either.

She wondered if the "rich man in his castle" did welcome the "poor man at his gate". The words of the hymn embedded in her since childhood seemed appropriate on many levels. For the first time in her life Frances quietly questioned whether God really did order everyone's estate. Her father would have been shocked to think that his daughter questioned God at all.

They wandered around the back braes, surveying the workers cottages, which had been hurriedly constructed to cope with the influx of bridge workers and their families. After the bridge was finished some workers decided to stay in the town, and many had growing families. Living conditions became very cramped and the landlords were under considerable pressure to improve the sanitary arrangements. Still, Frances contemplated, at least the children were now able to go to school for part of the day. If they could learn to read and write well they would stand a much better chance of a better life, elsewhere.

As they walked by the village school they were both thinking of the boy who drowned. They felt sad as they watched the children in the playground. They appeared to be having a group photograph taken, and were dressed in what they assumed would be the children's Sunday clothes. But there would be one child missing from the photograph.

'Wait until Charles is off to school,' Alfred said. 'We need to get his name down soon.'

Frances felt a shiver down her spine. She hoped that Alfred wasn't thinking of sending Charles away to school. She hadn't thought about it until then. She had made a vow to herself that she wouldn't take a back seat any longer. She would become more involved in her son's education and his future.

Gently reared, and mostly insulated from the outside world, Frances did realise that the world was changing fast.

What had been considered suitable for her family, and people like them, would not be sufficient for Charles. He would need to learn about the wider world, where he would have to encounter people of every social class, religion and political persuasion. Frances truly hoped that her son would make a really valuable contribution to society. He would have to earn his living somehow.

In spite of the inheritance from Alfred's father, they would not be outstandingly wealthy. Comfortable, is how Alfred described it.

Their new found situation meant that they could each afford to spread their wings a little, and follow their personal interests and aspirations, in a way that was never thought feasible before.

Alfred fully intended to relinquish his dreary position at the *Gazette*. He felt that even more strongly after visiting this part of Scotland. Alice could be supported in her dream of training to become a teacher, and Frances would take her time to find challenging and interesting charitable things to do.

Chapter Five

There was a little time to spare before the London train, so Frances had her promised visit to Jenners. Alfred would have happily purchased anything that she desired, but she declined all suggestions. She showed Alfred the chosen shawl for Alice, a toy for Charles and a box of crystallised sweets for Mrs Cole. Pleased with the modest purchases they made their way to Waverley station.

The return journey seemed much quicker and less tedious. Alfred couldn't stop talking, and Frances reflected on everything they had seen. Alfred was glad that it had been a worthwhile visit for both of them, except of course the tragic event of the boy who accidentally drowned. Neither of them would ever forget that.

They examined the sketchbooks.

'It's really difficult to choose the best, isn't it?' Frances picked out her favourites.

'I wonder which ones Frederick will like, or indeed use. I suppose it will depend on the slant of opinion that *The News* will want to promote?'

Frances liked the pretty, picturesque views of the river, and the harbour ones were very fine. She thought the ones of the fisherwomen were very descriptive, but, weren't they a little rough to put in the paper?

Alfred laughed at her perception of the job in hand.

'Well, that's the whole point Fran. *The News* is renowned for showing real life, warts and all!' Frances raised her eyebrows and pursed her lips, rather like Miss Appleton used to do.

'Anyone who finds my drawings offensive, or the subjects uncouth, should stick with the *Gazette*. No pictures to worry about there, just boring columns of text, hardly big enough to read.'

Alfred had been wondering how to broach the subject of his father's will reading, and the house in Kensington. He had practised several ways of introducing the subject to Frances, none of which seemed appropriate, and it never quite seemed the right time. But now, he had her full attention, and she seemed to be in a much brighter state of mind. So, he seized the opportunity.

'How about it, Fran? It will be a wonderful opportunity for you, designing all the re-decoration, and the garden. We shall have electricity, and a telephone.'

Frances listened intently, but said nothing. She had thoughts of her own, but she would keep them to herself for now. Alfred interpreted her silence as disapproval, so he added a further enticement.

'We could employ a gardener handyman. He could make a safe place for little Charles to play. Would you like that?'

She gave a half smile before she nodded off to sleep. The bracing air of the Fife coast, and the long walks around the harbour had proved to be invigorating. Her cheeks had more colour than usual, and she had eaten very well, too. She wasn't really sleeping, just dozing and dreaming.

Alice was waiting for them at King's Cross. She beamed and ran towards them, hugging her sister.

'Hello, Alice,' Alfred gave her a kiss, 'How are you? How are things at home?'

'Everyone is fine, just fine. Ellice is great fun to be around, Charles loves her already, but I'm not sure Mrs Cole approves of her.'

'Oh dear,' said Alfred, 'I hope it won't be another situation like the one we had with Miss Appleton.'

Alice giggled irreverently.

'No, not at all. Ellice is wonderful with the baby, and I like her. She's just... well... a trifle unusual.'

'In what way, "unusual"?' Alfred was intrigued.

'Well, she's… er, a little bohemian.'

Frances was amused to think that a niece of the very proper Miss Bell could possibly be described as bohemian.

'Her clothes are just a bit quirky. Not terribly feminine. She wears a trilby hat, and rides a bicycle,' Alice gabbled.

'I can't wait to meet the lady,' Alfred laughed, 'and aren't we going to have fun deciding who is Alice and who is Ellice? How did she get a name like that?'

'Well, her parents and Aunt Bell were devotees of the Bronte sisters. They wanted to name her after Emily, but being a touch well-progressive in their thinking, they chose to use Emily's pen name, Ellis. That sounded too much like a man's name, which is why Emily chose it, of course. So they had to re-think the spelling. There. Simple, wasn't it?

Over the next few weeks and well into the autumn months the entire Richards household experienced a kind of sea-change in their lives.

Alfred joyfully left his position at the *Gazette*, and became a freelance artist for the *London Illustrated News*.

'Marvellous pictures,' Frederick Ingram had congratulated him. 'We want to see a lot more like those, vivid and true.'

'It's not like work,' he told Frederick, 'I'm in my element doing this.'

Alfred was much sought after to document important events: historical, sporting, political. He relished in the variety of work he was presented with. More often than not he was working with news reporters, with whom he shared ideas and suggestions. He felt a new lease of life and sense of energy and excitement, so much so that he had little time to oversee, or "interfere" as Frances put it, the work she had earnestly begun at the Kensington house.

'I think you have a great sense of liberation don't you Fran? The old sparkle and spirit is re-awakening isn't it?'

Alice was pleased. They could all relax more. Frances seemed amused that her younger sister was speaking to her as though she was the eldest, more like her mother.

'You still need to be careful, not to become too over tired.' Alfred had given Frances a free hand with the house, which had looked much the same for the past two generations. Alice thought it was an enormous task, but Frances had set about it with a great sense of order and method. She had gone through every room with her notebook, writing down everything which she thought needed replacing, and, skilled as an artist herself, she even drew little sketches of how she envisaged the place to look, once it was all finished.

She kept the notebook from Alfred, on purpose, but she allowed Alice to have a peek at some of it.

'What will you do with the library? I don't see anything about that yet?'

Frances had a glint in her eye, and touched her lips, as if to say 'It's a secret for now!' Alice was intrigued.

On the rare occasions that Alfred found himself free to visit the house, to see how things were progressing, Frances ushered him to the garden first. If he said he was short of time, she would engineer things so that he had little time to see what she was doing to the house.

'Yes,' he observed, 'it has all become overgrown. It's hard to distinguish one shrub from another, and the hedging has grown out of all control. We'll get the gardener here in the autumn, not long now, when things will die back naturally. By next spring it will all be in much better shape.'

Alice joined in, 'By then Charles will be walking. It will be lovely for him to have a safe place to play won't it?'

Frances agreed. She was able to look ahead now, and think of others, not just herself. She was glad that Alice had a friend in the new nanny.

Miss Appleton had been difficult to befriend, but now, they all realised that her problems had been insurmountable. It left them feeling guilty that they had not noticed from the start. It was a relief that the poor woman was now receiving the care she so badly needed.

It was fortunate that Ellice Bell was nearer in age to Alice and they shared many common interests. They were both avid readers, though Alice preferred the classic novels of Jane Austen and the Brontes and Dickens. Ellice was well read in the classics, but now her entire reading was concentrated on politics and social conditions, especially women's issues. Their binding interest was music. They both loved to sing. Alice sang in church as she had since childhood. Ellice never ventured to church, but they both sang in a choral society where, much to Alice's amusement, Ellice would gladly sing Handel's *Messiah*, with great gusto, like her Aunt Bell.

'Well,' she would pronounce, as justification, 'Handel surely wrote the best choir tunes.'

Frances regarded Ellice as a kind of unofficial chaperone, a role now rapidly going out of fashion. Ellice would not thank Frances for regarding her as such. Nevertheless, it was re-assuring to the family to know that Alice didn't have to venture out on her own, especially at night. Alfred had warmed towards Ellice, but had many reservations about her political activities, and he didn't care for the way she called Alice "Al".

Frances wasn't the only one with secret plans. Alice had plans too, but since she was not yet twenty-one she had to rely on Alfred's approval and support. First she tackled him about the house.

'Alfred,' Alice pleaded, when she finally managed to get him on his own, 'I really want to stay here at Highgate when you move to

Kensington. This has always been my home. Ellice could live here with me, if you didn't mind?' She posed this as a question.

'Well, shall we discuss it with Frances?'

Alice was a touch apprehensive. 'Suppose Fran needs me at the other house? I'll never have a life of my own. It's not that I don't love you all dearly, but you must see that I need to forge my own path now?'

He grinned. It wasn't exactly how he had imagined life to develop for Alice. He still regarded her as a child, under his care.

'I don't think you would have been asking me this a few months ago. I recognise your new friend's influence here. Am I right?'

'It's my own idea, Alfred. Ellice just happened to be here and we get on so well together. It seems a sensible solution for both of us. Don't you agree?'

'And what happens if you marry, either of you?'

'Huh,' Alice laughed, 'Ellice says she's never going to marry. She doesn't want to do the bidding of a husband. Besides, she wants to be the first woman in Parliament.'

'And what of you, dear sister?'

'If I do marry, it will be a very long time ahead, Alfred. I'm going to be a teacher. I've decided. I can't think of anything better than to help children be the best they can be.'

Alfred was suddenly immensely proud and surprised that she had planned so far ahead. Little Alice, wanting to be an independent young woman now decided things for herself. After much questioning and wrangling, but mostly good natured banter, Alfred and Frances agreed that Alice and her friend could live in the house together, but only if they agreed to offer Lily Cole the job of housekeeper, to look after them. Mrs Cole would move to the new house when the time was right.

It was mutually agreed that Ellice would be Charles' nanny for five days and Mrs Cole would help out at the weekends. Frances was determined she would manage the baby through the night now that she was well. After all, she said, many women had no option but to do just that. She realised how lucky she was.

Alfred realised there was no holding Alice now. He gave her a brotherly hug, wished her well, and promised his support.

'I'm glad you aren't going to be a nurse,' he quipped.

'There's nothing wrong with being a nurse, Alfred. It's a very honourable profession.'

'Yes, I know that, of course it is. I'm just glad you have chosen something that you will enjoy. You'll be able to use your music and all the other things you are so good at. I hope one day you will teach Charles to sing and play the piano.'

Frances nodded her agreement to that.

'I can't wait for him to be old enough,' enthused Alice.

CHAPTER SIX

Life became more settled. Ellice Bell rode her bicycle every morning through busy London streets, to her new charge. She became very adept at finding quieter roads, and avoiding the carriage horses. She would park her bicycle behind the house out of sight and then change into her white apron, ready for work. Slightly eccentric and bohemian she might be, but she was a positive and very hard working young woman, with a mature outlook and many aspirations. She was like a breath of fresh air in the Richards' house. Ellice's character had been largely shaped by her politically motivated father, who had taken her along to socialist party meetings since she was a very young child. He thought nothing of it. Ellice had listened and absorbed much.

Alice, by stark contrast, had been educated at a church school, along with mostly middle class children who had the benefit of tutors in art and music, with a smattering of foreign languages too.

Alice was fascinated with her new friend.

'Won't you find being a private nanny very mundane after your work in the hospital?' Alice asked her.

'No, not a bit. It will be absolute bliss. Much less tiring. It isn't that I disliked nursing. St. Thomas's is a wonderful place. It's simply that I have other ambitions. Whilst I'm trying to study this job will be less stressful, and I'll be able to study in the evenings. Besides, Mr and Mrs Richards will only need me until Charles goes to school, and by that time I will know my future more clearly.'

Some people felt a little intimidated by Ellice. She was very outspoken, and cared little for social convention. Alice was excited by her, and felt encouraged. She felt a sense of urgency about her own life.

'You know such a lot Ellice. How come you are so informed about the world? I wish I was,' Alice confessed to her friend.

'Come on, Al, don't be silly. You know a lot about creative things, music, art, literature. I'm just a beginner at that sort of thing.'

'But you know about people, government and important things like caring for the poor and needy.'

'If you're going to be a teacher, Al, you will soon encounter more than you could have imagined, believe me.'

Alice felt inspired by Ellice, and determined that she would learn more about social issues. Frances cautioned her to tread very carefully in social matters, and not get too enthused by her friend's political leanings. Alice was fully aware that Frances and Alfred might disapprove of that side of Ellice.

'We read the newspapers,' Alfred said, 'we know about the women's movement in Europe and America. Do you know that in Australia they now have their first woman in Parliament?'

Alice wondered how long it might be before Britain had a woman in Parliament, but she didn't voice her thoughts just then. She was quite certain that if Ellice had anything to do with it, there would be women in Parliament right away. It isn't just about social care,' Ellice told Alice, 'it's also about women being equal citizens in every way.'

'I must admit to a feeling of trepidation about teacher training,' Alice revealed, 'I know that most of the other student teachers will be men.'

'Don't worry, Al. You would not have been accepted if the board hadn't recognised your qualities, believe me. You will bring something to the job which most men will be quite unable to do!'

Alice laughed. 'You don't like men much, do you, Ellice?'

'I don't think about them in that way,' she said.

Alice began her training. The institute had allocated her to a council board school, where she would be responsible for a class of forty children, aged between six and ten years. She would, from time to time, be monitored by visiting tutors, who would oversee her progress. At the same time she would have to report to the school's headmaster each week, for his assessment. It was very daunting.

Teaching was exhausting. Rising early took its toll on Alice, at first, and she had not reckoned with spending most of her working day on her feet. If she wasn't writing on the blackboard, she was walking the rows of desks, or conducting the children to recite their times tables aloud, and in noisy unison. Many didn't know their numbers and deliberately upset the flow of the task. It tried Alice's patience in the extreme.

'I don't know how to keep them quiet enough to teach anything,' she complained to Ellice, 'I don't think I'll ever be a good teacher.'

'Nonsense Al,' her friend said in a curt, school-ma'am-ish kind of voice, 'you are going to be a fantastic teacher one day. It's early days yet, you'll see. It's all a question of organisation, and letting the little blighters know who is boss.'

Alice bemoaned the fact that the visiting tutors, when they did appear, simply sat at the back of the room writing. They offered no help or suggestions.

'They just expect you to do it.'

'Sounds just like nurse training. Students are always thrown in at the deep end. It's "Nurse, go here, do this, empty that". You certainly learn by your mistakes. I learned early on about self-preservation. You had to find the quickest way to get a job done, then get it right the first time.'

'I will give more thought to my organisation, and I'll try to be more positive. Thanks Ell. You are a great leveller when I'm feeling down.'

'That's what friends are for.'

Alice persevered. With encouragement from Alfred and Frances, and forthright words from Ellice, she managed to develop a greater self-confidence, resourcefulness and patience. She grew to realise that she was the only teacher in the school who was responsible for such a large group of children. She felt a great sense of unfairness but was unable to do anything about the situation. She fraternised little with the rest of the staff, other than saying 'Good morning' as they arrived at school. The staff were mainly elderly gentlemen. There was one widowed lady, and a seemingly shy young man called Edward, a second year trainee, like herself. She was determined to speak with Edward at the first opportunity, when they were unlikely to be overheard.

She had expected teaching to be like her Sunday school class, where she taught bright, clean and biddable children. Some in her school class were from very poor homes, and they could not help that, of course, she told Alfred.

'But, Alfred, they often come to school bleary-eyed and hungry. Some fall asleep at their desks, and their clothes smell awful. Some don't even have proper shoes on their feet. The smell is awful, Alfred, it makes me retch.'

Alice developed a plan of action. No wonder the children couldn't learn, if they were hungry and tired. She persuaded Mrs Cole to bake a large batch of gingerbread biscuits for Monday mornings. She gave the biscuits to the children with the cleanest hands.

'Needless to say,' she told Ellice, 'there has been a furious bout of hand-washing, even face washing on Mondays.'

At least the week started well, with clean, shiny faces and hands, and a better working attitude all round. She could do nothing about the state of the children's clothes, but she would give it some thought. Window monitors were chosen, and on all but the coldest days the windows were opened to "refresh" the room.

As the year progressed, Alice came to realise that the tutors and the headmaster were not going to help her at all. So, determined to succeed, she set about dividing her very large class into smaller groups. She devised ways of hearing reading whilst other children were writing. Rotating the activities worked much better than having them all engaged in the same thing at once. That way she had a better chance of seeing who had progressed. Her sense of frustration lessened somewhat, but she decided in one of her less happy moments to pluck up the courage to voice her concerns with Edward, her young male colleague.

'We all have the same problems,' he admitted, 'we just have try to survive the daily grind of teaching them to read.' He sounded very bored, and clearly had no suggestions of his own.

'Do you know anything about the children's backgrounds?' Alice asked.

'Good Lord, no. I imagine most of them live in the courts across the way. I wouldn't go walking there by yourself,' he warned, 'the smell is indescribable, and you have to watch out for dogs running wild, and pickpockets.'

Alice told him about the children who fell asleep in her class each morning.

'Ah, they'll be the ones who work before school, selling papers and matches. Some of them hold horses for the toffs. At night they earn pennies sweeping up in the workshops and the market, or they run errands fetching jugs of beer. The smart ones work in the tailors' shops, unpicking, tacking seams, pressing.'

'Smart ones?' she queried.

'Yes, at least they are indoors, warmer in the winter, and they are unofficially learning a trade while they work for the bosses.'

Edward had actually observed a great deal about his pupils but he appeared unsympathetic to their plight, and not a little jaded himself.

'I just try to get through each day without any major mishaps, and I relish my evenings and weekends.'

'What about the lesson planning?' she asked him.

Edward laughed. The first time she had seen him smile.

'I used to do that, but I've done it for a year now. I keep a written record, and then repeat everything. It will get easier.' Edward thought that in order to stay sane it was important to have something to look forward to in your spare time.

Alice agreed, and at last, having managed to get Edward talking, she seized her chance, as Ellice had encouraged her to do, to ask what he did in his spare time. Miraculously, Edward's demeanour became much more pleasant and light-hearted.

'I sing, act, dance. I'm in a musical society,' he enthused.

'How wonderful!' Alice was thrilled to hear about it.

'I've always got some concert or play to be looking forward to. You might like to come sometime?' Without waiting to hear her response, he went on to tell her about the long summer holidays, not so far away now.

'In July I take off to France, with my bicycle. I pick fruit for some money, and then enjoy myself until September.'

Alice was surprised by Edward's revelations about himself. To look at this serious young teacher, dressed in his formal day clothes, unhappy in his work, no one would suspect that he had a very enjoyable time elsewhere.

'If you dislike teaching children, Edward, why did you enrol to begin with?' Alice asked him.

'It was my mother's idea. It was either that, or work in a bank, and that would have been too tedious.'

Having struck up a polite friendship with Edward, Alice discovered that she was quite good at getting him to talk. The other teachers might as well have been invisible. No one talked to either of the young teachers. The only time they encountered the headmaster was in moments of crisis, such as flooded toilets or classrooms.

Alice developed her own strategies for getting through the days without too many mishaps, and as the first year came to an end she had warmed to some of the children in her care. Their reading and number ability had improved, as did their interest in learning. Her kind, but firm attitude had borne fruit.

Edward and Alice found themselves responsible for most of the arrangements for the end of year prize-giving day, designed largely to please the governor and the few parents who managed to attend.

The leavers, usually aged twelve or thirteen, would be presented with a small red book, beautifully inscribed with their names, and a list of subjects which they had studied to the required level. Each class would receive a special prize for arithmetic, and another for reading. During the ceremony the pupils who were chosen to recite a poem, or sing a solo, would be presented with a volume of Dickens, chosen by the headmaster.

'These books are far too difficult for them,' Edward remarked.

'Perhaps,' said Alice, 'but they are wonderful books, and maybe they will inspire the pupils who receive them to work hard at their reading so that one day they will be able to appreciate them.'

Edward was responsible for marshalling the pupils into the main hall and into their rows, while Alice played Schubert's *Soldier's March*. They all sang the national anthem, followed by the youngest pupils' rendition of *All Things Bright And Beautiful*, and just for once Alice thought they all had tried to look bright and beautiful. Then it was the turn of the older pupils, who tried hard, but there were a few painful moments, when boys with breaking voices tried their hardest with *To Be a Pilgrim*. Alice was quite sure that in spite of the great gusto, and the rousing tune, the children understood few of the words. The prize-winners were allowed to march out before the other pupils and guests. Alice played *Land of Hope and Glory* to bring the ceremony to a close.

'Well done, Miss Combe, and you Mr Gardner, a very satisfactory afternoon,' boomed the headmaster, who gave Alice a glowing testimonial at the end of her first year.

'I feel more optimistic now, Edward,' she confided in her new friend and colleague. Alice, though exhilarated with her success that afternoon, felt really disappointed that it would be six more weeks before she would see Edward again. She needed the break though, and was looking forward to spending time with her young nephew, and helping Frances in the new house.

Edward Gardner was coming out of his reclusive shell too.

'Well done, Alice. You are fantastic with the children, and a very fine musician. I hope you will come to one of our concerts, after the summer. I shall miss you,' he said, shaking her hand, gently.

Alice thanked him, and said she would love to be at one of his concerts. Suddenly, it was she who blushed, and found herself searching for the right words as he held her hand just a moment too long for the handshake to be purely business-like.

'I shall miss you too, Edward.'

They went their separate ways, for now. Edward, lighter of step and in his demeanour, even stopping to converse with the headmaster.

Alice lingered a little longer at her desk, mulling over all the events of the past year or two. She had become an aunt, a godmother, had lost her temper with Miss Appleton, comforted and cared for Frances, and re-kindled a new friend in Ellice Bell. Perhaps another friend in Edward Gardner. Alice was still trying to decide whether the brief conversations which she and Edward had shared, as well as the gentle handshake, could constitute the start of a real, proper friendship, or whether he was just being polite. She would be filled with hopeful anticipation until September.

CHAPTER SEVEN

Edward Gardner wasn't the only person enjoying France that summer. Alfred was intrigued by Peter Lawrence's telephone message, and his urgent request that Alfred check whether his passport was up to date.

'Can you be ready to meet me at St. Pancras on Friday?'

'Yes, Peter, but what is so urgent?'

'I'll explain on Friday. We'll just need the weekend, tell Frances. Or, better still, don't tell her it's France, not yet, anyway. Say you are on another assignment. It's the truth in a way.'

'Very well, Peter. I hope this isn't a wild goose chase?' Alfred had to trust Peter Lawrence, although sometimes he wondered whether his lawyer really was fully competent, or whether he just chose to give people the impression that he was very laid back, and casual in his dealings.

Frances never questioned Alfred about anything he was doing, especially for his paper. There were times when he was suddenly called to go to some event, or a sudden catastrophe. She was used to him packing his sketchbooks and writing things, even an overnight bag.

Alfred was like a cat on hot bricks for the next few days, he couldn't imagine why he had to keep the visit to France secret.

He was relieved that things were working out well for Alice, now happily living at Highgate with Ellice, and Lily Cole as their housekeeper. Ellice, forthright and pragmatic, was proving to be an excellent nanny, nursemaid, whatever they liked to call her. She didn't care really about titles. She was there to do a job, and she would do it to the best of her ability. She was good for Charles. She made him laugh. She taught him to walk, to sing nursery rhymes, and to throw a ball and catch it again. In time she would teach him how to speak. Frances and Ellice would work together on that.

Whatever reservations Frances might have had about Ellice, she grew to value her because she was very good with Charles, and besides, Ellice spoke well. If Frances was happy, then he was too.

In time he felt sure that he would be able to accept more commissions to faraway places.

Happy that all was well at home, Alfred set off to meet Peter Lawrence that Friday morning. The trains were crowded with passengers, and it was impossible for them to have a quiet conversation until they were safely in their private cabin on the cross channel boat.

'Now, Peter, what is this all about? I must be mad to follow you on this journey where I know I shall be sick. It had better be worthwhile. Where are we off to, a naughty night in Monte Carlo?'

Peter Lawrence laughed.

'I'm surprised you even know where Monte Carlo is, Alfred. How do you know about that?'

'I don't know about it. I must have heard my father mention it on one of his trips abroad, ages ago.'

Peter Lawrence looked him straight in the face, looking quite serious.

'Can you remember when he might have talked about being in Monte Carlo?'

'Good grief, Peter, I haven't a clue. It must have been years ago. I didn't know about any of his postings in the past ten, twelve years or more. We had very little to do with each other after I left school and went to work at the *Gazette*.'

'All right, Alfred. Listen. What I discovered going through your father's strong boxes might give you a bit of a surprise. For now I must urge you to keep it to yourself. Don't let on to Frances or Alice, until I've finally sorted things out. Things may not be as difficult as I anticipate. That's why I need you with me on this. I don't think I can handle matters by myself.'

Peter Lawrence spoke in hushed tones, although there was no one else to hear what he had to say.

'It would seem that Captain Richards, your father, had a small, remote cottage on a hillside near Grasse. The lease is in your father's name, and has been for the past ten years. The lease expires in six months' time, and everything has been paid until then.'

'Grasse, where is that? Why didn't we know anything about it?' Alfred was completely shocked that his father should have had secret property abroad, and why was it in France, a cottage half way up a hill? Perhaps there was a hidden mistress. Surely not? Alfred could not imagine such a thing. There must be some plausible explanation.

'I might have had the information sooner,' continued Peter Lawrence, 'but the bank have been very slow to release all the papers to do with the captain's estate. The Kensington house is all sorted now, and you and Frances are the rightful owners under the terms of the will. All the bequests and monetary issues have been dealt with. It's just that after I had concluded the financial affairs with the bank, I was told that there was a separate box, held in the vaults, but there was no key. Personal effects, I understand. The reason for confusion and delay is that the new bank manager did not know that your father had left the box separately under the name of Alfred Richards. That's you, old chap!'

'So how did you find the right key then, Peter?'

'Well, there's the puzzle. I'm afraid I had the key all the time, but I didn't know it. Your father left a bunch of keys to my safe-keeping, until he died, and I would then have access to his safe box. I'm afraid he never let on that there was a second box, and I assumed that the key was, along with the others, for the Kensington house. Well, I just assumed it was for something there.

'But why,' said Alfred, 'wasn't there a label on the key? I thought they were all labelled. My set of keys has labels on.'

Peter Lawrence showed Alfred the key.

'Did you have a key that looked like this one?'

'No, I told you, all my keys were clearly labelled.'

'Well, it's certainly a bit of a mystery.'

Peter Lawrence explained that the new manager at the bank had been able to verify signatures, and realised that the second box did indeed belong to the captain, so the search had begun for a key to open it.

'Well, Peter, are you going to stop pussy-footing around, and tell me what you found in the box?'

Peter Lawrence handed Alfred a sturdy brown envelope, tied with string. He took out the two papers which were inside the envelope, and yet another key ring with two keys attached.

'It's a photograph of the cottage, and an address. Look, there's another sheet of paper. What on earth does this mean?'

'Plums ripe in orchard 3.' Peter Lawrence scratched his head, and Alfred was completely baffled by everything, 'I have absolutely no idea what this can mean, Alfred. That is why I had to have you travel with me. We need to find out. What did you tell Frances?'

'I explained that I had to go to France on business, with you, and it might take a few days.'

'Good. I suspect this might take more than a few days.'

Alfred was sick on the overnight crossing to Calais. He had hardly slept. So, by the time the boat docked he was feeling tired, hungry and worried about what they were going to find at the other end of their journey. Peter Lawrence seemed much less worried than Alfred. He had been organised enough to book their return boat and train fares, and he seemed to know exactly where they were going.

He hadn't realised that Peter Lawrence was such a seasoned traveller, or perhaps, since he was a highly thought of Gresham Street lawyer, he had done all of his preparations, well in advance, leaving nothing to chance.

The Paris train hurtled through the French countryside, much faster than the trains from London to Edinburgh, as Alfred recalled. He relaxed once he felt safe and very comfortable. He was soon fast asleep, having hardly slept on the overnight sea crossing. Peter Lawrence didn't wake him. He was content, for now, that Alfred was not awake and asking more questions.

They reached Lyon, where the train stopped for much longer than it should have. Supplies were placed on board, but still the train was kept waiting. Alfred roused from his sleep.

'Where are we?' he asked

'We're at Lyon, more than half way to Marseille by now, I guess.' Alfred tried to sleep again, but they were both surprised when their compartment door opened and they were addressed by a gendarme and another man, whom Alfred assumed was a railway official.

'Passports and papers please, gentlemen.'

They both handed over their documents, assuming that this was a normal procedure.

'What is your destination?' asked the gendarme.

'We are travelling to Marseille, and then on to Grasse,' Peter Lawrence explained. 'Is the train delayed? We need to be there in daylight.'

There was no answer to his question. Just another question.

'What is your business in Grasse?'

'A few days' holiday,' Peter Lawrence was quick to answer.

The official closed their documents and gave them back to both of them.

'Don't forget to buy perfume for your wife,' the gendarme said. 'Especially if you intend finding your way to the casinos.'

Alfred Richards smiled his response. Peter Lawrence appeared to breathe a sigh of relief, when the two men left their compartment and the train set off again, towards Marseille.

Much to their annoyance, the train was late arriving into Marseille, and by then it was dusk. They had missed the connection into Grasse, and the last local bus of the day. They would have to stay in Marseille overnight. A moderate small hotel was found, not too far from the station.

'Sorry, Alfred, old chap. But at least we won't have far to walk in the morning, and we will have rested.'

The two men left their luggage in the hotel, and decided to stretch their legs with a walk into town in search of a decent cafe. Alfred realised that they were not in the most salubrious part of the town. It wasn't long before they were approached by more than one "lady of the night", offering their services. Peter Lawrence pushed them away.

'No, thank you. We are here on business,' he told them. Alfred was shocked. He knew that prostitution existed in most cities of the world, but he had never actually been approached directly, even in London. Obviously, the French didn't care.

'We show you very good business,' one of the women yelled.

She ran her hands over Peter Lawrence's hair, and down his shoulders.

'No. Go away,' he insisted, and pulled her hands away.

He turned to Alfred, 'Don't be shocked. It's quite usual here. This is a busy port city. They're mostly here for the sailors who come off the ships. It's a hotbed of wild women, smugglers and all kinds of exiles or fugitives from all over Europe. Dubious characters can find a cushy hiding place here, at a price, to do whatever business they find profitable.'

Alfred was quite bemused. His face was a picture of incredulity.

'I'm glad Frances can't see this place,' he said.

'You're certainly having your eyes opened, eh, Alfred?'

They avoided the many bars and other houses of ill-repute, and found themselves in a small, family cafe enjoying a huge bowl of fish soup and bread.

Alfred was glad to leave Marseille and board the smaller, local train, which took them almost to Grasse, the hillside village where his father had, apparently, had a small cottage for several years, without the family having any knowledge of it.

'What kind of place is this?' he asked.

'It's a medieval town, with a beautiful twelfth century cathedral. I believe there are a number of historic houses, and museums. They have Fragonard and Rubens' paintings here. We must try to see them.'

Alfred's eyes lit up with excitement.

'I'd really love to see those paintings, and the cathedral,' he said, suddenly much more interested, and not minding the long walk from the train.

'There's the hillside, Alfred. Now we have a choice between a steady uphill trek on foot, carrying our bags, or if you prefer, we can try and find a bicycle to hire, or a man with a cart and horse.'

'I can't ride a bicycle!'

'Then a man with a cart it will have to be.'

'How do you know we can find one?' Alfred wanted to know.

'Well, there are several cottages on this side, and most of them have a small orchard, or olive grove. They must sell their produce, and get their own supplies somehow.'

Alfred was agog that once again, Peter Lawrence, a stuffy, London lawyer, should have such knowledge of French hillside farmers.

He left Alfred sitting on a low, stone wall, looking after their bags, while he went to investigate their likelihood of finding transport of one kind or another, up the hillside.

He found what appeared to be a general store-cum-post office-cum-bicycle shop. The windows were boarded up, but the front door was open. Alfred saw him go into the store, and re-appear a few minutes later with a young, dark-haired man, of about twenty years of age. He took off his grocer's apron, and indicated to Peter to follow him to the back of the store. He beckoned Alfred, who was left to pick up all the bags, and stagger towards them.

The dark young man from the store brought his cart and pony to the front of the building, and loaded the luggage for Alfred. It was a steady, careful climb up the narrow path. There was a turning point about fifty yards from the white painted cottage. The driver of the cart said that he couldn't take them right to the door. They would have to walk the last bit up to the house. Peter Lawrence mumbled something in French to the young man. Alfred had no command of the language, so he wasn't able to understand what had been said.

'I've arranged for him to come and collect us again tomorrow, just before lunch.' They waved the young man off to his business.

'Come, Alfred, let's go and explore your father's mysterious home from home.'

They reached the cottage and Peter Lawrence fumbled in his wallet to find the front door key, the largest, ornate key on the key ring.

'Let's just walk round the cottage first,' said Alfred, 'before it's dark. I would like to see the whole way round if we can.'

They left their bags by the doorstep and had a slow walk to the back of the place.

'There's an orchard. I thought so, Peter. Look, there's apples and some plums, and the grass has been cut.' Alfred was perplexed. The front of the cottage was, by comparison, rather rough looking, because it was on a slight slope downwards, a rocky, uneven mass of wild grasses and lavender dotted here and there. The smell of the lavender was quite strong, and made up for the rather desolate looking, rocky incline up to the cottage.

They reached the door, and as Peter Lawrence tried to turn the key he realised that the door was already unlocked. They knocked on the door before opening it fully. The smell of freshly brewed coffee wafted towards them as they stepped inside.

'Hello. Is anybody there?'

'Hello. Alfred Richards here.'

'*Entrez*, Monsieur Richards. Come. Come.'

A tiny, elderly man shuffled towards them. He walked with difficulty with an uneven gain, wincing now and then because of his arthritic hips. His hands too were badly affected, and gnarled.

He ushered Alfred and Peter Lawrence into the kitchen and invited them to sit at the table and take coffee with him.

'My name is Emile. I look after Monsieur George when he is here for his vacations. It is strange to see you here, monsieur. You must be the son of Monsieur George?'

'Yes, I am Alfred Richards, and this is my friend and lawyer, Peter Lawrence.'

Emile apologised for not getting up to shake hands. Peter Lawrence stood himself, and leaned across the large table to shake Emile by the hand, gently, regarding his pained joints.

'Emile,' Peter Lawrence asked him, 'has anyone been to tell you anything about Monsieur Richards?'

'*Non*.' He shook his head, 'Sometimes Monsieur Richards is away for many months. When he is expecting to arrive he sends Jean-Paul up with his cart and some food supplies. I think something is wrong that he has not been for some time, and here you are instead, looking for him.' The old man looked worried.

'Emile. Forgive me,' Alfred spoke softly to the old man. He had obviously been looking after his father for many years, and had regard for him. 'We have come to see to my father's possessions. I am sad to tell you that he has passed away in England. He suffered pneumonia and didn't respond to any medical treatment. He went very quickly.'

'I knew something had happened to him. I am sorry to hear that sad news. I will have to move out of this place.'

Emile spoke with resignation. He knew it would come one day, but he had thought to be the one to die first.

Peter Lawrence told Emile that the lease was all paid up until the end of the year.

'You are most welcome to stay here until the lease expires,' Alfred offered. 'Would you be able to renew the lease for yourself?'

'*Non*, monsieur, but thank you. It is time now. I will stay here until the lease is done. Then I will live with Jean-Paul, if he will have me. Do not worry about me. I will have the place cleaned up before I go.'

'Have you lived here a long time?' Alfred asked the old man.

'I have been here for over twenty years, before Monsieur Richards' time. I could tell you stories about this place, but my memory is not so good to remember everything. Before Monsieur Richards there were young men, a group of artists. They would come and go with their equipment, paints, easels, canvas, but I do not remember seeing them paint anything. They would sit in the olive trees, smoking, drinking and laughing. Sometimes they would have visitors who were not artists, smarter dressed. I would have to make supper for them.'

Alfred was intrigued to hear more, but Peter Lawrence was keen to examine the house, and particularly George Richards' private rooms.

'Did my father have many visitors? Who were they?' he asked. Peter Lawrence interrupted him.

'Can't you see Emile is tired, Alfred. He's had a shock, hearing about your father. Why not wait until after we've eaten. Then perhaps we can all sit among the olive trees, and enjoy the lavender?'

'Yes, of course,' Alfred agreed, 'let's do that later. Shall we look round the house? It will be very strange to be looking through my father's possessions again, after having to do it all in London.'

They were shown to the rooms of Alfred's father then Emile left them alone.

'How very Spartan,' Peter Lawrence remarked, 'though I didn't expect it to be terribly grand. A plain bed, a table and chest of drawers, and heavy brown curtains to keep out the strong sunlight.'

'Look here, Peter. There's a small dressing room with a single wardrobe and chair and a very small writing desk. That's all.'

Alfred opened the wardrobe expecting to find a naval uniform and some more casual clothes hanging there, but except for a worn leather jacket and a heavy wool sweater, there was nothing. There were walking boots, together with a walking stick and a leather hat hanging in an alcove, but no other clothes at all.

'How very strange,' Alfred said, 'it's all rather spooky. Don't you think, Peter?'

'Well, I guess the captain would leave his formal clothes on his ship, and come up here for relaxation, and to smell the lavender.' Alfred shrugged his shoulders, appearing to dismiss the matter, but he felt sure that Peter Lawrence knew a good deal more than he was letting on. Alfred was now so curious he was determined to find answers for himself. Sooner or later Peter Lawrence would do something, or say something which would reveal more about the true situation of his father's occupation of this idyllic place in France, which he had kept secret for years. He was curious to speak more with Emile, if he could get him by himself. Alfred was certain that he could shed more light on the situation.

Peter Lawrence had been busy whilst Alfred was exploring the bedroom and dressing room. He had gone straight to the locked desk and opened it with the smaller of the two keys that he had on the key ring, given to him by the bank manager in London. He invited Alfred to take out the envelope and package from the drawer.

'It's addressed to you.'

'It's in father's handwriting, to be opened after my death, it says.' Alfred was taken aback. He opened the brown envelope very carefully. It looked the same as the envelope he had received from the bank and it was tied with the same kind of string. Inside there was simply a short note asking Alfred to take the package home, to his mother Rose Maud. It was a "very special gift". A second piece of paper, much thicker, was a receipt in respect of a personal mail box, held at the post office in the village. Perhaps there might be mail to collect.

'Father must have placed this here a very long time ago, before mother died. Shall I open the package, Peter?'

'Well, yes, of course.'

Alfred removed the outer packaging to reveal an exquisitely wrapped box of very expensive perfume.

'Frances will love that, won't she, Alfred?'

Peter Lawrence explained that the town of Grasse and the surrounding area had a world famous reputation for producing the most sought after perfumes in the world.

'Yes, film stars, rich Middle Eastern ladies, and people who spend a fortune at the casinos along the coast at Monte Carlo all buy perfume from here. Maud would have been thrilled to receive such a gift.'

'That's very true, Peter, but would she have been so thrilled to discover that Father had a secret hideaway, and especially here?'

Peter Lawrence didn't answer him, and quickly changed the subject, taking the envelope from Alfred, he gave the paper another careful look.

'We'd better check whether your father has any mail lying there in the post office, hadn't we? We'll do that tomorrow, shall we?'

'Yes, we should, but who would be writing to him here?'

Again there was no answer or even casual conjecture from Peter Lawrence. Alfred decided that he would keep his own counsel from then on. He was determined to find out the circumstances of his father's reasons for being at the cottage in Grasse.

Emile had managed to find some cold ham, bread and cheese for their supper, which they took outside to eat by the olive grove.

'It's only cheap wine, monsieurs. If you plan to stay a few more days I will have Jean-Paul bring some better stuff.' Alfred laughed, and warmed to this kindly old man. He felt sure that Mrs Cole would have liked him too.

Emile had found two spare beds of a sort, for Alfred and Peter Lawrence. Alfred was so tired and had drunk rather too much of

Emile's cheap wine to bother about what sort of bed he had to sleep on. He awoke with a blinding headache, and resolved not to have any more wine. His companion didn't seem to be affected by the wine at all. Perhaps, thought Alfred, he was more used to it.

The breakfast Emile had prepared for the two of them was not eaten by Alfred. He couldn't face it. Instead he got up and dressed and went out for a walk by himself to look at the olive grove again, and the surrounding orchards of the neighbours. The air was cool, but it was what he needed to clear his head. Jean-Paul would be back within the hour to take them down the hill again.

Through the olive trees Alfred saw three men. They were sitting on the grass in the neighbouring orchard, eating their rolls, but he was sure that they kept looking in his direction. Alfred didn't know why, but he felt a little uneasy, and certainly didn't try to wave, or beckon them over to join him. If he was French he surely would have done so, but not he, a reticent Englishman.

'There you are, old boy,' Peter Lawrence found him in the olive grove, 'didn't you want your breakfast?'

'Couldn't face it, Peter, sorry. I didn't mean to seem anti-social. Anyway the fresh air has helped to clear my head a little.'

'Shall we go in and decide on a plan of action for today?' Peter Lawrence had observed the three men in the next orchard, but he too chose not to mention them, or to make contact. They went back inside the cottage, to George Richards' old bedroom.

'Well there's nothing here to pack up, no books or anything,' observed Peter Lawrence. 'We could just call at the post office and make our way back to Marseille, and home. What do you think, Alfred?'

'I thought you were going to show me the Fragonard and Rubens' paintings in Grasse. Have we time?'

'We'll see. Wait till we get to the village.'

'What do we tell Emile?'

'Leave it to me,' Peter Lawrence assured him, 'I'll make sure that he isn't out of pocket. We can do no more here, unless you want to stay longer?'

'No, thank you. Lovely it might be, another time, but we didn't come prepared for a holiday, and Frances would worry. She is under the impression that we should only be gone for the weekend.'

'Very well. I'll go and find Emile. Have you packed your bag?'

'There isn't much to pack, just the perfume. I mustn't forget that. I wonder when Father purchased it. So many questions left unanswered.'

'Perhaps Emile might know about the perfume.'

Alfred lingered a little longer in the fresh air. The men in the orchard had disappeared and he thought no more of it just then. Maybe they were just casual farm workers, picking fruit.

He went in search of Emile, to thank him for his kindness and hospitality towards them, and for looking after his father.

'Peter has decided we should make our way home today, I hope he has seen you, Emile?'

'*Oui,* monsieur. It has been a pleasure to meet you both. You might come again, and stay longer?'

'I would like that, thank you. Emile, just before we go may I ask you something about my father?'

'*Oui,* monsieur?'

'Did my father have any ladies staying here, ever?'

Emile laughed out loud. Judging by his response to Alfred's question, it was obvious that it was a ridiculous idea. In a way Alfred was glad he had asked the question, because he would have always wondered. He couldn't have imagined his father having a mistress, but there was so much secrecy about this place he did wonder what his father had been doing there all those years.

Jean-Paul arrived to take them down the hill. They said their goodbyes to Emile, and set off to walk to the turning point where the cart was waiting. Alfred seized his moment. On the short walk they were completely alone, and couldn't be overheard by anyone.

'All right, Peter, are you going to enlighten me, at last, why we made this short trip to Grasse?'

'Simple, old chap. I had to tie up the loose ends of your father's affairs. I wasn't sure whether or not there were things here to dispose of. You had to accompany me in order to check the poste restante. There may be important things there which only you, as his legal heir, can sign for.' Peter Lawrence thought he had given him sufficient explanation, and hoped the matter would be finished.

Alfred wasn't going to let the matter drop.

'So, tell me the meaning of "ripe plums in orchard 3"?'

'You mean, "plums ripe in orchard 3".'

Alfred noticed how quickly and readily he had corrected the deliberate mistake. If he had only glanced the paper once before, he must have an extraordinary memory.

'It didn't really have anything to do with picking ripe plums Peter, did it?'

'I think we will find it is a message to do with the poste restante. I guess it is the box number for the captain's mail.'

'Well, we shall see soon enough,' said Alfred, not totally convinced that he had heard the whole story. Jean-Paul took them to the post office, and waited outside in case they should need him again.

'Here,' said Peter Lawrence, 'you had better have the ticket as they will need your signature in order to open the box.'

'What if there's nothing there?'

'Then we will have done our duty in coming here. We close the arrangement, and go home.'

Alfred handed over the ticket to the post master and followed him to the collection of mail boxes behind the counter. He was amazed at the large number of boxes, for such a small town.

'We do not deliver mail monsieur,' he was told, 'too many rocky paths up and down hills. Sometimes we get visitors who stay along the Cote d'Azure and Monaco, and they want their mail to be kept privately.' He watched the postmaster go straight to box 3. So, Peter Lawrence was correct.

'There is a box here monsieur, just the one. Please sign your name to acknowledge your receipt of the package. Just for the law I will need to see your passport, *s'il vous plait.'*

Alfred signed the slip and showed the man his passport.

'*Merci,* monsieur,' Alfred thanked him, and almost immediately Peter grabbed him by the arm and hurried him out of the post office to the waiting cart, without speaking.

'Thank you, Jean-Paul. If we hurry we can catch the next train to Marseille.' Jean-Paul set off at a faster pace than before, in order to catch the hourly train to Marseille. They arrived at the tiny station just in time. Jean-Paul accepted his money and turned the cart around, without speaking, but with just a nod of his head, and without a backward glance.

Peter Lawrence took the package from Alfred whilst he climbed the big step up onto the train.

'Here, I'll put it in my bag. You have more luggage than I have, and remember we shall have to find the Paris train almost straight away when we get to Marseille.'

Alfred was relieved that they would not have to spend another fraught night in seedy Marseille. He hadn't liked that at all.

'Aren't we going to undo the package, Peter?'

'I think it might be wise to wait until we are sure that we aren't going to be interrupted. Let's see if we can get a private compartment on the Paris train, eh?' Alfred agreed, although he had a very strange feeling about the whole situation. He noticed that the three men from the orchard had also boarded the train.

'They are probably working in Marseille, or perhaps they're sailors, off to their next ship.'

The three men moved along the train to the next compartment, so they were not interrupted, that was, except for an old gentleman seated in the corner near to the window. He was fast asleep and snoring now and then.

'I hope he isn't going to snore all the way to Marseille,' whispered Alfred, 'let's hope he gets off soon.'

Peter Lawrence smiled wryly. He was still clutching the bag with Alfred's package in, not daring to undo it on the train. The smaller of Alfred's two bags was sitting on his knee. It was the bag with the precious perfume in, and just for a few moments he closed his eyes and imagined that he was a much younger man, having been on a French vacation, and he was taking the gift home to his mother. He could see her face in his mind, but then, coming back to reality the vision he had was of Frances, his wife. She would love the perfume just as his mother would have done, though he was quite sure that there would be questions about why the captain had not brought the perfume home. He wasn't sure that he would ever have a satisfactory answer. One thing that his instinct was telling him was that his father certainly had a secret life, and whatever that entailed also seemed to suggest that his movements in and out of France were often sudden, and not necessarily planned. He determined to solve the enigmatic life of the captain, and at the first proper opportunity he would press Peter Lawrence, and he would not be fobbed off again.

They reached Marseille and Peter Lawrence moved swiftly to the ticket office to secure tickets on the next Paris train. He left Alfred by the *patisserie* shop so that he could buy them something good to eat on the train. They hadn't eaten lunch, and they might not manage to find dinner. Alfred, pleased that he had managed to buy something using his schoolboy French, successfully left the shop to find his companion.

He spotted Peter across the busy concourse, and he waved. Just then, losing sight of his luggage, for just a fleeting moment he was pushed heavily to the ground. His larger bag was gone. He had been robbed. As he hit the ground he hurt his shoulder badly. He called out for help. Not so much for himself, but for help catching the robber, who had seized his bag.

'Help, help! *Brigand voleur!*' which was it? He was annoyed that his French was so limited now, when he really needed it.

'Gendarme! Please someone, find the gendarme. I have been robbed.'

A few concerned people helped Alfred to his feet, but there wasn't a gendarme anywhere in sight. Peter Lawrence caught up with Alfred, but too late to apprehend the robber.

'Did you see his face, would you recognise him again?'

'I don't think so, Peter. But look, over there. Do you see those two men looking at us. They are from the train, and they were in the orchard at Grasse. Do you think we were followed, and where is the third man? Was it him?'

'I can't say, Alfred. Anyway, they're moving off pretty quickly, perhaps catching a train. They don't have any luggage. But let me look at your shoulder, you're hurt.'

'It's just a bruise. I was pushed hard, to the ground. I'll be all right. Thank God it wasn't the bag with the perfume in.'

'Yes, but now you haven't any overnight clothes for the boat.'

'What makes you think I shall sleep, after all that?'

The pair hardly spoke to each other on their journey to Paris.

The train was full and bustling. They didn't dare to move from their seats, for fear of losing them. Alfred couldn't have stood up on the journey. The fall and the robbery had really shaken him. He was greatly relieved when they managed to get to the boat, without any further mishaps. Now, Alfred had to face the possibility of sea-sickness, as he had experienced on the outward journey.

Mercifully, for Alfred's sake, Peter Lawrence had managed to secure a private cabin for the crossing back to Dover. The sea was calmer, and for a while Alfred just had to lie down and sleep. He was exhausted and feeling the bruised shoulder now, which meant he had to sleep on his other side. As he woke he was aware of Peter Lawrence standing over him, with a tray of drinks.

'Take your pick,' he said, 'I thought you might like some strong coffee, so I asked for some to be brought, along with some brandy. Shall I pour you a glass?'

'I'll take a large brandy, thank you, Peter. Then you can sit down and tell me what on earth this has all been for.'

'Necessary I'm afraid, old chap. Had to tidy up the captain's affairs. You know that.'

'Yes, I am aware of that. But I am not stupid, Peter. I also know that you have kept things from me, and I want to know everything. What more is there to come? What was in the parcel we picked up in Grasse?'

'Ah yes, the parcel. Good job it wasn't in your bag, eh? We would never have found it, or its contents.'

Alfred was beginning to lose his patience, as he so often did with Peter.

'You're prevaricating again Peter. This has to stop, if you wish to remain my lawyer. I mean it, sincerely.'

Peter Lawrence took a large swig of brandy, then took the parcel from his own bag.

'Very well. But I can tell you that if any of this becomes public I could be in very deep trouble. You mustn't even tell Frances.'

Alfred could tell from his demeanour that it was serious.

'I deliberately took the parcel from you because I feared that someone would try to rob you of it. You were seen signing your name at the post office, and there were people who knew what the parcel contained.'

'What does the parcel contain, Peter?'

'Money.'

'How much money? Is it illegal money? Are we smuggling?'

'It is government money, old chap. There's a great deal of money. I don't know how much it is. It's in all kinds of foreign denominations: German, Russian, French, Italian.'

'What was my father doing with it?' Alfred was horrified to think that his father was involved in shady dealings. Whatever else he had seemed as a father, he had always seemed so very proper, an upright and honest citizen, keen on people stepping up to the mark, doing their duty. Alfred's mind was racing.

'Your father was working for the government, Alfred.'

'You mean he was a spy?'

'Not exactly,' Peter said cautiously. He was finding it very difficult to find the right words. Now that he had let the cat out of the bag, so to speak, he would have to reveal more.

'He was a liaison officer, Alfred. He was responsible for making sure that British government agents received their due monies.'

'So Father worked with spies?'

'Not necessarily. These agents work in a very complex web. The people your father passed money to may have had to pass it to other people in the chain. I cannot tell you anything else, truly.'

'What were these other people doing then? Did they pass any information to my father?'

'I doubt it very much, but anything else I say is only my own conjecture. If it hadn't been for the mishap at the bank I might never have stumbled on this part of your father's existence. I was summoned to the Foreign Office to give details of your father's death, and it was there I was asked if I would be willing to go and retrieve the parcel of government money.'

'Are you in the government's employ, Peter?'

'Only this one time, and if anyone hears of it, I probably won't work at anything responsible again, Alfred. Understood?'

Alfred nodded. He didn't press Peter Lawrence any further, but he knew there was much more to it than he had been allowed to know, so far.

'I should just warn you, old chap, that when we dock I will be escorted by a policeman to a government office. Just ignore it. Make your own way to the customs hall, and wait for me there.'

'Will they detain you for long?' Alfred was worried.

'No. I guess it will be a case of handing over the parcel to a government official, and then I will be free to go.'

Alfred shivered, half through his nervous anxiety, and because he had left his warm waistcoat in the bag which was stolen from him.

Dover couldn't come soon enough. He would feel safe then. It was exactly as Peter Lawrence had described. A discreet policeman met him and they went into a different building. Alfred followed the other passengers to the customs hall.

'Passport, please, sir.' Alfred showed the passport.

'Is this your only baggage, sir?'

'Yes, I had my bag stolen in Marseille.'

'I'm sorry to hear that, sir. Did you have anything of value in the bag?'

'No, just clothes for travelling, and my tortoiseshell hairbrush. I'm sad to have lost that,' he told the customs officer.

Somehow the officer had missed seeing the box of perfume, and Alfred apologised that he had left a half-eaten sandwich and cake in his small bag. The officer waved him on as he searched for something to wipe his sticky hands.

Alfred waited for what seemed an interminable time for his friend. Eventually the same policeman who had escorted Peter to the private office came towards him.

'Mr Richards. I have a message for you from Mr Lawrence. He wishes you to proceed to London without him, and he will be in contact with you tomorrow. Good day, sir.'

Alfred was relieved to have left Peter Lawrence behind. He actually relaxed and was enjoying the train journey back to London, and familiar territory. It had been a very strange, bizarre experience travelling to France and back again so quickly. He was not sure that he would want to go there again, or anywhere else on a boat for that matter. He spent the rest of that journey thinking of how to explain himself to Frances, and how he would explain the lovely perfume, addressed to his mother, Rose Maud, which sadly, she never received.

He was looking forward to working again, and getting into a normal routine. Alfred had plenty of time to reflect on the past few days in France. He began to think of his father in a completely new light, but maybe his imagination was running riot. Whatever was in his father's past didn't belong to him. He had to look forward now. Of one thing he was sure, he would never have made a spy.

CHAPTER EIGHT

Alfred Richards returned to his work as an artist at the *Illustrated London News*, with renewed vigour and purpose. He had become a different person in a very short time. He had been shaken out of his cosy London existence, and he had glimpsed another side of life in Marseille, and then in Grasse. He had found it totally incredulous that his father should have turned out to be a government agent involved, at least in part, of helping to maintain a secret network of other agents, who seemingly came and went to all quarters of Europe and beyond, disappearing into the shadows of dark cities, and seedy backstreets, as well as infiltrating the dubious play grounds of the rich and famous in Monte Carlo, as well as Berlin and Rome.

He looked at people differently now, scrutinising faces, like his lawyer, Peter Lawrence, who until then had not seemed the least bit questionable. Now, Alfred looked at everyone through different perspectives. Everyone was questionable. He would not be caught off guard again, if he could help it. He had avoided meeting up with any of his father's former friends and associates, and he avoided all contact with the Freemason friends. He didn't want to belong to any organisation that he didn't understand. He couldn't quite find out how his father might have been recruited into the government service, but he guessed that army and naval personnel were most likely to be called upon. He would try to put it all to the back of his mind, and get on with his own life.

The more drawings he produced, the better he became, and was in huge demand. Sometimes it was all about society events, or sports fixtures, and he especially loved drawing horses. With his reporter companion they documented the opening of new hospitals, rail tunnels and bridges, and the new motor cars. Eventually they had to cover the troopships carrying volunteer soldiers to conflicts in Africa and elsewhere.

By the time Charles was three years old, Alfred was a major illustrator and artist. His career developed in leaps and bounds after his magnificent pictures of Queen Victoria's Jubilee. He was at the very front of the crowd as the queen's landau arrived at the steps of St. Paul's Cathedral. His deft fingers and keen eye for every detail ensured that he caught the exact mood, and captured this impressive moment in history.

Imperial pride and pomp, clear to see in people's faces, produced a major public event, regardless of the class of the spectators. Colourful colonial troops paraded along with smart rows of tightly drilled British regiments. There were Indian princes, whose bright dazzling costumes contrasted sharply with the British dignitaries, who were mostly attired in black morning suits and shiny top hats. It seemed to be a celebration of Britain and her achievements worldwide, or at least that's how many people perceived it.

'I wish I was holding Charles up high on my shoulders,' he said to his fellow reporter.

'Isn't he here?' his friend asked.

'Yes, he's here somewhere, with Alice. She has the day off from school today, so that the children can enjoy the parties.'

Private commissions for Alfred's work poured in following the Queen's Diamond Jubilee. He began to produce drawings and paintings, in sets, which wealthy businessmen and socialites clamoured to possess. His spirits were buoyed by his success and confidence that Frances, with all the help available to her, was happy in the house. She was always busy re-decorating, re-planning, making the best use of the space, while Ellice, and her schoolteacher sister, Alice cared for Charles.

Alfred's reporter broke the news of South Africa and their latest assignment.

'We're going to be honorary Scots Guards,' he joked.

'When do we go?' Alfred asked.

'We've got three days to find some tropical kit, and malaria medicine.'

Alfred was alarmed. The soldiers were making light of the possibility of stomach upsets, let alone malaria. Nobody seemed worried about sending two reporters to an area of conflict, let alone the chance of being ill. It almost felt that they were planning a holiday in the sun.

It wasn't until Alfred was feeling bilious on board the troop ship *Nubia* that they realised the importance and seriousness of the mission.

'Aye,' said one of the Scots soldiers, 'we're off to separate the Boers from the gold prospectors. They're scared we'll take their land too.'

In a strange way, being amongst a group of Scots Guards made Alfred feel better. He had warmed to the Scots when he visited South Queensferry, with Frances. He imagined that they were amongst friends.

The troopship was actually much less turbulent in the sea than the French ferryboat had been crossing to France. In his calmer moments he was able to sketch the soldiers at work, and resting. They were amused to see themselves being drawn for posterity, and there were many jocular moments, and much teasing.

'Don't you find your wide brims get in the way?' Alfred asked one of the soldiers.

'Aye, that's true enough, but not as bad as the creepy crawlies up the kilts, eh, lads?' They all laughed.

'The daftest thing we have to do is to polish our white gaiters, and the straps, then march through muddy plains and through water.'

'Have you been to Africa before?' Alfred wanted to know.

'Aye, this is ma second trip. It's a never ending battle.'

As Alfred sketched away, his friend wrote down much of what was said, except for the rude words and blaspheming. Alfred thought about Charles. He guessed that some of his drawings might find their way into boys' magazines. If they did then he would save them up until Charles would be able to read about them.

Most of the Scots soldiers were volunteers, but still the general mood amongst them was one of smug superiority.

'Aye, we'll soon sort the Boers out,' said one.

'I'd rather be digging for gold,' said another.

'You might get the chance, Mac,' joked his friend.

The soldiers seemed to have little grasp of the situation in the Transvaal, except for rumour and speculation.

'Most of us enlisted for a bit of excitement, and the pay isn't bad, when you consider that we get fed.'

'Yes,' said one dejected soldier, 'we're only cannonfodder really. What was it Kipling said? "For it's Tommy this and Tommy that, and 'chuck 'im out, the brute'. But it's 'Saviour of 'is country' when the guns begin to shoot".'

Any true sense of patriotism came from the young, commissioned officers, who were reluctant to converse with Alfred and his writer.

'Look, you two,' he addressed them impatiently, 'this is not going to be a Vauxhall picnic. You'd better keep well out of the way when the firing starts.'

Alfred nodded his acknowledgement, but his blood ran cold, especially as he thought of Frances, Charles and Alice, who he guessed would be holding things together at home. He was remembering how it was for his mother when he was a boy, and his father was away for much of the time. Nobody talked about it

118

then, at least not in front of him. It was just explained as "Your father has another important mission. He will be back soon". All he could really remember was that his father was often cross on his return and his mother was frequently tearful.

The only time that he remembered the house being calm and happy, was when his father left again, and he gained his mother's devoted and undivided attention. He wondered if his mother ever knew about Grasse, and that her husband, respectable Captain Richards, was a government secret agent. He was suddenly overcome by feelings of regret and guilt. He didn't want to be on the ship at all.

He was tired of drawing soldiers polishing their rifles, and spitting when they thought the officer was looking the other way.

'Come on, Alf,' his writer persuaded him out of his gloomy mood. 'We can't get off now, chum. Don't worry. They won't let us anywhere near the firing line!'

'Or prospecting for gold,' quipped Alfred.

'That's better, man,' his friend said.

He made a pretence of seeming to snap out of his low mood. Alfred Richards knew far more than the soldiers. He researched every job he was sent on. He knew that the Boers were well equipped with weapons, and their gold reserves had helped provide them with far superior firepower. It was inevitable that they knew the terrain much better than the British soldiers, and the prospectors were only really interested in gold. The Boers could out run and out shoot any of them, and they were helped by the farmers and their families who would shelter them in the countryside. They used sophisticated tactics and extreme cunning when they had to.

The British soldiers often had to live in hurriedly erected primitive shelters, or in the bush. Food supplies were erratic, and sanitation poor, or non-existent.

Often, against the odds, Alfred and his writer documented many skirmishes, Boer farms, and one or two concentration camps when the troops managed to root out their enemies, and burn the farms where they had been hiding. Extra volunteer soldiers were sent to patrol the camps.

'Good Lord, Alfred, what have we come to? What a hell-hole.'

'Now you know what it's like out here,' shouted one of the soldiers, 'I bet you don't volunteer full-time, eh!'

Alfred was too weak to respond to their jibes. Before the fever truly gripped him body and soul, he had felt duly humbled and ineffective. He had to recover. He willed himself. He had to get his precious drawings home to show how dreadful the conditions were for the troops in South Africa.

Medical orderlies did their best for Alfred, and he was truly grateful. He had little recollection of how many days he had been seriously ill.

'Come on now, sir, drink this. We need to get some food down you.' He took the soup and tried to swallow it all.

'What's in it?' he asked.

'Rabbit sir, and a few vegetables.'

Alfred grimaced, but he thanked the orderly. He felt slightly disorientated, but felt the fever had subsided, so he must be on the way to recovery. He tried to stand up, but fell down onto his makeshift bed.

'Don't worry, Alf,' said his writer, 'you are back in the land of the living, for now. They're making plans to get us out of here. Seems we've completed our duty.'

'What happened to you?' he asked his friend.

'I copped it in the jaw. Sniper's bullet. He got me while you were sick with the fever. I wouldn't mind, but I've lost some teeth. They've covered me in all this padding, so I look like a war wounded soldier.' He tried to make light of everything, but both men were dejected, worried and thoroughly worn down through illness, injury and deprivation.

There was no feeling of ecstasy on the journey back to Britain. There was no sense of victory, or pride.

It wasn't until they safely reached Tilbury that Alfred felt he could breathe properly once again, and he was able to telephone Frances.

He knew that Alice and Mrs Cole would have looked after Frances, and he had every confidence in Ellice looking after Charles. He couldn't wait to get home. It seemed to take an age from Tilbury to London.

When Frances set eyes on Alfred, at last, she was horrified by his appearance.

'Now, now, dry your eyes, my love. I am home safe. I will not be going away again,' he said, kissing her forehead.

'Let us find Charles. Where is he? I must see my boy.'

It was a very strange feeling, coming back to his childhood home, where his father used to return from naval duties, often in a silent and sombre mood. He remembered his mother ushering him away.

'Leave Father alone until he settles himself. Then he will speak with you.' He could hear his mother's voice, even now.

Ellice appeared, smiling, holding Charles by the hand.

'Good to see you Mr Richards,' she said warmly, and she let go of the boy's hand. He ran to his father and hugged him tight, and Alfred hugged him back.

'You have been very long, Father,' he cried.

'I know, my boy. I can't tell you how much I have missed you. I have missed you all. Everyone.' Alfred shed tears of joy and relief. It was a joy to be home and to know that everyone was happy to see him, however he looked, and relief too that he had survived the wretchedness of it all. It had been the worst imaginable nightmare.

Charles tugged at the rope around his father's waist.

'Yes,' he grinned. 'I have become thinner, and my trousers don't fit properly.' They all summoned a happy laugh.

Alfred was led upstairs to change, and to have a proper bath for the first time in many weeks. Mrs Cole had stayed on at the house, once she knew that Alfred was on his way home. She beamed as he met her on the landing. Weak though he was, he lifted her off her feet and gave her a twirl.

'Mr Alfred! Put me down! You can't do this. Come, we have to look after you now.' She was slightly embarrassed at this very changed man's behaviour, and shocked at his appearance, but she soon recovered her composure, and remembered what she had to do for him.

'It's so good to see you, sir. Come, your bath is ready and Mrs Richards has picked out some clothes for you.'

Charles clambered up the stairs, following his father.

'Did you bring me a present, Father?' the boy asked coyly. For an instant Alfred saw himself in the boy's face. He remembered asking his father the same question all those years ago, when his father had returned home again, from goodness knows what kind of mission.

'You will have to wait and see,' he smiled at his son.

'Come, Charles,' Ellice rescued him from his father, who was clearly very happy to be back in the arms of his entire family, except, he asked for Alice, and had to be reminded that she was a teacher now, and living at Highgate. Of course, he knew that, it was just that he was still slightly disorientated. He wanted nothing more that evening than to have something to eat and then to retire to his own comfortable bed for a long, uninterrupted sleep. He would look at the house the next morning and admire the efforts of Frances and Alice.

He was certainly going to be surprised. Frances hoped that he would approve of all the alterations that she and Alice had made together, without Alfred overseeing everything. She had felt a kind of liberation in the planning of one particular surprise, which she would try to keep until last. She would share that surprise with him when they were alone, that is, if she could contain her excitement.

Alfred tossed and turned for most of the night, despite being in his own bed with sweet-smelling linen. By comparison to South Africa, and the journey on the ship, he was now close to heavenly luxury. It was that he was re-living in his mind the whole ordeal. He had vowed to keep the worst parts from Frances. She would pick up a great deal from his sketchpads, in time, but he would try to keep the violent pictures from her, if he could. But Frances was an intelligent woman, and withdrawn most of the time, she could see well enough by the sallow, thin face that he had been ill for much of the time. She was convinced that with Mrs Cole and Alice's help they would make him well again.

Ellice was allowed to take Charles a little later to his kindergarten, so that he could spend some time with his father.

Alfred woke the next morning, though physically weak, and a tiredness had crept over him that he had never known before. Still, he felt almost re-born, happy and safe. He heard Charles running downstairs as fast as his legs would carry him and Ellice in hot pursuit behind him.

'Steady, Charles,' she reminded him. 'It's best not to crowd your father. You must be gentle, and go slowly.'

'Hello little chap, come and sit by me.'

Alfred took out the notebook that he had made especially for Charles; the drawings that he felt would be suitable for the boys' magazines. Nothing too scary.

'Cor! Is that the boat you went on, Father?'

'Yes, that's it. See the flags? When you are home from school we will look at it all properly.'

The boy was immediately captivated by the drawings of the docks, and the ships, the soldiers, the African countryside, and he laughed to see pictures of Alfred, and his writer, as they drew each other. He noticed the finest details, even the buttons on the soldiers' uniforms.

'He has a great eye for detail, Mr Richards,' Ellice said, anxious now to take Charles off to school.

'Just a bit longer Ellice,' Charles begged.

'Why aren't you wearing a uniform in the picture, Father?'

'That's because I am not a soldier, or a sailor. My job was to draw pictures for the newspapers here at home, so that all the people could read about the war, and see some of the action.'

'Did you see any lions?'

'No, I didn't actually see any lions, but we knew they were out there in the bush somewhere. We weren't allowed to wander off by ourselves. We had to stay close by the soldiers.'

Alfred was persuaded to show a few more pictures of birds and other animals.

'Were you afraid, Father?'

Alfred paused before he answered.

'I suppose I was a little nervous, more excited, some of the time. I was a bit apprehensive when there were snakes around.'

'Time for school, Charles,' Ellice was insistent this time. The boy left the table and did as he was told, saying goodbye to his father, and kissing his mother. Then he turned to Ellice.

'Mrs Cole calls me Master Charles.'

'Well,' she replied, matter-of-factly, 'if I call you Master Charles you will have to call me Miss Bell, or Miss Ellice. Which is it to be?'

He pondered for a moment.

'I think we will stick with Ellice, or shall I call you Ell, like my Aunt Alice does?' She nodded in return.

'Why is your name nearly like my aunt's?'

'Oh, young Charles, you ask so many questions.'

'Father says that's how you learn things.'

Ellice attempted to give Charles a satisfactory answer, but she doubted yet whether he was acquainted with the names of the Bronte sisters.

'My Aunt Bell named me after a famous author,' she explained. But Charles wouldn't let the matter drop.

'What's an author?'

'An author, dear boy, is a person who writes.'

'I write,' he said, perplexed.

Ellice was learning very quickly that she had to find a way of explaining things, without there being any need for further qualification. She guessed that Alice, as a school teacher, had to do this all the time.

'An author is someone who writes stories, or poems.' Now he understood.

'What is my father? Is he an author?'

'No, your father is an artist. Art is what can be drawn or painted.'

'Stories without words?'

'Yes, well done, Charles. You are so clever.' He grinned.

Ellice hurried back to the house. She had to change and then take her bicycle to the Working Women's College. She had passed her certificates in mathematics, English language and literature. Now she was determined to pass in Latin and Greek, not her favourite or easiest of subjects, but she was canny enough to realise that if she could pass in those subjects, she might get to university one day. If she couldn't do that in the time she had set herself, then she would take up German and geography and try for a place at the London School of Economics. It surely wouldn't be long before women were admitted.

Ellice was inspired by speakers like the Webbs and Keir Hardie. She remembered that Sidney Webb had forged his own way through education, through sheer dogged persistence. He had passed every exam he entered, and mostly self-taught. No patronage for him. He believed in self-improvement, for the benefit of the working class.

'Good morning, Ell, are you off to college?' Alice greeted her friend, and gave a little giggle as Ellice struggled to put on her bicycle clips. She looked very comical, but Ellice didn't care what she looked like, and ignored her friend's giggle.

'Hello, Al, what are you doing here? Why aren't you at school yet?'

'I have an hour's grace. I promised Fran I would come to see Alfred, now that he is feeling better, and to show him the big surprise. I hope he's going to like it.'

'I'm sure he will. You and Fran have gone to a lot of work, and imagination, to do this for him.'

'It's a dream fulfilled, for him. Well, we hope that is what he will feel about it.'

'What's your dream, Al?' she asked.

'I'm still looking for it,' Alice said, 'perhaps I'll meet my Mr Darcy and raise dozens of beautiful children.' She knew that would irritate Ellice, and there would be some cynical reply.

Ellice groaned.

'You can't possibly mean that? What a waste of a life! Come on, Al. You're a talented musician, a good teacher. Don't you want to scale the heights? Improve your lot, and that of womankind?'

Ellice was easy to tease. She was always so earnest, and quite serious. Alice thought she should have been born a boy.

'Don't you want a family one day, Ell?'

'Never, I've got far too much to do.' She waved to Alice. 'See you later.'

Alice found it difficult to believe that they were both very good friends, and trusted each other implicitly, but they were, in every way, different in their characters. Her ideas of romantic love were formed by the novels of Jane Austen and the Brontes. She had little real experience of men, or the outside world, as yet.

She was learning a good deal more since becoming a teacher.

She had once fantasised that Edward Gardner, her somewhat shy teaching colleague, might return from one of his French holidays, filled with longing for her, and make a dramatic proposal of marriage. In her more lucid, awake moments she knew it was just a silly, girlish dream. She realised this in one very down to earth moment, where she and Frances had attended a musical evening given by Edward's Music Society. Edward sang a romantic duet in Italian, with another tenor. The two blended so well that

Frances made a chance remark, which gave Alice much food for thought. It was clear, Frances thought, that Edward's romantic attachments were not biased towards women. Alice was shocked, and it cured her fantasy.

CHAPTER NINE

Glad to have Alfred home and safe, Frances was like a giddy schoolgirl. She was eager for him to have breakfast and then she could show him round the house, to inspect all of the alterations, as well as his special surprise, which she would leave until last.

Mrs Cole took a tray up to Alfred. She was looking tired, Frances thought, not her usual bustling self.

Frances had been grateful to Mrs Cole for her expertise in renovating things, especially in the library. She knew all about curtain hangings and measuring doors and windows, and about the hanging of pictures. She had too, a surprisingly good eye for colours. Captain Richards had never seemed to notice how dark and shabby the place had become. Some of the dark, heavy furniture had been replaced, and this gloomy, old church house, which had just become somewhere for the captain to sleep when he was at home, was now a much lighter and pleasant family home. The many trips that Frances, Alice and Mrs Cole had made to Marshall and Snelgrove had been worthwhile.

Alfred enjoyed being led around the house, though he hardly noticed the changed dining room. Mrs Cole, excited by her new kitchen had to show him everything.

'Look, we have a new gas stove, for cooking, and electricity everywhere. It's wonderful.'

'I'm so glad you like it, Mrs C.'

'Miss Alice has asked if I would teach her how to cook, sir.'

'What a good idea,' Alfred replied. Mrs Cole wasn't quite sure whether he would approve, so she was glad to have mentioned it.

At last, Frances took Alfred by the hand, and with Mrs Cole's help they led him to the old library.

'There, Mr Alfred, what do you think of that?' Mrs Cole couldn't contain her excitement. Frances smiled as she saw his face light up. She gave his hand a gentle squeeze and then left him to wander round at his own pace.

'It's simply magnificent,' he said, touching every polished surface, stroking the new velvet curtains, and smelling the huge bowl of flowers that Mrs Cole had placed there that morning.

'I'm glad the painters have gone now,' she admitted, 'the smell of the paint never left my nose. I have tried to air the place as much as I could.'

'You've all done splendidly. It is such a change. Everywhere seems more spacious than I remember, and so light. Thank you.'

Alice was only able to stay for a short time, to welcome Alfred home, and to show him where she had hung his best pictures, and some of those precious ones of his mother, brought from Highgate.

'What has happened to Father's books?' he asked Alice.

'We asked Mr Lawrence what we should do with them; I hope that was all right? With his help we packed everything in boxes, clearly labelled. They are all in the other room, waiting for you.' Alfred nodded his agreement, and said he would look at them later. Knowing what he had discovered on his frightening trip to France, with Peter Lawrence, it wouldn't have surprised him if Peter hadn't sifted through every paper, every book in the place, to see if there was anything of significant importance to the government. He couldn't face thinking of that now. It would have to wait.

'Perhaps you could take the naval books down to Greenwich, or to Dartmouth?' Alice suggested. He didn't reply, and the women decided it was best to keep silent for now. Alfred stopped by one of his mother's paintings.

'She would have liked that. It's come home,' he said.

Alfred, his body still aching in every limb, and with weakness in his legs, sat down carefully on one of the two new light-coloured benches. He admired its highly polished surface.

'What beautiful wood, Fran. Come and feel the surface. Did you choose the benches by yourself?'

Frances obliged and felt the smooth, new wood. She whispered something in Mrs Cole's ear, and then took her leave from the gallery, now so called.

Mrs Cole moved to stand by Alfred. She didn't want him to feel faint, or fall backwards because there was no back to the benches.

'Shall I tell Mr Cole that you are pleased with the benches, Mr Alfred?' she asked, her eyes twinkling. He looked quizzically in her direction.

'Mr Cole made them for you, sir,' she answered. 'He's very proud of them, but he would like to know if they please you.'

'Please me? They are truly wonderful. What a very talented man your husband is, Mrs C. I had no idea that he could make such beautiful things. Who does he work for? He is an artist equal to the likes of William Morris, or Rennie Mackintosh.'

Violet Cole had heard these names before, but she wasn't quite sure in what connection.

'He works by himself now,' she said quietly, 'since his terrible accident.' She was slightly embarrassed now that Alfred should be asking about her personal life. She had never spoken to the Richards family about her life, unless she was asked a direct question.

'He is happy to work at his own pace, and each piece he makes is individual, a labour of love, not just for the money.'

'Ah! A true Ruskin-ite.'

Alfred felt deeply humbled, but also heartened by such a lovely gift from Jim and Mrs Cole. He thanked her more than a dozen times during his first slightly wobbly day back home.

'When I am fully recovered,' Alfred promised, 'I shall make it my first priority to visit Mr Cole, and thank him personally and properly.'

'Thank you, Mr Alfred, but that isn't necessary. Please don't trouble yourself. It will be thanks enough that you like his work.'

Alfred would not be deflected. He made sure that Frances realised how much he liked Jim Cole's work and that when he was well enough he wished to visit Jim in his workshop. Frances would not forget.

During his long period of recovery Alfred had a great deal of time to think about his future. One thing was certain: he would never accept any more dangerous foreign assignments. He began to formulate other ideas about his drawings, and became determined to put the "gallery" and its anterooms to good use.

He decided that his gallery would, for now, remain a private one, open to invited guests, friends, associates, and interested parties from the artistic communities, and in time they would use the anterooms to provide a working studio for other artists, and perhaps a series of art and craft classes for people who were keen to learn, but who, otherwise, would be unable to learn in a college.

Alice was full of enthusiasm, on Alfred's behalf, and Ellice was ecstatic.

'Fantastic, Mr Richards. What an amazing idea. I can find you several people who will gladly come and use the space.'

Frances was apprehensive, to say the least. In principle she agreed, but after hearing Ellice enthuse as she did, she was not sure that she wanted "all and sundry" traipsing through her lovely new house.

It was many more months before Alfred recovered physically from his African adventure. The mental scars would stay with him forever, and one result of that experience was that he had been forced out of his comfortable, relatively secluded middle class life, with its social rituals, routines and expectations.

Now he had experienced every kind of person, both good and bad. He had encountered both cultured and rough, uncultured types, educated and simple, selfish and selfless. Mostly, now, he was trying to stay positive, as he remembered the many acts of kindness amongst the soldiers who had helped pull him through. He was remembering too the inexplicable sense of optimism amongst the troops, when everything seemed doom-laden and futile. He was lucky to be alive. Sadly, he had to come to terms with the loss of his writer friend, who succumbed to septicaemia, and his injuries, the day after they reached England.

'He was as brave as many soldiers,' he told Frances. 'I am so glad his wife has sent me his notebook. His words will be published.'

Frances felt his sadness too as she thought of the writer's family. She asked if there was anything they could do to help her.

'Before the world wars are all over, my dear, I'm afraid there will be many more widows and fatherless children to take care of. At least I do know that this lady has a large, extended family who will care for her. I will visit when it is reasonable to do so. I should attend the funeral, but I am not sure whether I would be welcomed. I will give it some more thought.'

Alfred, poring over the boxes of his father's books, realised that his father had always returned home uninjured from sea, or wherever else he might have been. His mother would have suffered the same worry and anguish as thousands more wives and mothers, until their men were safe home. He realised also, too late now to tell his father, that he could understand a little of how he must have felt, returning home from duty. He would have lost men, and will have felt the futility of war. Doing his duty had made Captain Richards a hard man, difficult for a child to understand.

Alice helped her brother-in-law to sift through the books. There were hundreds to look through, and Alfred found it very tedious work. It took many weeks of Alice helping when she was free to do so, and when the curious young Charles was in bed, asleep. Frances mostly kept out of the way. She could tell that Alfred was not enjoying the task, and for two pins, she thought, he might just be tempted to ditch all of the books, without looking at them.

'We have to look through them,' Alice persisted with him. 'There might be valuable first editions, or some with author's notes or messages. What if there is anything of a very confidential nature?' She looked curiously for Alfred's reaction. His finger stroked his chin, slowly. It was one of his habits when he was thinking deeply about something. He didn't reply to her, except to encourage her to get on with the job as quickly as they could.

'I suppose the best thing is to flick through the pages without reading the books themselves, not that I am very interested in most of them. I wonder why he had so many books about submarines?'

'Perhaps,' said Alice, 'we should just turn the books upside down, carefully, and see if anything falls out?'

'Yes, that's what we'll do. It will save time.'

Months later, having "vetted" all the books from the captain's personal library, Charles was allowed to help his father seal up some of the boxes. When the carriers arrived to take them to Greenwich Naval Library, Charles asked if he could go too.

The officer librarian thanked Alfred profusely.

'This is a very important addition to our library. Most generous of you to donate Captain Richard's collection. But what about this young man?' He looked down to Charles. 'Will he follow in his grandfather's footsteps? Or should we say sea-legs? Do you not want to keep some of the books for him?'

Alfred had anticipated being questioned. It was one reason why he didn't really want to take Charles with him. He had prepared an answer, just in case.

'Well sir, by the time Charles grows up everything will have altered. All the European navies are racing each other to build new and faster ships, new types of engines and weaponry. This will all be history by then, though from a historical point of view I guess they might be of interest to students and cadet officers.'

'That's very true,' the officer continued, 'though we are taking boys from thirteen now, you know.'

The officer attempted to tell Alfred about the Youth Training Establishment, near Plymouth. He was anxious to get away and hurriedly thanked the officer. A junior had been assigned to give them a guided tour of the building, and inevitably Charles wanted to be by the river to see the boats.

'Where are the boy sailors, Father?' he asked.

'This isn't the place, Charles. We'll talk about it later.' Alfred had forgotten how green and restful Greenwich Park was. He should have brought Frances. Perhaps he would do so another day, when there was nothing else pressing on his mind.

He had felt unsettled by their visit to the Royal Naval College, or rather by the senior officer and his comments about boy sailors. Of course the officer couldn't have known what a sensitive issue it was for him. He was only trying to be useful, and do his job.

They walked steadily, with Charles stopping every now and then to look at something which caught his eye, or to ask a question. He was certainly an inquisitive boy, interested in anything and everything. Alfred made sure that they visited the observatory before they left for home. Charles was fascinated and wanted to stay for much longer.

'We'll come another day, just for the observatory, and if it's a fine day we will bring your mother too.'

Disposing of his father's library had a strange effect on Alfred. At first he felt guilty for getting rid of things, but his father would have been pleased for the books to have been given to the navy. So, having resolved that in his own mind, he felt less guilty, and in fact it was almost a feeling of catharsis. He could go forward now, choose his own direction, and re-furbishing the house and disposing of the books had been instrumental in that decision.

'It's a good job finished,' he told Alice, 'thanks ever so much for helping me.'

'I was happy to do so, Alfred,' she said, 'now we have to get your gallery up and running, and find more of your good pictures to display. We will all help.'

He began to consider his work again. Assignment offers were coming in thick and fast, but he knew that he would have to become more selective. No more foreign tours, he told Alice and Frances.

'I can do more good here. I shall leave the gadding about to the younger members of my profession.'

He realised that there were more than strong rumours of wars across Europe and Asia, and his terrible experience in South Africa had brought home to him that his duty, for now at least, was towards his family. It wasn't that he was a coward for being reluctant to volunteer himself for anything dangerous. If things were to develop nearer to home he was sure to find a way of doing his bit. He was certain that he would not be put upon by any of his father's former military associates, or by Peter Lawrence, who he now regarded as somewhat of a shady character. Alfred was convinced that he was a spy.

Besides, he certainly didn't want to be drawn into an all-male dominated society. He had no interest in becoming a "club" person. He didn't gamble, and only drank alcohol in moderation, and he certainly didn't want to become one of the "country house set" where business deals, whether legitimate or underhand, were discussed. All that was anathema to him.

As Charles grew older, Alfred was able to talk with his son about his mother, Rose Maud.

'You would have liked your grandmother, Charles. She was a very talented lady in so many ways, and she was very wise too. She always knew the right thing to do.'

'Was she like my mother?' he asked.

'In some ways, she was, I expect that is why I married her. Though your mother had a much quieter life than your grandmother when she was growing up, that is why she is sometimes a little bit shy when she is with strangers.'

'Mother isn't shy with us, is she?'

'No, of course not. Like your grandmother she has a wonderful way of diplomatically telling you what she thinks, without seeming to be bossy!'

'What did Grandmother think?' the boy asked.

'Well, like your mother, my mother always believed that the most satisfaction and joy to be had out of life was when one survived through one's own talent, or ability, and used a lot of common sense to know how to use that talent, for the betterment of others, as well as yourself.'

'I will be a thinker, Father.'

'I'm sure you will be, my boy. Be a creative thinker. They are the people who can solve problems. They are the people who, like you, ask a lot of questions. They consider every aspect of a problem and then try to find the best solution. The world is in great need of creative thinkers just now.'

CHAPTER TEN

'He has a really good voice, Alfred,' Alice revealed. 'It is a pure, clear tone. I think he may have perfect pitch.'

'Might he be suitable for a choir school?'

'I will make some enquiries if you wish,' she said. Charles was full of enthusiasm.

'I know two boys at school who are trying for St. Paul's. If they pass the trial they will be going to the school. Could I try for St. Paul's, Father?'

'Maybe, we'll see what your aunt can discover. But don't count on it, my boy. You might end up being disappointed, and besides, you know that by the time your voice breaks, at thirteen or so, you could lose your lovely, pure tone. You certainly couldn't be a boy soprano forever. Some boys can't ever sing the tenor parts.'

'How do you know about that, Father?'

'Believe it or not, I used to be a chorister myself, but you would never know that now, to hear me sing.' They all laughed at the thought.

Alfred didn't want to dampen his son's enthusiasm, but he wasn't too sure that he wanted Charles to enter that rarefied and privileged kind of background, but on the other hand neither did he want to be a dictatorial father, like his own had been.

He searched his mind for reasons to dissuade Charles. Certainly he would receive a good education at the choir school, but there would be less emphasis on sporting pursuits, and probably more pressure to excel in Latin, Greek, and history, with only minimal attention to science and the arts. He was not sure that those subjects would prepare Charles for the challenges of the twentieth century. He would continue to mull it over.

Making the right decision caused a great deal more consternation than Alfred had thought possible. Frances was in favour of a grammar school for Charles, an academic career. He could be a doctor, or scientist, was her suggestion. Alice disagreed.

'He's such a creative boy, a thinker, not too keen on the duller things like mathematics, or even science. It would be cruel to load him up with mountains of academic work when his heart was not in it.'

Alfred paced up and down, stroking his chin. It was his thinking mode.

'We'll give it some more thought,' he said, eventually.

'I know,' offered Charles, 'Why don't we ask Ellice what she thinks about it?'

If anything would spur Alfred into a decision it was the thought of any strongly felt socialist ideas coming from Ellice. Much as he liked her as a person, he was relieved that Charles was grown up enough now not to need a nanny. He would see Ellice when she and his aunt were together for concerts, or other outings.

Alfred thought, to himself mostly, that Ellice's influence was better from a distance.

The matter of Charles and his senior education was soon resolved. They had missed the entry date for the choir school, and Alfred was reluctant to appeal. So, for the time being Charles would finish his time at the junior school, and then he would attempt the grammar school entrance exam.

'Your aunt will continue to give you piano lessons,' he told Charles, 'and, because Alice thinks you are such a good singer, we have arranged for Mr Cavalli to help with your voice.'

Charles was non-committal about Mr Cavalli. He had heard

from one of his friends at school about him. He was a very large, strict, Italian opera singer. Charles thanked his father, but would reserve his own judgement until later.

Alfred's work gathered a frantic pace, *The News* always finding him interesting assignments. Private work too was plentiful, and Frances was in her element selecting which of his works would be displayed in their new "gallery". They decided to invite Jim Cole to the gallery, where Alfred made him a proposition.

'Welcome Mr Cole, do come in.' Alfred helped him up the steps and along the short passage to the gallery. He could see that his wooden benches were being put to good use.

'Your lovely benches are being admired all the time. We love the wood too. Frances and I wondered if you would consider making us some bespoke frames, for the pictures? Whatever design, carving, or moulding you thought appropriate?'

Jim was overwhelmed. He asked if he might sit down.

'Of course. How silly of me. We'll both sit.'

'It would be an honour to make the frames, sir, ma'am, but I must tell you that I am very lame now. I can't stand for too long at a time. I can work safely for a couple of hours, then I need to rest my legs, and my eyes too, if it's intricate carving work.' He sounded very apologetic. Alfred felt very humble. Frances felt deep sympathy for his condition, but she was careful not to make Jim Cole feel embarrassed.

'Well Mr Cole, may I call you Jim?... Jim, we are not in any great hurry to have everything completed at once. We just want the finest work and we know without the shadow of doubt that you can produce that.' He took Jim to view the workroom-cum-studio at the back of the house.

'It used to be a scullery,' Alfred told him, 'but we've had it converted to a workshop for artists, sculptors and other craftspeople. Look! We have large sinks, a lathe and workbenches. There's a cupboard for tools. Everything you could possibly need.'

'It's very fine, sir,' Jim said, admiring everything in turn.

'If you think it a feasible proposition, you would be more than welcome to work here and use the space for as little time, or as long as you wished. You could come for half a day, or a few hours on Saturdays. Your grandson might come and help you?'

Jim Cole thanked Alfred warmly. He was much more animated and excited than Alfred guessed he might be.

'I can't quite believe that I'm being offered such a place to work, a proper, decent, clean workshop. I will have to pinch myself, Artie,' he said to his grandson Arthur, 'do you think I'm dreaming?'

Artie just smiled. His grandmother had warned him to only speak if Mr Richards addressed him.

'I will go home and discuss it with my wife and daughter, sir, if you don't mind. I would like to accept your offer, if they are also in agreement.' They shook hands and Artie helped his granda, as the boy called him, out of the house, and in search of the horse bus.

Mrs Cole was pleased with Jim's news, but at the same time she felt anxious for his health.

'How long will you need to do the work?' she asked him.

'Who knows, Vi! It'll take as long as it takes. Mr Richards didn't specify a time limit, or how many frames I was to make. If they keep selling the pictures I might have a job for a long time. It's not the frames that take a long time; it's the carving if they want it to be fancy.'

She knew that Jim was more than capable of producing the most beautiful work, and it would be meticulously done. She did worry about the to-ing and fro-ing. It would be difficult unless Arthur could accompany him. Violet Cole was a sensible woman. She would wait until Jim made up his mind. Then she would give her view on the matter. Theirs had been a good marriage, with a lot of give and take, and sharing of household chores.

Jim never thought housework beneath him, like some men would have. It was just accepted that if Violet Cole had to be out all hours doing other people's housework then she shouldn't have to come home and start again. Lily took care of the laundry and the children, unless she needed a minder, and she fetched most of the family's food. Her mother was definitely the cook. Jim's role was to look after the fire, heating the water for baths, and mending anything that was broken. If he didn't have the right tool for a job, then he would fashion one himself. Even young Arthur had his chores. He watched Jim at his work bench and picked up all the wood shavings and odd bits of wood, the off-cuts. Every off cut was saved in a box, because it might come in useful for another job. Arthur was learning how to handle tools, and how to clean them and put them away safely. Everything had its proper place. Jim promised to teach him about polishing next.

Jim Cole's most vulnerable time was when Arthur had to be in school. His slightly dimming eyesight meant that if he dropped anything he couldn't always see where it had fallen, and if he did see it his bad leg might prevent him from picking it up.

Arthur would rush home from school every day, and the first task he had to do was to scour the floor for dropped wood, nails and other things which Jim had not managed to retrieve.

'You're a good lad, Artie. How would you like to come with me to Mr Richards' workshop on Saturdays?'

'If Mr Richards will let me.'

'Of course he will. He suggested it. It'll earn you a bit of pocket money. You'd like that, wouldn't you?'

'Would I have to give it to Ma, like the pop money?'

Jim hadn't realised that the money the boy earned on a Friday night for helping the lemonade deliveryman was going straight to Lily.

'We'll see about that,' his granda said, crossly.

Arthur didn't know whether to tell his granda about his older brother, Jim Jr. He had a job as a butcher's boy. He had to deliver people's meat orders to their houses. He liked the job because the butcher let him use a bicycle. It had a posh plate beneath the cross bar with the butcher's name painted on it in scroll writing. He didn't much care for wearing the apron. It was too big for him and no matter how he tried to tie it round himself, it always got in the way of his legs when he was riding the bicycle. The butcher yelled at him if he took the apron off.

'It shows the customers my name, and that we are clean!' Arthur asked his brother if he had to give his butcher's wages to his ma.

'She lets me keep a bit of it, but I'm saving it up, and it's a secret. You keep your mouth shut and don't tell anyone I told you about it.'

'What are you saving up for?' Arthur wanted to know.

'Never you mind. You'll know soon enough.'

Lily Cole, the boys' mother, was now working full time as a housekeeper for Alice, and her friend, at Highgate. She didn't have to worry about the boys so much now, or, mercifully, her errant husband, who had at last been apprehended by the police, and jailed. Her life was more tolerable now that she wasn't being knocked about. She didn't mind working hard if she was treated well, and she was treated very well at Highgate, and at Kensington when the Richards family needed extra help.

She hadn't told the boys about their father. As far as they knew he had joined the army and gone off to Africa, with his regiment. That was the story they were to tell, if anyone should question them. Nobody ever did ask.

'There's no need for you to take the lad's pennies.' Jim told his daughter one night when they were alone. 'You are earning enough now, Lil, and so are we. We're never going to be rich, but we have sufficient, and we have a better life than most.'

Lily tried to argue with her father, saying that she still had to clothe the boys, and buy new boots every year as they grew.

'The boy will learn the value of money when he has to be responsible for it. Let the lad buy his comics and a bag of sweets if that's what he wants.' Lily remained silent. She couldn't win.

Arthur decided that he would do as his brother did. He would save up. He didn't know what he would save up for, but that is what he would do. It made him feel grown up. Jim made Arthur a wooden moneybox, with a sliding top and a secret compartment.

'I'll show you how to polish it, Artie. You'll be able to see your face in it when we've done.'

Arthur kept the moneybox under his bed, and covered it with a couple of jumpers. Nobody would know where it was. It was his secret. He wouldn't even tell his brother.

The Saturday arrangements worked well for everyone. Arthur helped his granda onto the horse bus, and off again at the other end. Some Saturdays Mrs Cole was required to work, so they all travelled together.

Arthur loved working with his granda, and Jim liked working with Artie. The boy learned quickly, and handled tools like an experienced carpenter. He knew how to cut and saw, to drill and plane, and he could name all the different types of wood which Jim used for his frames. He wasn't so confident reading written plans, or writing things down, but he had a good, retentive memory, and he possessed an instinct about wood. He could imagine a shape, or a length, and know just what to do with it. He had a steady hand and a good eye for things. Much like his grandma, who had never used a cookery book, but knew exactly how many ounces or pounds to use in a recipe. She was a naturally gifted cook.

Mrs Cole had been teaching Lily to cook since she was a small child. That was how they did things in the Cole household.

'You'll never be out of a job,' Jim Cole told his daughter and grandchildren. There would be no slackers in their house.

Some Saturdays, when Charles Richards didn't have to be at choir rehearsals, or singing at weddings, he would play in the garden behind the workshops. On a fine day he would take out his box of soldiers, and fight imaginary battles, or he might set up his model train-track on the concrete path. He preferred the train because you really needed two people to fight battles with the soldiers. If it was raining Charles would take his books and his drawing things into the little summer house, which had been almost obscured by climbing clematis and honeysuckle. It was his own private place.

That was, until young Arthur Cole discovered it. Arthur would take a tea break whenever his granda took his, and they would have ginger biscuits to keep them going until their next meal. That would be when Jim had worked for so long that he couldn't stand any longer. His hands and brain were willing to work all day long, but his legs were not. During the long school holidays Charles became bored playing by himself, so he would tentatively ask Arthur if he would play soldiers with him. Arthur was a few months older than Charles, but seemed much younger.

'My proper name is Arthur, but my granda calls me Artie.'

'Why does he call you Artie?' Charles asked him.

'I don't know. It's just his special name for me. Don't you have a special name?'

'No, I'm always called Charles.'

'You could be called Charlie.'

'I don't think my parents would like that,' Charles told him, 'and my grandparents are both dead.'

'What about your school pals?'

'We all have to use surnames. So I'm called Richards, and my best friend is called Anderson.'

Arthur pondered for a moment.

'We only get called by our second name when we're in some kind of trouble.'

Arthur hated school, and he told Charles how he regularly had his fingers rapped with a ruler for getting his sums wrong, or if his writing was untidy.

'I'm good at arithmetic,' Charles boasted, 'I'll help you if you like.'

Arthur shrank from Charles's offer. His school teacher had already ruined his confidence. He certainly wasn't going to show himself up in front of Charles Richards.

Charles hadn't meant to sound boastful, it wasn't in his nature. He would think of a more subtle way of getting Arthur interested in numbers. A few months later, and as their friendship had blossomed, Charles found an opportunity to inveigle Arthur into helping him with the train set.

'I've bought some extra tracks,' he told Arthur, 'do you want to help me make the tracks go through the bushes?'

Arthur had to think about it.

'Look,' explained Charles, 'if we put a station, or a level crossing every eight or ten bits of track we can make the train go along the path, through the bushes and back again. What we need to do is to number each bit of track so that we always get the right bits back in the same place every time.' He asked Arthur if he wanted to number the track pieces, or the train map he was creating.

Arthur thought hard. It seemed whichever he chose he would still have to get the numbers right.

'I'll tell you what!' said Arthur, suddenly enthusiastic, 'you number the track parts and I'll follow you round with the plan and I'll copy each one onto the plan when you've done your bit!'

'Ingenious, Art,' said Charles, coining his own new name for Arthur. He knew all the time that his ploy would make Arthur more interested, and it did.

Arthur was thrilled to be allowed to share the train set. He'd never seen anything like it. Sometimes though, his granda would drag Arthur away, on a pretext. He wasn't quite sure how the Richards would feel about his grandson playing so often with Charles. Nothing was ever said on the matter, by either side, but Jim was astute enough to manoeuvre Arthur into other activities, or jobs. It wouldn't be long before the boy would have a whole weekend job, like his brother.

'As long as he doesn't have to handle money. He just can't seem to fathom it,' Violet Cole warned Jim.

'He'll have to work with his hands,' said Jim, 'he can stay on with me as my apprentice, as long as I have work. But what will he do if I can't work anymore and he's not fully trained? He spends too long with Master Charles. That young man will be off to college before much longer, and Artie will miss him.'

Violet worried less about Arthur than she did about Jim.

'We'll think of something, I'm sure about that. The lad will be all right, don't you fret.'

That summer passed and the two boys enjoyed each other's company as long as the sun shone, and they could drive their trains through imaginary countryside, picking up their model passengers, who were travelling to exotic destinations. The garden flourished and the undergrowth, wild in parts, provided them with ideal places to play "lookouts". It was probably the last real summer of their boyhoods, though neither of them would recognise that until much later in their lives.

The gallery flourished too. Frances appeared to come slowly, if diffidently at first, out of her emotional shell. She enjoyed being the hostess on "friends" evenings, and Mrs Cole enjoyed wearing her best dress in order to serve refreshments.

Alfred had grown into his unexpectedly good fortune with his career. He was trying to look to the future in a more positive frame of mind. Charles would finish grammar school, then university, perhaps Oxford or Cambridge. That wasn't quite decided yet, but there was no urgency about that. It would wait a little longer.

'Life has been such a roller-coaster, Alice,' he confided in her at one of the gallery functions.

'But you have a lot to be thankful for now, Alfred.'

'I don't know how we, I, would have managed without you Alice.'

'Don't be silly,' she teased him, 'we are all family, and we share our problems and try to help each other the best way we can.'

'You have been wonderful with Frances, and patient, and I do realise she has been difficult to deal with.'

'Well she is certainly making an effort now, Alfred. Try to be proud of her, and don't underestimate what she can do.'

'I know all that. I just don't want her to have a relapse.'

'Why should that happen?'

'Frances has been shielded from many things, me going to Africa and returning so ill. I daren't tell her the seriousness of the situation, and then there was France.'

'What about France, Alfred? I thought that was to retrieve your father's belongings.'

'Well, yes, except there was a good deal more to it than that. I don't want to burden you with it, but neither do I want Peter Lawrence blurting things out like he did once before.'

'Try not to worry Alfred. Frances is stronger than you think, now. She has been mollycoddled all her life, I'm afraid.'

'And what about you, dear sister? How is the teaching going?'

'It has its ups and downs, but generally I love teaching the children. It's the other teachers I find so frustrating, except for one.'

Alfred's eyed twinkled. He gave her a half-smile and raised his eyebrows in expectation.

'Tell me about the one who doesn't frustrate you, Alice. Would that happen to be young Edward Gardner?'

Alice blushed.

'How would you know that, Alfred?'

'Stands to reason. All the other teachers are very aged, apart from the lady teacher, whom you have said is not very friendly, or talkative.'

'Well, I understand Edward's point of view, although I don't share it. He is not inspired by the children and he is less interested in the other teachers, who have shown little interest in him at the start of his career. He has had to find his own way. By contrast, I am daily inspired by the children. Some of them are from extremely poor homes, and often arrive hungry and dirty, but they are keen to improve, and when they make the least effort I feel a sense of achievement.'

'Frances and I are enormously proud of you, Alice.'

'Thank you, Alfred.'

'So what is it that inspires Edward Gardner? What does he do when he is not at school?'

'He is very involved with his musical theatre company. He sings and acts. Apparently he is very talented at the light musical comedy. Ellice and I might go to see him one day soon.'

'Why doesn't he teach music in school? He might enjoy it more if he could employ his talents that way too?'

'I don't think that would go down very well with the governing body, or the head teacher, Alfred. I'm the only one who is asked to do any kind of music, and it's only hymn singing, and marching into prayers, to music which I play on the piano. But, rest assured, I have it in mind to cause a "revolution" soon.'

'That's more like it! Good for you, Alice.'

Alfred didn't want to push his curiosity about Edward too far, just yet, but he sensed in Alice more than an inkling of interest in Edward. Alice, in turn, did not wish to be too exuberant about her feelings towards Edward. It would make Alfred too excited, when really she wasn't completely sure about Edward, herself. She wasn't quite sure whether it was that he was different, out of school, and had an interesting pastime. By all accounts he could have made a career in the theatre. She wondered why he hadn't. She was intrigued by him. For now, she was happy to maintain a friendly, but carefully managed relationship with Edward.

Later that year, near to Christmas, and before Ellice would become involved in her political rallies, she accompanied Alice and Charles to see Edward perform in the latest Gilbert and Sullivan operetta. Charles giggled the whole way through the performance.

'It's very funny, Aunt Alice, seeing all those grown-ups dressed in Chinese costumes. It's just like pantomime, but with more music, isn't it?'

'I'm glad you enjoyed it, Charles. I'm not sure if Mr Cavalli would care for it though.'

'He would say it is not proper music,' said Charles.

'It's good to let your hair down once in a while,' said Ellice, 'it was a great hoot, and of course it had a hidden message.'

Charles couldn't stop giggling, and neither Alice nor her friend recognised the joke in Ellice's remark about hair.

'Letting your hair down,' Charles giggled, 'you know, pigtails down their backs.'

'Charles!' reprimanded Ellice, 'I am surprised at you.'

'Sorry, Ell; Aunt Al.'

'Now that's enough cheek, young man.'

'Actually,' Ellice continued, 'I prefer proper, serious opera. You can't beat Mozart. He used political message too, you know.'

'And good tunes,' joined in Charles.

'I prefer piano and song recitals, myself,' said Alice, 'Lieder, Schumann, Brahms. Wonderful music. Don't you agree, Charles?' Alice knew that Charles was now a fine lieder singer and Mr Cavalli would have him perform before long. At last, Mr Cavalli had found something which excited Charles, and in which he would excel. Charles was relieved that he didn't have to sing any more Italian arias, which Mr Cavalli had foisted upon him for long enough. He thought they were too flamboyant, and loud.

'Will you come to hear me sing, Aunt Alice, Ell?'

'You just try to stop us.'

Charles was a good student, like Alice, he was willing to learn about everything presented to him. He would have great difficulty deciding what his degree should be when it came to select courses in a year or so. Of course, everyone else thought they knew what was best for Charles, but he was determined that when the time came, he would decide for himself. Young Arthur Cole, his friend, would have no such difficulty. He had his life mapped out for him by force of family circumstances. Jim Cole had trained the boy well. He could make small items without supervision, and he was especially good at making children's chairs, even the high ones with a tray.

He couldn't carve like Jim. It was a gift, but Arthur was able to make perfect handles, finials and sets of drawers. He would always be able to earn a living, and one day he might have to take over when his granda could no longer manage.

Ellice Bell was relieved that she no longer had to look after Charles, though they remained great friends. Charles treated her like a second aunt. Alfred hoped that her influence was not going to rub off on Charles, much as he liked Ellice as a person.

'She's too opinionated about the Labour Party for my liking,' he told Alice. 'Do you think she will influence Charles?'

'What if she does, Alfred? He will go away to university and there will be all kinds of political influences there. He has to learn about politics and then decide for himself where his sympathies lie. One thing is for sure, he will not remain neutral, I'm sure of it.'

Alice's prophecy came true much sooner than anyone expected. Since Ellice had become seriously involved with the women's movement, and the Labour Party, she saw less and less of her at the concerts with Charles, and the musical plays with Edward.

'I do miss Ellice,' Charles told his aunt, 'she is such a fun person, isn't she?'

'She can be, when she isn't involved with politics, then she is very serious and will have no time for frivolity.'

'So is it correct to say that commitment to her friends will depend upon which political activity she is involved with at the time?'

'That's about it, Charles. But we mustn't be too disappointed. We should be proud to have her as a true, loyal friend, and admire her courage, even if we don't understand her political persuasion.'

'What is there not to understand, Aunt? I would have thought that you would want to see better conditions for the families of the children you teach, and what about votes for women? Is that not a good thing to bring about?'

'Yes, of course it is, Charles, it's just that all this flag-waving and marching, shouting in public, well, it's undignified, and could be dangerous. Ellice needs to be more careful.'

'She has a rally in Hyde Park next week, Aunt; do you think we could go? I am interested to see what happens at meetings.'

Alice had to think carefully. Alfred wouldn't approve of it, and whilst she was curious, Alice wasn't sure if her school governors would approve of her being there either.

'I'm not sure Charles. It could get a bit rough, you know.'

'I could go by myself. I'm old enough now, and I wouldn't get too close to the shouting, and the pushing and shoving.'

'Well, you don't need my permission, that's true.'

'I could go, like Father, as an observer, even a sketch artist.'

'That might be worse, Charles. If people thought you were a reporter you could be mobbed.'

'But how would they know whose side I was on?'

Alice felt very uncomfortable having such a conversation with Charles, not that she disapproved of what he was curious about, but because she felt quite out of her depth. She had never had to think about politics before. Still, Ellice was right. Women were getting a raw deal, and why shouldn't they have more say in running the country? She had observed much about the way poorer families had to live, since she had become a teacher. It had opened up a whole new world to Alice. She decided that she should take more of an interest.

'We'll go together, Charles, but keep it from Alfred, for now.'

'Really, Aunt? Thank you! I can't wait for Sunday.'

During the course of the following week, Alice learned that several speakers in the House of Lords had deprecated the growing expenditure on education, when more money was needed to build warships and arm troops, in case the threatened war did happen. This was the single motivating factor to galvanise Alice into more positive action.

'Wrap up warm, Charles,' Alice suggested, 'we might be standing around Hyde Park for some time. It isn't too warm.'

Alice was well covered, partly from the breeze, but wisely from possible prying eyes. Her hat and shawl covered most of her face.

'You looked dressed for the Arctic, Aunt.'

'I'd rather be warm,' she said.

They chose a spot near to the speaker's stand, but not so near the front where policemen had begun to gather. As the crowd increased, Alice and Charles lost sight of Ellice, who was passing through the crowds with pamphlets and newspapers. Alice was soon approached by a small group of women, dressed in dark green and wearing the suffragists' banners. One of them thrust a pamphlet into Alice's hands.

'Are you a member, Ma'am?' she was asked.

Alice dithered, but then accepted a membership card from one of the women.

'Fill in your details' she was told, 'and post it back to Red Lion Court.' The woman touched Alice on the arm and smiled.

'Do it today, please.'

The crowd swelled to hundreds of people, and there was much pushing and jostling as people wanted to be nearer the speaker's stand, some to listen, and others to heckle loudly. Alice shivered and thought they should move away.

'I think we should go, Charles, things look as though the might get out of hand.'

'Oh, just a while longer, Aunt, it's just getting exciting.'

'Dangerous, Charles.'

'We'll be all right if we move this way,' he suggested. Away from the suffragists' corner there were several other speakers emerging, each had brought their own box to stand on.

'Those aren't suffragists, Aunt, are they?'

'No, Charles, they're politicians.'

Charles was anxious to listen to the politicians, but as each one started to speak, the crowds of hecklers grew even larger and noisier. The speakers had to shout even louder in order to be heard at all. Some of the suffragist women had left their own group and had infiltrated the political speakers' groups.

'The Commons should decide on taxes, not the Lords!' shouted someone.

'Women should have the chance to vote. We're half the population.'

'Prevent real waste,' shouted another woman. 'Women are the ones to sort out the economy and conduct fair dealings.'

The arguments back and forth became more heated and angry. Insults were not the only thing to be thrown. A group of trouble makers began to throw stones; others threw fruit at speakers, or at members of opposing groups. When the police summoned reinforcements on horseback Alice pulled Charles away.

'We definitely have to leave right now,' she told him, crossly. 'We can't stay here safely, Charles.'

They pushed their way through, mostly through people coming in the opposite direction, towards the troublespots. Alice was relieved to have reached a safe distance out of the park. She and Charles tidied themselves, and Alice discovered that she had lost a glove.

'It must have been when I was accepting the card from the suffragist lady, how annoying. My best pair.'

They couldn't possibly find it, and Alice was glad that they had escaped from the crowds.

'Look!' shouted Charles, 'the police are bringing vans in.'

'I hope they are rounding up the ruffians who threw stones at the speakers,' Alice said.

'And the ones who are fighting. Look, Aunt!'

'I can't bear to look any more, Charles. Come. I hope you have learned a lot from this afternoon's excitement?'

Alice had fully intended to keep the trip to Hyde Park secret from Alfred and Frances, but Alfred, keen-eyed man that he was, noticed how dishevelled the returning pair looked.

'Charles, where on earth have you been? Your boots are extremely dirty, and so are your hands. Go and clean yourself up immediately.'

'Yes. Father, but–'

'No buts, go and wash. I will speak with you later. Alice, you too look rather unkempt if I may say so, do you have an explanation?'

'Alfred, I am not a child!' she retorted, 'And I resent being spoken to like that. If you must know Charles and I have been to Hyde Park.'

'To the rally of suffragists?'

'There were other speakers too, Alfred. Charles wanted to know what it was all about and I agreed to take him.'

'This must be Ellice's doing?'

'No, actually. She did not know that we intended to be there, neither did we meet her there.'

Alfred stormed off. He would deal with Charles later. Alice decided to make her way home to the Highgate house, but looked in on Charles before she went.

'Don't worry, Charles. Your father will calm down. Make your apologies, and blame it on me.'

'But it was down to me, I insisted. Sorry, Aunt Alice.'

'It will blow over, you'll see. But in future we will have to be honest with your father before we go on any more excursions.'

Ellice didn't return home that night, and Alice lay awake for most of the night worrying about her. Concentrating at school the next day was difficult. Only Edward Gardner noticed that she was not her usual self.

Alice rushed home to find Ellice fast asleep in her bed and looking very bruised and dirty. She was shocked to see her friend in such a state, but guessed that she had fared badly at Hyde Park the day before. Alice closed the door and left Ellice sleeping. She would prepare soup for Ellice to have later.

Noises in the bathroom told Alice that her friend had woken. It was some time before Ellice appeared.

'Don't say "I told you so",' Ellice said, sleepily.

Alice said nothing. She had never seen anyone look as bad as Ellice had looked the moment she had returned home, and found her sleeping.

'I will have to tell you, dear Alice, because if I don't, you will surely read it in the newspapers. I'm afraid that I spent last night in prison.'

Alice gasped.

'It's all right. I wasn't charged with anything. There was this massive demonstration, scuffles at first, but then trouble makers throwing things, people badly cut, and so on. The police couldn't identify the culprits, so everyone was rounded up, like cattle into the police vans, and carted off to prison. This morning the women were brought before the magistrate. Those who could pay a £10 fine for affray, were released, the others have to remain in prison for three days.'

Alice didn't know what to say. She thought it best to reveal that she had taken Charles to Hyde Park.

'We were there, Charles and I. We saw the start of the fracas; then I persuaded Charles to come away home. We had no idea that you were mixed up in the violence.'

'Does Alfred know that you were there?' she asked.

'Yes, I'm afraid so.'

'He will think that I persuaded you.'

'No, he doesn't,' Alice assured her.

It was some time before Alfred could see his way to forgiving the incident of Hyde Park, and things cooled between Ellice and Alfred, in spite of Alice defending the whole situation.

Nevertheless, it was time, Ellice decided, for her to leave Highgate. She took lodgings nearer to Labour Party headquarters, because now her destiny was clear. Her commitment to both the women's movement and the Labour Party had wavered back and forth, but she had now made up her mind.

'I've been obsessed, Al,' she told her friend, 'one minute I wanted to lead a group of suffragettes, the next I wanted to be the first woman in Parliament.'

'So what has made you more positive?' Alice asked.

'I still care passionately for the rights of women, Al, especially now I've seen how they're treated in prison. Do you know they will force-feed women who refuse to eat?'

'Why do they refuse food?'

'Some women feel so strongly for the cause they threaten to commit suicide, so that Parliament will listen to them.'

'And you, Ell, how strongly do you feel?'

'I think I can do more good out of prison, than inside.'

'How will you work now?'

'I shall share an office at Labour headquarters. They've trebled their vote now, the Tories have lost half their seats, and the liberals have overtaken them, so I feel more optimistic about the coming of a better welfare state. I'm going to work for Mr Keir Hardie.'

Alice hugged her friend, and persuaded her to let her tend to her cuts and bruises.

'I don't hurt, physically,' she told Alice, 'and I'm fired up with enthusiasm, more than ever now.'

The country was experiencing a great deal of political turmoil, first one party, then another. It was swings and roundabouts as the various governments each tried to do what it thought was right for the working poor. There was much uncertainty, not only in London, but on stock exchanges the world over, especially with the increasing prospect of war.

Alfred Richards had noticed, for a while, that his wealthier clients were not buying so many of his paintings and drawings.

They too were being cautious.

The Highgate house felt very empty after Ellice moved out to pursue her political career, so Alice was glad for a short respite from the feeling of loneliness when Alfred was sent on another important assignment for *The News*. She decided to stay with Frances, to keep her company while Alfred was away.

Portsmouth was Alfred's destination this time, but he wasn't about to embark on another mission overseas. He was there to cover the launch of the most powerful warship yet to be built, anywhere in the world.

'*Dreadnought* is thought to revolutionise naval power,' he explained to Charles, 'the Germans, especially, are rushing to match her power and weaponry.' Alfred did not like the assignment. He had a great sense of foreboding, since rumours of war had been circulating for some time.

'Do you think there will be a war, Father?' Charles asked.

'I don't know Charles. Most people think it's just dangerous chatter, and wars are fought somewhere else, a long way away from here. Let's hope so, eh?'

'Yes, Father.'

Charles was almost an adult, and intelligent, blessed with intuition, like his father, and often there was no need for them to discuss things. They knew what each other was thinking.

Alfred had read alarming reports about Russia, where the first democratic parliament had been squashed. The Russian peasantry were starving in mass numbers, and the situation there was worse than anyone in Britain could imagine.

Alfred did his duty. He sketched the pictures of the warship's launch. Someone else, a reporter, had the job of describing it.

He drew the sailors, the engineers, the dockyard and the watching crowds. He couldn't understand why people wanted to stand there and watch this war machine being launched. His job completed, he returned to London as quickly as he could. He didn't want any more of it. In fact Alfred found excuses, reasons why he wasn't able to be responsible for any further pictures of military events.

He would concentrate on domestic scenes. There was plenty to expose among the London poor and starving children. There were many more people now, demanding votes and better treatment of women. There were even marches and demonstrations in front of Buckingham Palace.

'I am militant in my own way,' he would tell Alice and Charles. 'Social justice and care is what we must work for, not war.'

Whilst Alfred Richards had decided that he was a pacifist, young Jim Cole Junior, (named so for his granda), had been fired up by the images of the *Dreadnought* being launched. Of course he had no idea of what being a sailor on such a warship might entail. He was curious about the sea and ships, and he longed to escape his humdrum, boring life. He wanted to escape his mother, Lily, who bullied him, though she didn't recognise that she did so. She was having a very tough time herself, hiding the truth about her husband, working in other people's houses all the time, and worrying about her own parents.

'You kids don't know the half,' she often told Jim Jr. and Arthur, 'you'll find out one day when you've a family of your own.' Jim Jr. was old enough, at thirteen, to realise what his father had done, though it was kept from young Arthur, in case he blabbed it to his friends at school. Jim Jr. knew that things were unlikely to change for his mother. She would always have a life of "drudgery" as she called it, and scraping her money together to give them a decent life. *Well,* he thought, *now I'll make life easier for her.*

Approaching his fourteenth birthday, and knowing that he would have to leave school before very long, he decided to run away. That's what he was saving his money for. He had heard that boys could join up in the navy, or the army, when they were fourteen. That's what he was determined to do. He would get himself to Portsmouth and see if he could join up, and maybe, just maybe, he dreamed he might get to sail on the new *Dreadnought.*

Jim Jr. walked out of London, took an omnibus to the coast, walked some more, hitched a ride, slept in barns and fields, walked some more, and finally found his way to Devonport.

CHAPTER ELEVEN

By the time Jim Jr. arrived at the naval base he was looking very untidy and rather dirty after sleeping rough in his clothes. Albeit they were his best Sunday clothes, he was looking bedraggled and not nearly as clean and tidy as he would have looked on Sunday mornings, when his mother would have scrutinised every bit of him.

He approached the recruiting officer.

'What's your name, boy?' the officer bellowed.

'Jim Junior… I mean, Jim Wilson, sir.'

'Well, are you sure? Which is it, Junior, or Wilson?'

'It's Wilson, sir. At home I'm just called Jim Junior, after my granda, I mean, my grandfather.'

'So, who is your father?'

'He's called Eddie Wilson, sir.'

'And your mother?'

'Lily Wilson, sir, but she prefers to be called Lily Cole. That's her maiden name, sir, before she got married.'

'Unusual that. Why doesn't she want to be called by her married name?'

Jim didn't really want to tell him the story about his father being in prison, for defecting.

'Because my father left us. He went off to join the army in South Africa. He's never come back, sir.'

'Why do you want to be a boy sailor?' Jim was asked. His eyes lit up as he answered the officer.

'I've seen pictures of the *Dreadnought* and I want to sail on her one day, if I can, sir.'

The officer grinned. He asked Jim for his birth certificate, and wanted to know his age. Jim hesitated, but decided that he had better tell the truth. He admitted that he had forgotten to bring his birth certificate, but told the officer truthfully, that he was thirteen, but very nearly fourteen.

The officer paced up and down to consider the situation.

'Are you a bright boy, Jim Wilson?'

'I think I am, sir.'

The officer sent him to wait outside the door to reflect on whether he might have muddled up his birth date. The officer gave him a very concentrated, knowing look. Jim was a bright enough boy to pick up the officer's silent message, though he struggled whether he should actually say the word fourteen.

He knocked on the door and waited until he was told to enter.

'Ah! Young Jim Wilson, come in,' the officer beckoned.

'Remind me, did you tell me that you were fourteen or thereabouts?'

'Thereabouts, sir,' Jim nodded.

The officer sat down and filled in some application forms, using the information provided by Jim. Of course, since his father had not featured in the boy's life for some years he could hardly be called upon to sign the form giving parental consent. His mother would have to be called upon. It was at this point that Jim was relieved that he had at least left a note for his mother to find. He hadn't told anyone else, apart from the butcher, where exactly he was heading.

Lily found Jim's scribbled note the next morning. She could hardly believe her eyes. She was stunned to read his words.

Dear Mother,

*Just so you don't think I've come to any harm I am writing to
tell you that I have decided to join the navy. I am hitching to
Devonport to sign up. Don't worry about me. I will be O.K.*

Your son, Jim.

Lily's shock and amazement soon turned to anger. *How dare he just
take off like that, without a word to anyone. Surely he wasn't old enough to
sign on,* she thought. Lily wondered if anyone had put him up to it.
Perhaps he wasn't alone.

At first she couldn't decide what to do. Her immediate instinct
was to go and find her son and bring him home. Then she realised
that she would have to tell her parents, and Arthur would have to
be told too. She would need their help. Lily's head was in a whirl.
She tackled Arthur.

'Did you know that Jim was going to disappear like that?'

'No, Ma, but I knew he was up to something.'

'How? What was he up to? Come on, tell me the truth!'

'I don't rightly know Ma, but he was saving up.' Arthur was
vague in the information he could offer. 'He said he was saving up,
and I wasn't to tell anyone. He said that I'd find out soon enough
what it was for.'

It was clear that she wasn't going to extract any further information
from Arthur, so Lily hurried to the butcher's shop where Jim had
worked as an errand boy. The butcher was surprised to see her, and in
such a state. He was taken aback at her anger and frustration.

'He gave notice to quit,' the butcher told Lily. 'I paid him up,
and he said he was off to Plymouth, or somewhere. Said he was
joining the navy. I thought he'd gone with your blessing. I'm sorry,
missus.'

Lily calmed down a little when she realised that it wasn't the
butcher's fault. Jim had planned everything very carefully.

'I've got to find a new lad now,' the butcher said, 'what about your other boy? Can he ride a bike?'

Lily had to think quickly.

'Well he's been helping his granda at the weekends, but I dare say he could manage your Friday rounds, after school. Shall I send him round?'

'Yes, that'd be grand. Just so long as he's not going to run off to join the army or the navy.'

'He's too young yet!' she yelled. 'I'm not letting him go anywhere. I need him here.'

Lily stormed off. She was seething with anger at Jim's deviousness. *He obviously takes after his father,* she thought. She was angry and upset, but at the same time worried for him. One minute she felt like shaking him, the next she was tearful and anxious. These mixed up emotions were different to anything she had felt when her husband Eddie had mistreated and betrayed her; betrayed everyone in fact. She was glad to have got rid of him from her life. She never wanted him to return, even if he was released from prison. The problem now, for Lily, was that she'd to be constantly working, to keep herself and Arthur.

Jim's disappearance had caused more problems for Lily than she would ever comprehend. For one thing, she couldn't leave Arthur by himself when everyone else was working. Her mother, gem that she was, and willing, was constantly at the Richards' beck and call. Jim Cole worked steadily for as many hours as his legs would hold him, and as long as his eyes could see.

Lily broke the news to her mother first. She would know what to do, even if she would be cross at what had happened.

'Well, my girl. I can't say that I am really surprised the lad wanted to leave home. I'm only shocked at the way he chose to do it. It was cowardly to leave you a note, and then disappear.'

'What can I do to get him back, Ma?'

'If you want my honest opinion, Lil, I would let the lad go and do his basic training. Let him see what hard work it is. He'll probably want to come home after that.'

'And if he passes the training?'

'If he passes the training and signs up for the navy proper, then they'll make a man of him. That's more than his father will ever achieve.'

It wasn't the response she had expected from her mother, and since Arthur had already told his Granda Jim, she felt she had to get his opinion too. She regretted having to cause any more distress for her ailing father. He was fragile in health, though he remained mentally very alert and capable. It was he who suggested that Mr Richards, with his father's naval background, would know someone who they could approach for reliable advice.

When he heard the news, Alfred Richards was the first person to offer his sympathies, and help. He lost no time at all in using the telephone. He spoke to someone at the Royal Naval College, at Greenwich, who in turn put him immediately in contact with the Youth Training Establishment in Devonport.

'Yes, it was correct,' Alfred was told officially. 'A boy known as Jim Wilson, of Kentish Town, aged fourteen, or thereabouts, has signed up for a trial period. I'm afraid you will have to sign the parental consent form,' he told Lily, 'or the boy will not be allowed to remain there.'

'Right,' breathed Lily, with some sense of relief. She felt more positive now that she knew her son was safe. She thanked Mr Richards for his help.

Determined to resolve matters, she asked Alice if she might take leave on the Friday and Saturday of that week, so that she could take the train and find the naval base herself.

'That's very brave of you, Lily, to contemplate the long journey there, by yourself.'

'I will be all right Miss Alice,' she said.

Somehow, the anxious Lily found strength and courage to arrange things, so that she could travel from London to Devonport alone. She would find a small boarding house where she could stay the night. It was too long a journey to go there and back again in one day, especially if she managed to spend time with her son.

Her temper subsided, though she still felt a great sense of indignation and insecurity. Until now Lily had been quite certain of her role in life, and her destiny as daughter, wife, mother and skivvy. Now, her father was becoming frailer, and her mother worked all the hours day and night, whenever she was wanted. Her errant husband was in jail and her elder son had absconded. It wasn't so much that she felt sorry for herself, but she felt a great sense of unfairness in it all. She had tried to do her very best for everyone, to the detriment of her own personal satisfaction. She longed for something good to happen. It didn't have to be anything world shatteringly beautiful, or expensive, just a bit of pleasant respite from all the worry and drudgery.

Friday came and Lily made her way to Paddington Station. She had only been on a train once before, on a day trip to the south coast, to Brighton, when she was a child. She wasn't so excited this time, and she felt nervous climbing aboard the train by herself.

She was relieved to have found a seat in the ladies only carriage. It would be a longer journey than going to Brighton. She closed her eyes, although she wasn't really sleeping. She was rehearsing in her mind exactly what she would say to the officer in charge of new recruits.

Suddenly, the compartment seemed to be filled with a group of blowsy, common women, laughing and talking loudly about their sons. By coincidence it appeared that they were all heading in the same direction, but these women had made the journey many times before.

'Is this your first time, dearie?' one of the brazen women asked Lily. The other women broke into a group cackle of laughter.

'You ought to re-phrase that, Pearl,' said one of the women.

'I do beg your pardon, miss, or is it missus?' the first woman calmed herself down, realising that Lily was not like them. 'I meant to ask if you had been to Plymouth before.'

Lily thought that she had better answer something.

'No, I haven't been to Plymouth before. I am going to see my son, who has just enlisted in the navy youth establishment.'

Lily was determined that she would not discuss her son any further. What business was it of those awful women? She had to remain pleasant, but didn't really want to converse with them at all.

Pearl made pretence of being a respectable and dignified woman. She straightened her clothing, and sat up straight herself.

'Oh! Isn't that interesting, Ruby?' she addressed one of the other women. 'We're all going to visit our boys, aren't we?'

She winked at Ruby and the group broke out into fits of laughter before feigning some better behaviour when the ticket inspector appeared.

'Good morning, ladies,' he said seriously, before joking with Pearl and Ruby.

'On our way to Plymouth again are we?' He turned to Lily and became serious again.

'I can tell that you're not with this lot, Ma'am.' Lily gave him her ticket.

'Have a good journey to Plymouth, ladies,' he grinned. The blowsy women left Lily alone and chattered amongst themselves. Of course, Lily, eyes closed pretending to doze, heard every word of their coarse banter. They were on their way to collect half their son's wages from the navy paymaster. They were going to the same office as Lily. She thought it was a long way to travel, just to pick up a few pounds.

'They should let us have all their wages, then we wouldn't have to work so hard, eh, girls,' Pearl joked.

What Lily would shortly discover was their "pickings" were to pay off court fines, and it wasn't all they picked up at the navy base.

The women were there with the express intention of frequenting the local taverns, where they would entice off-duty sailors to part with their wages too. Lily was shocked beyond belief as she listened to their babbling. To think she had travelled all the way from London with these awful creatures.

Lily presented herself to the Recruiting Office as soon as she arrived at Devonport. The women went in the direction of the nearest tavern, for which she was grateful and relieved.

'Good afternoon, Madam,' greeted the desk clerk. 'I suppose you're another one after your son's wages? Name?' Lily was surprised, and rather insulted by his manner.

'The name is Mrs Lily Wilson, and my son will not have any wages to collect, yet, thank you.'

'Ah, yes,' he said in a more civilised manner. 'I remember now. Yours is the lad from Kentish Town, named Junior, for his grandfather.'

'Yes, that's correct,' Lily replied.

'Well Ma'am. If he's staying with us we need to have your signature, and his full home address.'

The clerk pushed the papers towards her.

'I was hoping to see my son first,' she said, 'suppose he has changed his mind, and wants to come home with me?'

'I can assure you that he wants to stay. He's gone off happily to swimming training. I can't reach him now. He's off the base.'

The clerk, seeing that Lily was genuinely worried, explained that her signature was not on a legally binding document. If the boy wanted to leave he could do so, after the trial period.

'We need these details in case of illness or other difficulties, so that we can contact you, if necessary.'

'His father can't sign it,' she said crossly.

'That's right, so I understand. South Africa was it?'

Lily just nodded. She didn't know whether a nod, in this instance, constituted a lie, but she didn't offer any other details.

Lily reluctantly signed the papers.

'In that case Ma'am, you are within your rights to claim half the boy's wages, once a month, if you so need.'

So that was it. That's what the bawdy women were doing,

collecting their son's wages, claiming they had no husbands to bring family money in. Lily felt quite degraded. She told the clerk that she would not be claiming the boy's wages, but asked if he would be able to make her son save the money in a bank, for his future.

'Indeed Ma'am,' the clerk said, altering his tone to one of absolute admiration. 'We have a post office here, and a bank. Rest assured, he will get the message that you wish him to bank his money. We will do our best to take care of him.'

Lily was uneasy about leaving her son, but she agreed to the trial period. She would leave him be, for now.

She decided to take the next train back to London, even if it was late when she arrived home. She couldn't bear to find that she might be lodging, even overnight, anywhere near the blowsy women she had encountered on the train. She made her way to Kentish Town, and her parents' house. Alice would not be expecting her back until Sunday or Monday.

Expecting the house to be empty, Lily was surprised to see her mother sitting alone in the parlour – "the room".

'Ma! Ma! What is it? Where's Arthur? And Pa?'

'Lil, your Pa's in the hospital. He took ill just after you left. They don't know if he will pull through. His heart's giving up. I've been waiting for you to come home. I didn't know if you were staying away for the night.'

'I changed my mind, thank goodness. I'm here now. Where's Arthur?'

'I've left him with your friend, Jenny.'

'I'll go and fetch him then we'll all go to the hospital.'

'Wouldn't he be better left where he is, Lil?'

Lily didn't answer. She fled along the road, tired though she was after her exhausting train journey, to fetch her boy. Nobody was going to take him away. Ever. She cried tears of tiredness and worry. No words were spoken between mother and son, just a quick hug, and a gasp for breath. Arthur had told Jenny about his brother running away, and now Lily's friend knew about his granda too.

Violet Cole, Lily and Arthur sat beside Jim's bedside through the night. At first light they knew that he had lost his fight for life. The nurses had to wake Arthur up. He was still holding his granda's hands. He would be inconsolable when the truth sank in. There were just the three of them now, to care for each other.

Violet had long expected Jim's demise. She was surprised that he had lasted so long. His crippled leg and failing eyesight were only the visible problems he had. He had been in constant pain with one thing or another, for years, and he had hidden it well. The only thing which had dulled his pain was his nightly ale. Not that he ever became drunk and incapable, and he was never violent. It just helped him sleep through the night. That way Jim Cole had got through each day without complaining. His was a dogged determination to finish his next piece of work, another piece of beautiful furniture, or another exquisite piece of carving, and then there was his Artie, of course.

Jim had taught Artie a lot about wood, but he also taught him the value of patience and persistence. Doing a job well, so that you could be proud of it.

Arthur was devastated by the loss of his granda, and he kept trying to remember all the things he had said to him. He was going over and over it in his mind. He never wanted to forget. He wanted more than anything to make his granda proud. He believed that his granda was still watching over him, guiding him, and telling him how to do the right thing.

He begged to be taken to the workshop. He became obsessed with wanting to finish something for his granda. Alfred Richards and Frances were more than happy to let the boy spend time there where he was his happiest, and where his granda was too.

Lily and her mother made all the arrangements for the funeral. They would work as usual up to the day of the funeral, but Arthur didn't go to school. He couldn't even bear to think about it.

So what if he was in trouble with the school board inspectors. He didn't care, and just for once, neither did Lily.

When Charles Richards came home from his school he was allowed to sit quietly at the end of Arthur's bench, ostensibly completing his homework. He watched Arthur like a hawk, but he didn't talk unless Arthur wanted him to.

Every now and then Charles would look up from his books and notice a few silent tears coursing down Arthur's face. Charles was afraid to say anything, and he knew that if he even touched Arthur's arm, the floodgates would open, and Arthur would not be able to help himself.

Arthur worked steadily on. He had cut the length of elm to the right size. He shaped and smoothed it, then spent a very long time carving a simple, but perfectly balanced design on the top. By the third day of that terrible week Arthur had varnished the wood as well as any professional artist; almost as well as his Granda Jim.

'I'll have to leave it to dry now,' he told Charles. 'I'll come back for it tomorrow. Will you be here?'

'Yes, of course I will. See you then, Art.' Charles admired the boy's work.

'See you then, Charlie,' Arthur replied with a wry sort of grin.

Neither boy was upset or offended at the other using their familiar, common names.

Arthur finished clearing up, and he was allowed to go to the scullery where his grandmother Violet made him a mug of cocoa.

Alfred inspected the workshop. He was impressed that Arthur had made a very good job of cleaning the place. He had tidied away all the tools, just as his granda had taught him. He'd cleaned every possible surface. Not a thing was out of place. Alfred's eyes caught sight of Arthur's work. It was the most beautiful and impressive walking stick. Arthur had carved on the handle "For Granda Jim".

'It's to go in his grandfather's coffin,' Charles quietly told his father. Alfred was overcome with emotion for the boy and his family.

'We'll try to look after him,' he said, as he put his arm around Charles' shoulder.

Alfred found Mrs Cole as she was about to put her coat on after her day's work. She had gone through the motions of her daily routine, but now was resigned to having to think of other things. She was expecting to meet the undertaker to visit her home that night, to finalise details for the funeral. Out of sight of the boys Alfred pressed an envelope into her hands.

'Mrs Cole, please take a few days off now. We can manage by ourselves. You have kindly left us plenty of food. Please take this for Jim,' he said, 'spend it as you wish. If there is anything we can do for you now, you only have to ask and it will be done. We treasured Jim too. He was a fine man and a fine artist. We will miss him.'

Mrs Cole thanked him with her look. She couldn't speak.

Chapter Twelve

The undertaker brought a temporary coffin. Jim's body would lie in the darkened parlour until it was time. The day before the funeral the undertaker would bring a proper coffin, and he would seal the lid.

First there was the harrowing job of sending out cards to relatives and friends. Arthur helped to inscribe the black-edged cards with his grandfather's full name, the dates of his birth and death, and then the funeral details.

'Should we put R.S.V.P. on the bottom?' he asked.

'Yes, of course,' said his grandmother, 'we need to know how many will want tea afterwards, so we can order the ham.'

'What about Jim Jr.?'

Lily had no idea whether Jim Jr. would be allowed to come home for the funeral, or how he would behave if he did. He might feel very awkward, though Lily was sure that no one would have a go at him on such a sombre occasion.

'I'm not sure it's such a good idea,' said her mother, 'it could be the cause of people arguing, and I don't want that, and anyway he might not want to go back afterwards, then he'd feel bad. Why not let him decide for himself?'

It was decided. Instead of asking Mr Richards if they could use his telephone, they would send one of the black-edged cards and a letter, with the train fare. Then Jim Jr. could decide for himself, and he would have the letter and card to show his training officers.

Black clothes were brought out of the cupboards, where they had been stored since the last funeral. Arthur had grown quite a bit since then, so he would need a new suit and boots. Lily and Violet Cole made their own hats, each with an unostentatious veil.

'What about the flowers, Ma?' Lily asked.

'Jim used to like the ones with a glass dome. He said they were worth buying because they could sit on the grave for months and maybe even through the winter time.'

'That's what we'll do then, I'll see to it,' said Lil.

Jenny, Lily's friend since childhood, and who knew and liked Jim Cole, had been round all the neighbours to gather contributions for some floral tributes, and when all the flowers started to arrive, emotions overflowed.

The day before the funeral Uncle Joseph arrived from the Kent countryside. He had left his farm in the care of two labourers for a couple of days. He brought James with him.

'We don't know where Frank is in the world,' explained James, Violet and Jim's eldest son, 'so we couldn't send word to him. I'm sorry, Ma.'

Violet Cole just nodded. She had never cared much for Uncle Joseph, and his rough manner, but he was honest and decent, and he had taken her two boys in at the worst time she could remember.

She wondered what young Arthur would make of them all.

'He's too upset to worry about Uncle Joseph and James,' Lil told her mother, 'he might just hide away by himself, go into his quiet shell. He does that sometimes.'

As arranged, the day before the funeral, the undertaker brought a proper coffin for Jim Cole. Everyone left the parlour while his body was carefully and reverently placed inside. He had been wrapped in a white satin shroud. His face looked calm and pain free, at last. The family gathered round to say their final farewells. Violet, resigned and calm, stroked Jim's cheeks and bent to kiss his forehead. Lily couldn't cry as she kissed her father, but when young Arthur placed the beautiful walking stick, which he had so lovingly crafted, inside the coffin beside his granda, Lily's tears were unstoppable.

Arthur just gazed sadly at his Granda Jim.

After everyone had finished their goodbye rituals the undertaker returned to secure the coffin lid. It was then that Arthur broke his calm. He rushed forward to the coffin.

'No! No! Don't shut the lid,' he screamed, sobbing his heart out, uncontrollably.

He had to be gently removed from the parlour, away from the coffin. He was led to the kitchen where Lily held him tight, and she rocked him back and forth, until he quietened down.

After his terrible ordeal, and the commotion it had caused, the front door opened. Standing there, holding his sailor's hat, was Jim Jr. He looked awkward, but more grown up. He didn't know what sort of reaction his presence might have on his family, but he had risked coming anyway. He would try to behave himself, and to be dignified. The funeral was not about him. Everyone agreed it was not the time for recriminations.

That night, the night before the funeral, Jim Jr. sat on the floor beside Arthur's bed. They didn't say much to each other at first. Then Arthur said, 'Why didn't you tell me you were going to run away?'

'Well, I wasn't exactly running away. I left Ma a letter telling her what I was going to do.'

'You should have asked her first.'

'I know I did it the wrong way round, but she might have said I couldn't go. Anyway, she doesn't mind now.'

'What's it like then?' Arthur asked, more out of politeness than curiosity.

'It's good. I'm really glad that I did it. I didn't like the first couple of days. We had to polish brass fittings, and clean up everywhere. But we are going to learn about engines and things. We have football teams, and I've learnt to swim properly, not just the doggy-paddle. I can dive too.'

Arthur braved a wry sort of grin.

'I suppose if you're going to be a proper sailor you'd have to be a good swimmer, just in case you fall in.'

Both boys laughed hysterically, and the anger dissipated. The two brothers decided to walk together behind the horse drawn hearse. The adults, thanks to Mr Richard's generosity, followed in two carriages. The black plumes of the horses waved in the slight breeze. Friends, neighbours and onlookers lined the pathway, or they followed on foot, to join the family in the church. Much to Violet's surprise the church was overflowing with people who had come from far and near to pay tribute to Jim Cole. Even Mr and Mrs Richards, Alice and Charles were there. Arthur felt too choked to join in the hymns, but he could hear Charles Richards singing above the rest. Arthur felt warmed and inspired by the sound, and by the presence of all the people.

The Richards family shook hands with the entire Cole family, including Uncle Joseph, then made their own way home. Invited friends and family returned to Kentish Town, for their ham tea. There was much discussion about the merits or otherwise of the day's proceedings, the vicar, the horses, the weather, and of course the fact that poor Jim was now free of all pain and had gone to a better place.

Arthur wasn't sure what "a better place" meant.

Jim Jr.'s better place was Devonport. As soon as he could decently leave the house after he had consumed his ham tea, he received a stern telling off from Uncle Joseph, and kissed his mother and his grandmother Violet, then made his exit.

Arthur walked with his brother to the omnibus.

'I wish you weren't going,' Arthur told him.

'I'll be getting leave soon, a proper long one.'

'Then what?'

'Then I'll be assigned to a ship somewhere. You could join up too, you know. When you're fourteen.'

'I can't swim.'

'They'll teach you,' said Jim.

Arthur waved his brother off and made his way slowly back to the house, where people were beginning to disperse. He didn't go in at first. He sat outside on the wall, thinking of his Granda Jim. Arthur hoped that he was in a better place, whatever that meant.

Working life would have to return to normal for the Cole women, even though they would still traditionally be in mourning. Arthur would have to return to school. He didn't think he would ever feel normal again.

CHAPTER THIRTEEN

The death of Jim Cole turned out to be a kind of watershed. It had upset Alfred deeply and so he did his best to help young Arthur to find his place in the world. It caused Alfred to question everything in his own life, and both he and Frances decided that they would open up the whole basement area of their house to provide a number of different facilities for people wishing to improve or learn new skills, which were going to be vital in the days to come.

An air of uncertainty pervaded the whole country, not least because of the fluctuating political climate. One minute being governed by the Tories, then the liberal landslide, and a growing new socialism was taking hold of working class people's imagination and hopes for the future. Alfred sympathised with their plight.

'Alice, I think I am becoming a socialist, without realising it.'

'I think the same, Alfred. You do not surprise me.'

'I'm not sure whether my new ideas will go down too well with my employers, but I think *The News* is gathering momentum among working people now.'

'I agree with you, Alfred. It's very interesting seeing your pictures of new road vehicles, aircraft and so on, but times are difficult for many people and you are right to try and highlight more social conditions.'

'I'd never have got away with drawing slum housing at the *Gazette*,' he remarked.

'Or the soup kitchens,' reminded Alice, 'I was shocked to see your pictures of the seemingly never-ending queues there.'

'It was all true, Alice. We only publish things as they are.'

'Well done, Alfred. I'm very proud of you.'

'And I'm proud of you, trying to cope with all those poor children on a daily basis. You look exhausted.'

Alfred Richards took himself to the very poorest places to draw pictures of the most harrowing scenes of deprivation, hoping to shame the powers above to spring into action to try and alleviate poverty and distress. He exposed unscrupulous landlords and businessmen who were charging exorbitant rents and rates, and he cited many cases of sick people who couldn't pay either their rent, or buy food and medicines. Alfred would often return home feeling very dejected after one of his assignments, but he struggled on while ever he thought there was a cause which needed to be exposed.

'This workshop gives me some sense of hope,' he told his wife, and Alice, who often came to help with some of the evening groups. 'You are so good, Alice, to come here and help, especially as you will have had a hard day at school.'

'Nonsense, I love to help. Come and look. I'll show you what we are doing so far.'

Alice walked Alfred round the various groups of women and young girls. Some were her former school pupils. She pointed to the groups.

'This group of ladies are making garments for the soldiers who are being sent overseas, warm gloves and hats. Some are clever enough to make socks too.'

'I'm very impressed,' Alfred said.

'And these,' Alice was sounding especially pleased, 'these younger ladies are being taught how to sew and knit, so they will eventually be able to make things to sell for themselves.'

'Where are you getting the wool and materials from?'

Alice hesitated. She didn't really want to divulge that her friend Ellice, who was the most resourceful person she had ever met, had persuaded some of her more affluent suffragist ladies to donate cast-off dresses and wool garments, which could be carefully unpicked and re-used.

'They have unpicked a lot of the donated garments.'

'That's very enterprising, Alice. Well done.'

Alice was glad that she had managed to avoid bringing her friend Ellice into the matter. Not that Alfred would have objected on this occasion. It was just that Ellice had been in trouble with the police over the women's demonstrations. Alice thought it would be more diplomatic to avoid mentioning her just then. Actually, she saw less and less of Ellice now that she seemed to be taking on a slightly less confrontational role in her activities. Her imprisonment had opened her eyes to the treatment of women by the authorities, and she left prison, quite undaunted, determined to find a way of improving things, without getting herself locked up.

'I shall try to do things in the traditional manner. I will run for Parliament myself,' she had announced.

True to her word Ellice began to work for the socialist cause, and took on a lesser public role with the suffragists, though she was not undimmed in her support of them. She would work alongside the Webbs and support Mr Keir Hardie in his pursuit of a place for the Labour Party, in government.

Much to Alfred's relief the two friends did eventually drift apart, not through any kind of disagreement, but because Ellice had to work all the hours available to her, day or night. She decided to take rooms near to the London School of Economics, where she would always be on hand, for the "party".

Alfred couldn't resist making some kind of comment.

'Well, at least we won't have to worry about bricks being thrown through our windows now, Alice.'

'Alfred! What an awful thing to say. Ellice is a very kind and helpful person. She is the one to turn to in a crisis.'

'She will still come to concerts, with Charles and I, but probably not quite so many. You should bring Frances along. I'm sure she would love the music.'

'Yes, the music. I'm afraid Fran isn't quite ready yet to face the crowds. She is happy where she knows people; in her own environment. I'm so glad that she has taken to helping the women and girls in the sewing classes. She's very good with them.'

Alice continued to take Charles to concerts, mostly by herself. On rare occasions Alfred would manage to persuade Fran to come too.

Charles was thrilled when Frances agreed to come to the Kreisler concert.

'Wasn't that wonderful music?' he reminded Alice. 'We were so lucky to get tickets for the first performance of the Elgar Concerto.'

'We were very lucky. Do you remember how you went home and tried to pick out the themes on the piano?'

'Yes, Aunt. It was the only time I wished I had learned to play the violin. It doesn't sound the same on the piano.'

'You're quite right Charles, but you can't do everything. You are a fine singer now, and people love to hear you.'

'I like singing lieder best of all,' he told her.

Alice laughed with him. His relationship with Mr Cavalli had been rather tempestuous, but his teacher had finally relented and ceased to force Charles into singing Italian opera. Frances was pleased to hear Charles singing his beautiful lieder, but was a little worried that maybe, in the present world climate, he ought not to be singing in German!

Alice made quite sure that she was at every performance that Charles took part in. People often saw them together and assumed they were mother and son. They would receive nods of acknowledgement and Alice liked the feeling. She didn't disillusion anyone.

Alice had watched Charles develop from a premature, almost lost baby, into a shy schoolboy; a gangly but affable youth, with his head always immersed in a book, then blossoming into a caring, confident, and well-rounded, socially aware young man. She was as proud of the way he had turned out as if he had been her own child. She had convinced herself that she didn't really mind too much if she was destined to remain a spinster aunt. She had probably let too much time elapse before even thinking of marriage and children. She had often wondered if her sister Frances had ever longed to have more children, but she didn't dare to ask her about it. The traumatic birth of Charles had been an overwhelming, terrible experience for her. It was never spoken about.

Charles had a very different upbringing than either of his parents, and they felt it was all to the good. Yes, he had an excellent education, and a myriad of experiences in sport and music, and had often accompanied his father on interesting assignments for the press. He was un-blinkered about life, and through the friendship with Arthur, in fact the entire Cole family, he had developed an unusual empathy with people who might not be so fortunate as himself. He had quite happily volunteered to help in the soup kitchens, alongside his mother, and at the hospital. Ellice had introduced Charles to the children's ward. He would read stories to some of the frightened children, and hold their hands. Sometimes he was allowed to spoon-feed patients when they couldn't manage it for themselves.

Alfred and Alice often discussed Charles and what career path he might consider. They didn't often include Frances, and of course whatever the boy chose to do, it would inevitably mean that Frances would miss him.

'Yes,' remarked Alfred on one of those discussion days with Alice, 'ultimately all this character building experience has simply given Charles more problems, when it comes to making a choice.'

'You're right, Alfred,' Alice said, 'one minute he wants to be a children's doctor, then he wants to be a professional musician, or a writer, how realistic is that?'

Alfred remembered the vehement arguments he had experienced with his father. Alfred had to listen only to his father's views. He was not allowed to voice his own opinion. Even his beloved mother, Rose Maud, knew when to keep silent.

'It was fortunate for me,' Alfred reminded Alice, 'that when the time came for me to do something with my life, my father was sent away on extended naval duties.'

'So how did you manage to get the work at the *Gazette*?'

'Luckily, one of father's friends sent a letter of introduction to the editor, and I was offered a trial period. It did prove to be a good compromise.'

'So what are we going to do with Charles?' Alice asked.

'It's very strange. I find myself in the same position as my father was, with me. I want to encourage Charles into something safe, and with long future prospects. Any father would do the same, wouldn't they?'

'Yes, of course, but times are very different now. You have allowed us all to benefit from this new, liberal way of thinking, and express our individual views. You are to be praised for that.'

'Thank you, Alice. I hope Frances will see it that way.'

'How about us having a family discussion; all of us together?' Alfred felt relieved once the family conversation got under way, and of course Charles took complete charge, from the start.

'I used to think that I would like to be a musician,' he began, 'but I wouldn't want to end up like Mr Cavalli, or be a school teacher, like Aunt Alice.'

'Charles, that's very unkind. Your aunt is a wonderful and respected teacher. She does an amazingly good job. She has a gift for finding the best in children.'

'Sorry, Aunt, I didn't mean that to sound so rude.'

'Carry on, Charles. I forgive you,' Alice said.

'Thanks, Aunt. I mean, if I were to be a singer of any repute I would have to be prepared to travel the world. Right now that doesn't seem a sensible thing to do. Besides, I would miss you all. I shall keep music as my lifelong passion. I'll never lose it,' he reassured them.

Everyone nodded in agreement, but nobody spoke. They were all impressed with Charles's very mature analysis.

'I am very fascinated by history,' he continued, 'and there are many things I would like to write about, but I don't want to go to university to do that. From what I have heard from other chaps, it is all very formal there. I'd like to take my time, researching and travelling a bit, perhaps. What does anyone else think?'

'It would be wonderful to travel, Charles, and to write about your foreign exploits,' Alice offered, 'but where could you go that is now a safe place?'

'It doesn't sound like a career, just a holiday,' Alfred said. Charles reminded his father about his time in South Africa.

It wasn't a good idea to bring that up just then.

'I was rather forced into that,' Alfred reminded them. 'Well, Charles. I don't want to dampen your enthusiasm, but if you do have an extended travel period, to follow your interests, it could be more difficult for you to find a permanent position somewhere in London.'

Alfred thought he was beginning to sound like his father, and wished he hadn't said quite so much.

Alice lightened the mood.

'Why don't you write down all the things you are really good at doing, and consider each in turn? You might surprise yourself with the possibilities?'

'That's easy,' laughed Charles, 'I'm good at music and creative writing.'

'And mathematics,' chimed Alice.

'And what about your great gift of compassion?'

Alfred had thrown another, previously unthought-of idea into the discussion.

'You're not suggesting I become a priest, Father?'

This caused great hilarity, especially the thoughts of Charles in clerical robes. Alice thought it time to be serious.

'Actually, Charles, your Grandfather Combe was a wonderful parish priest.'

They all spent a few moments in quiet reflection. Then Alice patted Charles on his arm.

'We have time. Charles has time. Nothing has to be decided right now. At least we have opened up the conversation to ideas.'

'I'm luckier than Arthur Cole, aren't I? He had to leave school early, but he is grateful to you, Father, for helping him into the carpenter's apprenticeship.'

'He is a gifted boy too, but in a different way,' Alfred acknowledged the gift that Arthur had inherited from Jim.

Before long, a temporary, stopgap occupation was found. Charles was offered an unpaid placement in the offices of his father's lawyer, Peter Lawrence.

Charles didn't care much for Peter Lawrence. He seemed a pompous man, dismissive of people he didn't think of as important. But, Charles was prepared to stick it out for a while. He would keep his head down, learn how a lawyer's office was organised and take from the experience whatever he could.

Peter Lawrence was away for much of the time, much to Charles's relief. He had been entrusted to the care of Mr Hugh Greenford, the office manager. He was quite different to Peter Lawrence, a very quiet, unassuming man but with a wry sense of humour on some occasions.

'You need a sense of humour to work here,' he once told Charles, 'we see all kinds of people, but we have to remain impartial, and deal as efficiently as we can, with everyone, no matter who they are. We just have to get on with the job, pass no opinions, do as you are told, and everything will be fine.'

Charles warmed to Mr Greenford, but he found the days interminably boring.

'I mostly have to double check pages and pages of figures, accounts which somebody else has already checked,' he told Alice.

'I expect it's an important part of the job,' she sympathised.

'Sometimes I get to copy lists of client's names and addresses into various large coloured ledgers; the only bit of excitement is when I am on a postal route, delivering brown envelopes to other places around London. Then I manage to get some fresh air, and stretch my legs.'

'At least you are learning about a lawyer's office.'

'To be honest, Aunt, the only thing I've learned is that being a lawyer's clerk is a very tedious job.'

Alfred made no comments. He was just thankful that Charles had not been in the company of Peter Lawrence, except for a few days at the beginning of his time there. Knowing a little about Peter Lawrence and his connection with the government agents in France, he felt more than a little nervous about Charles possibly being inveigled into that murky world.

Charles Richards fulfilled his commitment of almost a year, working as a temporary legal clerk. He couldn't wait for the end of it.

'It has been extremely boring, Father,' he told Alfred that very last day, 'and you know it's a very lonely profession.'

'He's been a very quick learner,' Mr Greenford reported.

'Too clever to stay a law clerk, if I may say so?'

'Why don't you study law then, Charles?' Peter Lawrence added to the conversation.

Charles was far too polite to say that he would find all the studying at university equally as tedious as the daily grind he had endured at the office. He kept his real thoughts to himself.

Wild horses wouldn't drag him back to any kind of office work. He had definitely had enough of that.

'I'm leaving all my options open for now, thank you, sir.'

Alfred Richards praised his son when they were away from the lawyer's office and no one could overhear.

'Well done, Charles. You haven't particularly enjoyed it but you've had the courage to stick it out, and it has shown you how other people function in their lives and work.'

'I can't tell you how great it feels to have escaped, Father, I don't know how people like Mr Greenford manage at all.'

'You can get used to anything if you have to. Many people have little choice, Charles.'

'Yes, I understand that, Father. I think Arthur will be enjoying his work with wood, won't he?'

'He found his vocation, through Jim, didn't he?'

'It must be wonderful to know exactly what your life is going to be, but then, where is the challenge, Father?'

Glad to have escaped the office work, Charles remained very unsettled. Schooldays and school chums were left behind, long since, and he missed Artie too, in a funny sort of way.

Charles was almost eighteen, not quite a man, but no longer a boy.

'If you're feeling at a loose end Charles, would you like to come and help me choose some new photographic things?'

'Yes, Father. How exciting. But er... you, and photography?'

'Photographs are the next new thing, Charles. I can foresee the time when newspapers will be reproducing photos in the papers, and when that happens, I'll be out of a job.'

'But you are the leading sketch artist, Father.'

'I hope there will always be private buyers of my work, but honestly, I think pen and ink drawings now have a limited appeal. We'd both better learn about photography, especially if you decide to go travelling.'

'What about *Punch* father? Could you draw for them?'

'I'd rather depict real life, as it happens. I don't feel I have the talent for satire, especially if it's political.' The two made their way to the Knightsbridge store, where all the latest cameras and equipment were being demonstrated. They even had their portraits taken, both separately, and then the two of them together. They would have to wait until the next day before the prints were available.

They looked for some special frames in anticipation of collecting the prints the next day.

Charles found some silver frames.

'Do you think Mother would like these?'

'Yes! I am certain she would.'

They were both remembering Jim Cole at that moment. How sad, Alfred thought, that they would never have any more of Jim's lovely frames, with their unique, special carvings.

'Do you think of photography as art, Father?' Charles was curious. He was surprised that his father was prepared to embrace the idea of this modern, time-saving invention.

'It would take you a long time to paint pictures such as we have seen in the photographs, wouldn't it?'

'True,' replied Alfred, 'I suppose you could call it a lazy man's art. All you do is click a shutter and the work is done.'

'Is that all there is to it?'

'No, not really, Charles. I'm being facetious. It's just a very different way of producing an image. Surely a good photographer would still need to consider the light source, the sort of background desired and the placing of the subject in the most appealing way.'

Charles was fascinated and thanked his father for the new camera. He couldn't wait to try it out.

'Perhaps I could be a photojournalist, Father?'

'So you'll be happy to put real artists out of a job, then?' They hurried home to show Frances their new cameras, and a lot of other bits of equipment too. They took everything to the workshop, to find a special place for it all.

'If we develop our own photographs, Father, we will need to make a dark room, won't we?'

'There's plenty of room here.'

They shifted tables and benches around, and found a spare corner which could be cordoned off, for now. As they were busy measuring up they were interrupted by Arthur Cole.

'Hello,' he said chirpily, 'I hope you don't mind me having a last look at the old place. Mrs Richards said it would be all right.'

Alfred beckoned him in.

'Of course, you're very welcome, Arthur. Come in.'

'Nice to see you, Arthur. It's been a long time.' Charles greeted him with a grown-up handshake and a pat on his shoulder.

Alfred enquired about Arthur's apprenticeship.

'It's been good, sir. I've finished now. Qualified carpenter. I might have my own business one day, like my Granda Jim. I came to say thank you for everything, Mr Richards. My Ma said I should come before I go away.'

'Where are you off to, Arthur?'

'I'm going to be a ship's carpenter. I'm joining up. Going to try and find Jim Jr., if I can.'

'How does your mother feel about that?' Alfred asked him.

'She's all right about it now. She's glad I've got a trade. She's got herself a new fella. He's all right too. He treats her good, and he treats me good too. Like his own son, he said.'

Arthur, now also grown-up and much more confident, dared to ask Charles what his next move would be.

'I expect you'll be one of those city gents, going off in your posh suit and bowler hat,' he teased Charles.

'No! God forbid!' Charles told him, 'It's the very last thing I want to do.' He told Arthur about the lawyer's office, which he had hated, and which had put him off any kind of business career.

'I want to travel, at least I do when the world is a more settled place. I want to explore other lands and people, oceans, mountains, wild animals and forests.'

Arthur was in awe of him.

'Yeah! That'd be great,' Arthur said, in wonderment.

They sat there daydreaming, and reminded each other of the train set which they had made go through imaginary forests. They both fell silent, just sitting there, enjoying each other's company.

'You could always follow me to Devonport, Charlie. I mean, not to join up, proper. They want educated people, like you, to be writers. They work for the navy, in the offices by the dockyard.'

Arthur began to tell Charles about the youth training place.

'It's where Jim Jr. ran off to. He pretended he was fourteen. Well, he was nearly, but they let him in all the same.'

Arthur thought the writers must be good chaps, because they played football and billiards with the boys, and taught them how to swim.

Charles interrupted him.

'I suppose a lot of the city boys had never had the chance to learn to swim. They'd have to do that first.'

'Yeah! Or they'd fall in,' joked Arthur, the same words he had used jokingly, with his brother Jim. Charles felt like a brother, and strangely Charles thought that Arthur would be fun as a brother.

'What do they do then, these writers?' Charles asked.

'They have to keep records of everything, accounts, orders, taking reports to officers and the medics. Jim said that one of the writers taught him how to read properly. The writers need to be good swimmers too, because sometimes they have to go out in small ships with the boys, before they get posted to the big ships.' Arthur was so enthusiastic that it didn't take very long before Charles was enthusiastic too. He wouldn't care for doing accounts, but he could cope with that if there were lots of other interesting things to do, and he would be near the sea. Arthur had persuaded him. He would apply the very next day, after he had spoken with his father and mother, and Alice, of course. She was really his greatest ally. She would back him up.

Alfred was relieved, in a way, that Charles had found something that excited him, but he was secretly filled with apprehension. War seemed to be inevitable, if the papers were to be believed.

The most worrying sign, to Alfred, was the public bickering between Winston Churchill and the First Sea Lord. More battle ships were being built, in seeming haste, and the British fleet was being expanded in the North Sea. Thousands more men and boys were being recruited into the army and the navy, and the latest he had heard was that Churchill was insisting on re-furbishing old battleships, in case they would be needed.

'There seems to be little cohesion of thought between the senior politicians and the military experts, or at least those who think they are experts,' Alfred was trying to draw Charles into a serious conversation, before he embarked for Devonport.

'Don't worry, Father. We have the best soldiers and sailors in the whole world. It won't come to anything.'

Alfred and Frances took Charles to Paddington Station. Alice couldn't bear to wave him off, but in any case she had to be in school, so she had said her tearful goodbye the previous evening. She had given him a silver pen, engraved with his name.

'Be sure to write some amazing things, Charles.'

'I will, Aunt, I promise.'

Alfred comforted his wife, as they waved to Charles.

'Well, my dear, he's not going to be a regular sailor, like my father. He'll be shore-based. We will be able to visit him in Devon. You would like it there; the countryside is very pretty, and we would be near the sea. We can look forward to his home leave as well.'

Frances nodded and bravely fought back her tears.

Two weeks elapsed before Frances received her first letter from Charles. She had anxiously waited for the post every morning.

'Here we are Mrs Richards. This is what you have been waiting for.' Mrs Cole smiled as she brought in the post. 'My boys never wrote to me, and neither have Lily's two, except for the leaving note when Jim Jr. took off.'

Mrs Cole left Frances to her letter.

June 30th 1912

Dearest Mother and Father,

Just a short note to let you know that I arrived safely. I am

well. The base is very large and spread out. My quarters are
comfortable. The only drawback so far is having to rise at 6.00 a.m.
or I should say 0600 hours, to the sound of a bugle.

Much love,
C.

Frances left her breakfast. She couldn't wait to write a reply to
Charles. She hurried to find a pen and paper, as though it was of
vital importance to write there and then. Alfred didn't dissuade
her this first time, but he knew that it would be wise in future to
delay a few days between letters. Charles needed to adjust to his
new life, and frequent letters from home might just cause him less
likely to settle. He might feel lonely or homesick. Even at eighteen
and intelligent though he was, he had been used to having
everything done for him by the family, or Mrs Cole, their kindly
treasure.

Charles didn't feel lonely, or homesick. He soon learned to
fend for himself. He was excited by this new world, if slightly
daunted by the regimentation of it all. Everything had to be done
either by the clock, the bugle, or the bells. Still, the writers and the
petty officers had their routine and regular responsibilities. In
between, they were allowed to go off base or help the boy sailors
with their swimming or sporting endeavours. Many of the boys
had come from pitiable backgrounds; they had lacked food and
needed building up. Some of them just lacked even basic, raw
skills in reading and writing. They had just enough to scrape into
the navy. Charles saw this as a worthwhile challenge, as well as the
rest of his clerical work and report writing.

When it came to writing letters home he wasn't quite sure how
much information he was allowed to pass on. Nobody had told
him. He decided to keep details of his work as brief and general as
he could, just in case his letters were scrutinised.

30th October 1912

Dearest Mother and Father,

I trust you are both well and keeping busy in the craft workshops. Apologies if my letters seem very short. I do have to write a lot, during the daytime. It's a wonder I don't have writer's cramp. I have to keep a detailed log of everything which happens here.

I don't mind the timetable now. Up at 6.00 a.m. Rolls 7.20 a.m. and working parties at 8.00 a.m. Then God Save the King. On Sundays we accompany the boys to church. Tomorrow the writers are invited to dinner on board with the Marines. We have to wear white gloves. It's silver service, flowers, a band playing. Very civilised.

Much love,
Charles.

Alfred, Frances and Alice read the letter together, even calling Mrs Cole in so they could read her the bits about Charles having dinner with the Marines, and the white gloves.

'It does sound as though he has found an interesting job doesn't it, Alfred?' Alice was pleased to hear about him trying to teach the young boys to read and write.

'Yes. I think we can all relax a little. Charles does seem to be in his element.' Alfred was trying his best to keep up appearances for the sake of his women, but he was inwardly very worried for the future prospects of his son.

Alfred read the morning papers diligently, though now more out of habit; a daily ritual and not because he really was keen to read all the depressing news. When he had finished reading he threw the papers out, so that Frances would not be tempted to pick them up. Part of him realised that he was being very selfish and not a little chauvinistic. He would be in Ellice's bad books!

Charles's next letter home, in November, told of rumours about Germany and Constantinople. Officers seemed edgy, he said, but as far as he knew, life and leave continued as before. He had played in a billiards tournament, and won. To celebrate, he and a friend had found a classical concert at the Guildhall, in Plymouth. They had taken two young ladies with them. Charles had been so moved by one of the songs that he had copied out a verse, along with the tonic sol-fa, so that he could sing it for himself.

'Charles is good to be keeping up with some kind of music,' beamed Alice, 'fancy him remembering how to write the song out in tonic sol-fa. Perhaps he will sing it for us when he is home on leave.'

Alfred was pleased too.

'We're hoping Charles will be able to book us a place at the Sailor's Rest for our visit to Devon. It's a Temperance Hotel; Frances should approve of that,' he told Alice.

'Is it right that Charles could actually live in the hotel if he chose to do so?'

'Yes, he could. Apparently some of the more affluent writers have a permanent room there; others just book a room for their extended leave, when they want to escape from their offices. Charles says it is very comfortable, a home from home, with bathrooms, a writing room, good food, and evening entertainment. Sometimes a classical singer or duos are engaged and sometimes they have music hall artists. Inevitably young lady friends would be invited along for the evening shows. Frances hoped they were decent girls.'

'Well, they won't be inebriated if it's a Temperance Hotel, will they?' quipped Alice.

Alfred was becoming more philosophical about Charles being away from home. He thought it might be the making of him. Letters home became less frequent, now that Charles had access to a telephone, and they could speak to each other instead. Frances was in a much more cheerful mood after she had spoken with Charles on the telephone. She left little time for Alfred to speak with him, so Alfred engineered a time when Frances would be out of the house. This annoyed Frances greatly.

'Do you know, Fran,' Alfred related one such conversation to Frances, 'Charles spent thirteen shillings in two nights. He went to see Plymouth Argyle play Exeter City. Then he had tea at the Sailor's Rest with a friend, and went to a concert in the evening. He's still singing, Fran. Aren't you pleased? He's rehearsing *Worthy is the Lamb,* and his choir have several engagements to sing the full *Messiah* in December.'

'Wonderful,' said Alice, 'isn't that wonderful, Fran?'

That Christmas of 1913 proved to be anything but wonderful, and started out to be a rather sombre affair. Charles had his leave cancelled, and there was a great panic as Christmas gifts had to be bought and posted off to Devonport. The Cole boys had not been heard of for months. The two families did their best to keep things as cheery as they could, though none of them felt as though it was Christmas.

Frances and Alice, at Alfred's instigation, invited Lily and her mother to spend Christmas Day with them, and after a few embarrassed moments they all managed to relax in a fashion. The Richards family waited upon the Cole family.

'You are our guests for today,' Alfred said proudly. He raised his wine glass.

'To all of our absent loved ones,' he said.

'To all of our absent loved ones,' everyone repeated.

The Christmas meal, shared by the Richards and the Coles, heralded the awful rumblings of war in the year to come. It would be the end of their gentle, comfortable life, for some time to come. Thousands of young men would be drafted to fight in Europe, and beyond, and thousands would never come home. Women would find themselves having to do men's work in the fields and factories, in order to keep everyone fed, and the country functioning as best it could. Women would certainly have earned their rights, when the time came.

Ellice Bell never relinquished her fight for women's emancipation and the right to vote, but when the war started she returned to nursing, where she could be of immediate help.

One awful night, a zeppelin bomb fell on Kentish Town, where the Coles lived. Alice, fearing for their safety, insisted that both Lily and her mother came to live with her at Highgate, until the situation improved.

'What happens if the boys come home?' Lily wanted to know.

'They will know where to come,' Alice reassured her. Violet Cole was glad of Alice's kind offer, and glad too that Jim, her husband, was not alive to experience the war. Alfred and Frances were thinking the same about their own kin.

Charles was not allowed to use the telephone on the base any more, and the post became very erratic. Alfred lost track of the sequence of events which Charles had last related to them. He became distracted from everything else, but finding the last few letters they had received from Charles. He fumbled awkwardly to put them in order of the dates.

'Here we are Fran. Listen. Prince Louis had visited them with Winston Churchill. All the boys had to polish their boots and buttons until they shone. It was the next letter that he said he was being transferred to Chatham.' Alfred's eyes misted over when he found the third letter. He found it difficult to read the words. Alice took the letter from him.

'Would you like me to read it, Alfred?' He nodded.

Alice quickly read the letter to herself, before relating the details to them both.

'He was hurriedly upgraded, given a short service commission, and sent to board *HMS Goliath*.'

'It's one of the old pre-dreadnought battleships,' said Alfred. He had read about it in the papers, 'Churchill has pressed it, and others, in to service, without total agreement of the War Cabinet.'

'Can he do that, Alfred?' Alice was quick to ask.

'I'm not an expert, dear heart, but it strikes me that the army generals and the navy commanders do not talk to each other. They each think they own the war, but that is only my opinion.'

Frances looked totally bemused. Alfred tried to say as many comforting things as he could think of.

'Well, there was talk of sending ships out to the North Sea, to guard the fishing fleets. That's probably what it's all about. We need the food, don't we?'

Alfred walked away. He left the two sisters alone, to try to comfort each other, in their anxiety. He was sure there was one more letter from Charles that he had missed. He went back to his desk drawer and carefully sifted through everything he could find. There it was. He found the letter, but wished that he hadn't. *HMS Goliath* had been returned to Chatham, from the East Indies and from Africa, for a complete re-fit. It would be sent to the North Sea battle fleet to help the French. Its destination from there was uncertain, Charles had written:

... One good thing, Father, you will be pleased to know that Arthur Cole has joined the ship as a foreman joiner.

I have to keep inventory of all the wood his men use for repairs, even the stuff he throws overboard as of no use. Every nail or pot of varnish has to be accounted for. No word of Jim Jr., I'm afraid, but I'll be able to write home for Arthur now. He sends his love to his mother, and his grandmother, as I do to you all.

Your loving son,
Charles

P.S. An airship has just passed over the dockyard.
P.S. Later... it was Winston in a naval airship floating out of Arethusa. C.

There were no further letters from Charles.

Alfred read the dreadful news in the *Gazette*. He took the paper to the workshop, to read by himself. He was thankful that he no longer had to check the print, but he was certain that the facts would be correct, and officially verified, beyond doubt. There it was, in black and white, the news that he had been dreading. He felt very faint, and sick, but he forced himself to read it all, very slowly, and more than once:

"Anchored in Morto Bay, off Cape Hellas, alongside the ship Cornwallis, and a screen of five destroyers, a German-Turkish torpedo boat crew eluded the Beagle and Bulldog, through the thick fog, and closed on the ships. At approximately 1.00 a.m. on May 13th under cover of darkness, the Muavenet-i-Millet slipped down the straits of the Dardanelles, and fired two torpedoes, which then struck HMS Goliath simultaneously abreast the fore turret, and abeam the fore tunnel, causing massive explosions. Goliath began to capsize almost at once, and was lying on her beam-ends when a third torpedo struck another turret. Goliath rolled over completely, and began to sink by the bows. It is thought that 570 out of 700 crew were lost very quickly, including the captain, Captain Thomas Lawrie Shelford. Many of those who survived the blast are thought to have drowned. The Admiralty will publish precise figures as soon as they are available."

Alfred's blood ran cold, and a sense of numbness enveloped him. He was filled with fear and dread. He read the paper again and again, and eventually laid it in a drawer. He wouldn't say anything to Frances until it was official, until they received the telegram. Charles could be one of the survivors. He was an excellent swimmer, and over one hundred men were thought to have survived. Alfred tried to stay positive, and busy, when he wasn't praying.

Alfred Richards tossed and turned in his bed that night.

He hardly slept for remembering that May 15th 1915 was his son's twenty-first birthday. They had planned a special dinner, even though Charles would not be with them. He had been born just a few weeks later than Arthur, whose mother Lily had helped save his life along with Mrs Cole and Alice. It all came flooding back to him as he lay there, trying desperately to think of any words he might use, if the worst was to be confirmed.

They were all at the house together, preparing for the very special birthday dinner, when the doorbell rang. Alfred opened the door to the telegram boy, who took his hat off as he gave the telegram to Alfred. He gave the boy a shilling.

'There will be no reply, thank you,' he choked.

'Thank you very much, sir,' the boy said, and ran off.

Alfred shook. He had to open the envelope, though he knew its contents. He didn't need to speak. His ashen face said it all. Frances took the telegram from his hand, and as she read it she gave a piercing, heart-rending scream, like the scream that Alfred recalled from that night twenty-one years ago, as Charles was born.

Lily ran out of the house, screaming.

'I have to get to the Highgate house, that's where my letter will be.'

She had absolutely no doubt in her mind at all, that Arthur and Charles would be together.

Alice hugged her sister tightly. They were both utterly devastated, and for a few moments, unable to speak. Then, Frances let go of Alice, stood up from the green sofa, and whispered, 'They did their duty.'

Alfred nodded tearfully, and clung on to Violet Cole, as if she were his real mother.

CHAPTER FOURTEEN

Widespread grief and horror had consumed the nation for four and a half years. Almost every family had lost at least one of their members, or they knew someone who had. This had been known as the war to end all wars, though few people really believed that. Peace did eventually come to a war-weary country, and there were the most unprecedented scenes of jubilation in the streets, when on 11th November 1918 at 11.00 a.m., the documents of peace were signed in a heavily guarded railway carriage, in the French Forest of Compiegne.

At 11.00 a.m. on Victory Day, in London, the church bells chimed constantly, boy scouts cycled around towns and villages with their bugles, to sound the "All Clear" for as long as they had the breath to do so.

People thronged the streets in their thousands. They found flags to wave, and songs to sing. The king and queen drove through Hyde Park, waving to the people. Thousands more crammed into hectic Downing Street, to cheer Prime Minister Lloyd George, and the members of the coalition cabinet. Licensed bars ignored the law and stayed open until they had no beer left to sell. Any soldier or sailor, in uniform, who found himself on the streets, would very likely be hoisted on high, and carried to the nearest ale house.

In people's homes, the blackout screens and curtains were removed and suddenly everywhere seemed ablaze with light.

The Richards family were of course relieved that the war was over, at last, though they could not bring themselves to join the merry throng, out in the streets. Even though three and a half years had passed since they had lost Charles, and Mrs Cole and Lily had lost Arthur and maybe even Jim Jr., Frances particularly, lived each day as if she was repeating that fateful day of loss and heartache.

After the cruel loss of Charles, grief and sadness occupied the private thoughts of Frances constantly. Irrationally, in her heart, Charles was still alive, and would be coming home to celebrate his birthday with them. She clung to this belief, because it allowed her to give an outward semblance of normality. Alfred's strength and solace came mostly from Alice.

'Overwhelming grief and sadness does things to the people who survive,' Alfred told her, 'Alice, it isn't true that time heals the pain. One becomes anaesthetised, pushing sad thoughts into the background, so that you can give some appearance of carrying on.'

'I know what you mean, Alfred,' she said, 'I try my best to keep things moving at school, for the children's sake, but sometimes a child will tell you something, or they will be quietly crying, in a corner somewhere, trying to make sense of the world, and it will bring everything back to me, so that I have to go and find a corner to cry in.'

'Do your friends comfort you, Alice? How is Ellice these days and what about your young man; Edward, is it?'

'He's not exactly my young man, Alfred, and Ellice is a great help because she is so practical and down to earth, she doesn't really allow you to drown in gloomy thoughts for long, though she understands about the pain and loss.'

Alice reminded him about Ellice being a nurse during the war years and about Miss Appleton, the nanny who ran off with Charles that day, to Hampstead Heath.

'Do you know, Alfred, that when Ellice was nursing in the hospital, she arranged for Miss Appleton to be moved, so that she

199

would not catch sight of injured soldiers being in the wards. Her fiancé was apparently killed in South Africa and that is why she suffered the breakdown.'

Alfred remembered his awful time in Africa and how ill he was on his journalist assignment. He wasn't sure whether he had been told about Miss Appleton's breakdown.

'Why didn't we know about that at the time?'

'I understand that Doctor Ingram kept quiet about it, knowing how desperate you and Frances were to find a nanny, and Miss Appleton was in need of a job.'

'Alice, I am so sorry about the poor lady.'

'Ellice tells me that she is slowly improving, but, like Frances, she still chooses to believe that her man will return, and she will marry him, when he does.'

'We must try to help her, when she is fit enough.'

'Alfred, you are such a kind person. You would like to help the entire world, wouldn't you?'

'We must all try to help. There are so many destitute and damaged families because of the war, it is really difficult to decide how best to help in our own small corner, isn't it?'

'I'm quite sure you will find a way, Alfred.'

'Alice, I think I have an idea which will prove to be useful to soldiers, returning from the war, but I am going to need some help setting it up properly. I feel so weary myself; I can't really tell if I have the energy to keep it going; much as my heart tells me to get on with it and be grateful that I have a home, the trouble is, it is such a sad place just now.'

'I know, Alfred,' Alice comforted him, 'but we will all help in whatever way we can, even Ellice. Take courage, brother. We are all sad, and we will steadily find ways of dealing with it. I worry for Frances, so anything we can do to keep her involved would be a very positive step.'

Many months passed after Victory Day, and the house at Han Street still seemed eerily quiet. Frances had retreated into herself, hardly able to move her body. The shock of losing Charles was all-enveloping. She and Alfred were unable to find any meaningful words to say to each other. Frances could only search the skies for answers, and none came.

She had permanent dark circles around her eyes through lack of sleep. When Alfred tried to hold her gently, to offer some warmth and comfort, she pulled away from him, completely unable to respond. She was cloaked in her grief.

Alfred's sense of loss and grief manifested itself in real physical pain, from which he had little respite. His brief moments of warmth and comfort emanated from Alice, and from Mrs Cole. At times all three of them cried together, without them speaking any words. There was no need for words. How could anyone utter any words which could put their world right again?

Violet Cole's daily chores occupied her as usual, and in a strange way she needed the routine, and the fact that other people relied upon her, however she might be feeling. Work was her therapy. She was the first to recognise that people who had suffered deep shock usually lost their desire for food. The main thing was to find something not too rich or overpowering, to stimulate their appetites again, even if they were just going through the motions of what used to be normal mealtimes.

'Shall I make soup today?' she would ask Alfred. It was no use asking Frances. She was quite unable to focus on anything much.

At least Alfred managed to nod a reply, and sometimes a short answer.

'I'll make small, fresh rolls, instead of the large loaves,' she would mutter to herself, but at the same time knowing Alfred would have taken it in.

'I'm sure Mrs Richards would like that,' he would reply.

Mrs Cole set about her work, a handkerchief permanently in her pocket, for those moments of sadness, which crept up on her unawares.

Alfred mostly retreated to his craft workshop until he heard the bell to signal that a meal was ready. He would usually just sit there and think of Charles, and about the fine Jim Cole, master carpenter. He would never forget the day that young Artie had crafted the beautiful walking stick, and when it was finished, how tenderly he had placed it inside his granda's coffin. It was at that very moment that Alfred felt the complete loss of his faith in God. It all seemed so futile, now.

Alice, mainstay of the family, felt just as low and lethargic as everyone else, but she yearned to escape from them sometimes.

She travelled back and forth between her own house and theirs, just to keep an eye on them both. She often came away feeling that her visits had not helped at all. School was still very much on her mind. The end of the war had brought even more problems for pupils and teachers, alike.

The damage caused by the zeppelin bomb was still waiting for repairs, and in the meantime they were two classrooms short, and with many more children to accommodate, since the arrival of the refugee children from Europe, but mostly orphans from Belgium.

It was a daunting task, trying to maintain anything like a usual timetable, but now they were having to teach children who didn't understand the English language. Many of the children were in need of food, and warmer clothes.

'Edward, we just have to get some more practical help. A lot of these children are so malnourished and ill, that they will learn very little until they feel well again.'

Alice and Edward had arrived early at school that morning, and decided to investigate the lasting damage, to report once more to the council. There was a biting, cold breeze, and the pair of them clambered carefully over the frosty rubble.

'Here, take my hand Alice,' Edward offered, 'be careful how you tread, it is quite dangerous here.'

They walked gingerly through the ruined quarter of the building to discover leaking water pipes, and ruined kitchens.

'We can't deal with this by ourselves. It's too big a job; that much is certain, Alice.'

'Do you think the council will rebuild the school for us, Edward?'

'I doubt the council will have funds for any re-building yet. It will be a case of making the place safe, and giving us some new cooking facilities. That must be the priority.'

For once, and sensing Alice's deep distress, Edward was to take the initiative. He was shaken out of his former complacency, much to Alice's surprise and relief.

'Right,' he said, rubbing his hands against the cold, 'I will count the new children, and make a register. I will have them all in the hall. When the other teachers appear I will attempt to divide the children between us. It's the best we can do.'

'What can I do to help?' Alice asked.

'Could you telephone the works department again? Tell them it is more than pressing now. The water leaking has ruined the food store, and the kitchens. They have to be seen to, and food for lunch today is vital. We have none!'

Edward Gardner lost no time in dividing the children into suitable groups. There was a certain amount of groaning and grumbling from staff and children. The mostly elderly staff didn't relish the thoughts of bigger numbers, 'Especially if they can't speak English,' said one. The children, especially the refugees, didn't want to be separated from their friends. Alice decided to be brave and take on the rest of the staff concerning their grumbles.

'Listen everyone. This is important. We have to work together, and safely. We are not the only damaged school in the area. We may have to wait for help, like everybody else. If it transpires that we can't cope, we will be forced to send the children home. We have spoken with the council and the fire brigade. The pipes will be fixed, and we will be receiving some barrels of fresh water by lunchtime. As to food, we hope to have something, even if it is just a sandwich, for today.' There were more groans from the staff. Alice was deeply disappointed in the response. Grown teachers should know better than to behave in such a manner. It made her cross.

'And before you go, ladies and gentlemen, and children, I would like to remind you that some of our new children have been sent here for safety reasons, and to recover from what must have been a nightmare experience in their own countries. It is up to us to make them feel wanted and cared for. Thank you.'

The teachers moved away. The majority of the children sat cross-legged on the floor, many just looking dazed. Others cried quietly, or held hands with their friends.

'Alice, you were absolutely magnificent! I bet some of the old chaps had never heard a woman speak like that before.'

'Well, their attitude made me so cross. I couldn't help myself.'

Edward was filled with admiration for Alice. They worked well together. They would make a good team, he thought.

Whatever Alice had managed to convey to the council and the school board official, had certainly been noticed.

Later that morning a school board officer arrived accompanied by Ellice Bell, now also a board member.

Ellice was laden with several baskets of food, emergency rations, she announced, 'Dried soup, bread, cheese, and some other stuff; cleaning supplies, I think.'

'Thank you, so much, Ell. This is very much appreciated.'

'That's all right. You must call me anytime. I can often find a way to obtain things, you know. Just ask and I will be here.' Alice saw her friend out of the building, and thanked her again.

'I'll be back later, when I've finished my official visit,' she said, 'you should have enough there for today, at least.'

Alice, feeling more resolute, returned to the hall to select "volunteers" from the older children, to help fill the water jugs and bottles. Some were taken by other teachers to see if they could rescue any crockery, or utensils from the wrecked kitchens. It was decided to keep the new children together, in the hall.

Books were found, and reading groups were swiftly set up, so that the children could return to some kind of normality. Older pupils were persuaded to take groups of three or four younger ones to listen to their times tables.

Alice realised, with some joy, that they still had the piano.

It was undamaged, and playable. She made a mental note that she would use the piano later on, when everyone felt a bit more settled, and the children were calmer.

Some of the older boys made a game of filling the water jugs, seeing who could fill the most without spilling the water all over the yard. Nearer to lunchtime Alice let the children help unpack the food which Ellice had brought from the council.

'Ooh, look miss!' shouted one.

'We've got cheese. Loads of it... and bread!'

'And here's some corned beef.'

'Mmm,' pondered Alice, 'I don't know if we can find a tin opener. We might have to improvise on that.'

Setting up the temporary food trestle tables, and feeding the children had occupied most of the morning, but Alice, Edward and the other teachers were relieved that every child had at the very least a small snack of something, to fill their empty stomachs. Water bottles were passed round in relays because, as yet, they had not managed to find enough drinking beakers.

After their sparse meal the children were encouraged to run around outside, even though the temperature was dropping. They did not seem to feel the cold, in the way that the adults did. Alice was developing a cough, as were many of the children. She pulled her shawl tight around her neck and shoulders as she wandered round the playground, observing the children. Edward, now acting as head teacher, since the official head had become ill, wandered around the playground observing Alice. He was concerned about her.

Alice came across a small girl for whom the worry and chaos surrounding them was too much to bear. The child was huddled in a corner, alone, and sobbing. Alice helped the child to her feet and listened, trying to hold back her own tears as the child clung to her skirt.

'Me dad's not coming home, miss. He's been shot in France... and me uncle too. Me mam couldn't wake up this morning. I'm glad we got some food, miss. Thanks, ever so much.' The child ran off to find a friend.

'Shouldn't we be getting the children back into school now?' Edward found Alice looking tired, tearful and shivering.

'I think you have a temperature, Alice.'

She couldn't manage a smile, but followed him.

'Come, Alice, you are looking quite ill. Let's get you inside too. You have been absolutely marvellous with these poor souls, but you have to take care of yourself now. We all have to take care, or we shall be of no use to the children.' Alice staggered back into school, with the help of Edward's reassuring arm, all ideas of decorum forgotten for once.

She was so tired and shivery that she had hardly paid attention to the fact that suddenly Edward had become a different person, caring and considerate, and capable.

'What shall I tell the children about tomorrow?' Alice asked him wearily.

'I'll do it. You take a seat,' he said.

'Children. Listen to me carefully. Today has been very difficult for all of us. Tell your mothers that because of the pipes being damaged, we couldn't use the kitchens and we have had to have emergency food brought. If you could all bring something from home, however small, it will help us a great deal.'

Edward dismissed the children, and as his attention turned to Alice, her friend appeared. Alice greeted her wearily.

'Ell, I can't thank you enough for the food you brought us earlier. We would all have gone hungry, otherwise.'

'You are very welcome. I'm glad we had something left in the stores. There are many schools in crisis. You will get the basic cooking facilities repaired, and food supplies very soon. In the meantime, here's another suggestion for you, as a temporary measure.'

206

Ellice handed Edward several pillowcases. He was bemused.

'They are quite clean,' she told him, 'If you can manage to get down to the grocer, just before he closes, my friend there has promised to give you the food which might otherwise be thrown out. Tell them I sent you.'

'Thank you again, Ellice,' they said in unison.

'I think lunch is probably the only meal some of these children have. I'll be glad when we can get the kitchens working again,' Alice said.

'It won't be long. It's a priority, Al.'

'Good,' said Edward, 'we can't have sick children here.'

'I'm afraid we already have Edward, and it's serious: some have persistent coughs. Most have pale, sunken faces and no energy. They fall asleep in class, but I can't be cross with them. I just let them sleep.'

She told Ellice about the child in the playground.

'Her mother couldn't wake up this morning, and the child had to get herself up and off to school, without breakfast.'

Alice thought she would take the child home, in order to investigate further.

'Are you sure that's wise, Al? You are not too well yourself, and besides, you can't go visiting every home, can you? Why not let Edward or myself go with you?' Edward nodded.

'If they know you are from the council, and the school board, they will become worried,' she told Ellice, 'I'll go after we have been to see the kind man at the grocers.'

'We will go together,' Edward assured Ellice, and excusing himself, left the two friends together.

'Edward seems to be shaping up now, Al?'

'Yes! He has certainly stepped up to the mark today. He has been a magnificent help. Usually he has to be told what to do; he doesn't naturally seem to think spontaneously. He has exceeded all my expectations.'

Ellice gave a wry smile.

'Male trait, my dear Alice,' but it is good to know that he is capable of responding when there is a crisis. I am pleased that he has agreed to go with you to the grocer, and then the child's house. But, think on, you mustn't go visiting all the sick parents. Leave it to the professionals.'

'I will,' said Alice.

'Good. Well, I mustn't stand here pontificating. I must leave you for now, Al. Meetings to go to, other schools to visit.' Ellice kissed her friend and wished her good luck at the store.

Just as Ellice Bell had predicted, the shop manager did save all his slightly stale bread for them, and some bruised apples, some hard cheese, which he had thoughtfully grated, and a large, slightly dry, ham joint.

'If you take this jar of pickle and add it to the ham, you won't notice the meat being a bit on the dry side.'

'Thank you so much,' said Alice, 'you are very kind.'

The manager said he was glad to be able to pass the food on, especially if it was for the children.

'Every time I throw food out,' he said, 'I have a problem with rats and mice, and other scavengers, sometimes the two-legged kind.'

'This feels very strange, us having to beg for food,' said Edward, 'I feel as if we are scavengers.'

'Let's just be grateful, Edward, that between them, the grocer and Ellice have helped us in our difficulty, for the next day or so.'

'Yes, of course. Let's hope we can soon be back to normal.'

'Thank you Edward. You have been a great help today, too.'

'You can call on me for anything Alice. Do not hesitate. It is my job now, to be helpful. I know I don't always respond at once, instinctively, but once I know what has to be done, I am quite ready and willing to help.'

'I know you are, Edward. I'm sorry if I sounded a bit haughty or condescending. I didn't mean to.'

'Of course you didn't sound condescending. I guess it's one

feature of my character that has prevented me from becoming married. I must seem to be rather selfish, but I certainly don't mean that either,' he joked.

Alice had never heard Edward speak like that before. She was very surprised that he had opened himself up to her.

'You see, my father died when I was very young, and my mother was incredibly demanding. I was never allowed to think for myself.'

Alice was quite shocked at Edward's revelations. She had known him for years, but never had the slightest idea that he could be the marrying kind, or that he had been so intimidated by his mother.

He could see that he had probably said too much about himself. He apologised if he had embarrassed her.

'I'm not embarrassed, Edward, not in the least, I am just immensely surprised. I always thought... well, you know... the acting, the singing musical comedy, your... friend.'

Edward laughed heartily.

Now it was Alice's turn to apologise to Edward if she had voiced anything embarrassing.

'I know exactly what you are trying to say. You find it so awkward. People have been thinking that I was a bit strange, may be that I was "batting for the other side" as it were, all my life. Theatrical people are often like that, always play-acting if you like. They often can't tell real life, from fiction!'

'So,' Alice dared to continue, 'why didn't you marry, then?'

'My dear mother would never have approved of any girl, so I gave up thinking of the possibility that anyone would find me a good enough proposition as a husband.'

Edward chanced that he wasn't being too forward. It was true that he didn't really know how to talk to a woman. But he was learning fast.

'What about you, Alice? Why haven't you found a beau good enough to marry? You are so good with these children; you would make a fine mother.'

Alice laughed the suggestion off.

'Well, it's too late now. I always thought I would be a spinster aunt, to my wonderful nephew, Charles. Then he was lost at sea. It seems like yesterday.'

Alice began to cry. Suddenly thinking of Charles like that had caught her off guard, and she lost her composure for a while.

Things were calmer the next day. The elderly teachers had all turned up for duty. Their former reluctance to help in their extraordinary situation seemed to have abated. It wasn't that they didn't care about the children, it was that they too had been shocked by the war, and found it harder to adjust to a new way of life, and circumstances that none of them could control.

Many of their sons, or grandsons had perished in France, Flanders, or elsewhere. The men left behind, because they were too old, or incapacitated to fight, suffered their own feelings of hopelessness, loss and, in some cases, guilt. Guilt, because they couldn't fight, or guilt because they had encouraged their young men to enlist.

Alice's outburst with the reluctant teachers had obviously had a positive effect, and they all worked together on the food sacks. The children's eyes lit up as they helped too.

'Cor look! Broken biscuits and apples,' they cried.

'Look, miss, look at these funny shaped carrots!'

The shop manager had thrown in quite a few misshapen vegetables, which caused great hilarity. It was good to hear the children laughing.

Alice had another surprise for the children.

'I know a very kind lady who is going to come into school today to show you how to make soup!'

The children cheered.

'We'll be like the dinner ladies,' a child piped up.

'That's right. A very important job,' Alice told them.

Lily Cole would bring lentils and pearl barley from Alice's own kitchen, to add to the soup. They had rescued some large pans from the wrecked kitchen, and the soup making got under way.

'We could go to our butcher miss,' shouted a boy, 'they have stuff to give away, or it's thrown out to the dogs.'

'Me ma always asks for bones,' said another boy. 'Me ma says ham bones give the best taste, and the butcher's always got a boxful.'

Alice was pleased that the children had entered into the spirit of the soup making with such gusto. She supposed it was partly the change of routine which had enabled the children to be so receptive of their condition. Producing proper handwriting and saying their daily prayers seemed quite irrelevant, when they were so hungry.

For the ensuing months, and over that harsh winter of 1918 Ellice continued to find other "co-operatives" of one kind or another, prepared to give food for several schools and hospitals.

'You deserve a medal,' Edward told her one day when she was visiting the children.

'No,' she laughed, 'I'm just the fixer. You are the gallant ones; trying to teach these children under such terrible conditions. Do you know, Edward, the government are now asking people to eat less bread because the wheat harvest has been so poor? And before very long, they will request people to have at least two meatless days each week.'

Edward was not really shocked by the news, but he was very disheartened by it.

'It's hard enough feeding the children as it is. Most have very little to eat at home. It's a feat of ingenuity sometimes.'

'Talking of ingenuity, Edward, I must tell you about Alfred Richards and his truly inspiring and enterprising project.'

'Really, what about it? Alice hasn't mentioned it.'

'Well, I might be speaking a little prematurely, but the craft workshops and gallery are being extended and, as well as needlework groups, he is allowing part of the premises to be used for cookery lessons, following the government's guidelines.'

'What a wonderful idea.'

'Yes, it is, Edward, but that's not all. He plans to give temporary work to a few returning soldiers, including army cooks. They know how to improvise and produce meals out of very little.'

'You seem to know all about it, Ell,' he said.

'I don't know everything about it, but I know the general ideas because Mr Richards has needed permission from the council to install cooking ovens and safety measures. I don't know how much Alice knows about it, so keep it to yourself until she enlightens you.'

'I will, of course, but I'm sure I will be able to help a bit, in some way.'

'That would be really good of you, Edward. I must fly now, so much to do. Give my love to Alice. I hope her throat is feeling better now.'

Alice had worn herself out, working at both ends of the day, with little sleep, and visiting sick people.

'I've just caught a cold, through being out so much in the damp air at night,' she explained to Edward, but when the cough became almost continuous, and she started vomiting blood, Edward was desperately worried.

He searched the streets frantically for a carriage to take Alice home to Highgate. Some of the drivers heard her terrible coughing and wouldn't take her on board. Eventually one cabby did stop, but insisted that she keep her mouth and face covered from him.

'I've heard that cough before, and it's bad!' he said. 'I'll be as quick as I can if you don't mind a fast ride?'

'No!' yelled Edward, 'The quicker we can get her home and call the doctor, the better.'

Edward covered her as best he could manage. He went to kiss her forehead, and realised that she had a raging fever. She could hardly speak, and Edward was in a way glad that she wasn't too aware of the rough ride to Highgate.

Doctor Ingram, now a frail old man himself, sent his young assistant doctor for Alice.

'I'm afraid she has diphtheria,' he said, seriously.

'What does that mean?' asked Edward.

'I'm sorry to say that Miss Combe will have to be by herself, isolated from other people. It is very contagious. Has she been in contact with the disease recently?'

'She has been around a lot of sick people, I'm not sure if they had diphtheria, and there are many sick children at school.'

'Well they shouldn't be at school, passing germs around. The hospitals are full of really sick people and very few places to isolate people with something of this nature,' the doctor said.

Edward and Lily stood there waiting for the doctor to perform some sort of miracle to make Alice well again. He insisted that both Edward and Lily wear a facemask to cover their nose and mouth.

'Sadly, I am lately having to carry a supply of masks around with me. I fear we are seeing the start of an epidemic.'

'What can we do, Doctor? We don't want her to be in hospital.' He turned to Lily.

'Are you here all the time?' Lily nodded.

'And what about you, sir?' he asked Edward.

'I won't leave her side until she is well,' he said, 'half the school are sick, teachers too. I can be more use here.'

'Very well.' The doctor warned both of them that Alice could suddenly take a turn for the worse, if the membrane closed over her throat.

'You need to keep her cool, by using a wet flannel on her face and forehead, and at all costs, try to keep her sipping fluid, a small sip at a time.'

'We will take it in turns, between us,' Lily assured the doctor.

'How will we know if the membrane causes problems?'

'You will know immediately because she will not be able to swallow. Telephone me immediately if that should happen.'

Lily took the first watch over Alice, while Edward used the telephone to inform Alfred and Frances. He telephoned Ellice too.

'You mustn't come here; any of you,' he said, 'the doctor says it is highly contagious. Lily and I are taking it in turns to cool her fever, and give her sips of water. There is nothing you can do, but pray,' he told them all in turn.

That didn't go down well with Ellice, a confirmed non-believer. Alfred felt the same. Frances prayed, morning, noon and night, for her beloved sister.

Edward sat beside Alice's bed for almost two weeks before she roused at all. The cough gradually subsided, and she had taken only water and fruit juice, in little sips. Then one day, at the sight of a tiny smile from Alice, Lily raced to the kitchen and brought Alice some chicken soup, which she had carefully strained so that there were no bits to get lodged in Alice's throat.

'Come on, Miss Alice; see if you can manage a spoonful or two.'

Edward, very tired and weary through sleeping on the bedside chair, forgot his own aches and pains, found another pillow so that Alice could sit a little way up in her bed. Her weak, little voice could only manage a few words, but she smiled at them both.

'How long have I been here?' she asked.

'Two weeks, miss,' Lily told her.

'And why are you wearing face masks?'

Edward took her hand. 'I expect we can remove them now that you have stopped your coughing. You have been terribly ill, with diphtheria. The doctor agreed to you staying at home, because the hospitals are full of extremely sick people, and you needed to be isolated.'

'Mr Edward has been here all the time, miss,' Lily said.

'And so has Lily,' he added.

The young doctor returned that evening, to find Alice sitting in the chair.

'I can't tell you how thrilled I am to see you on the road to recovery,' he said, 'your two friends here have saved your life, Miss Combe.'

She could only smile and squeeze Edward's hand.

'You need some nourishment now,' the doctor insisted, 'you will not feel too keen to swallow much, but I urge you to get some good, wholesome food down you. We have to build up your strength before you can even think about returning to school.'

'The doctor is quite right, Alice,' said Edward.

'I expect your legs will feel quite wobbly at first, miss,' Lily guessed correctly.

'Yes,' she said quietly, 'but I want to be on my feet when Alfred and Fran come. They will come, won't they?'

'Of course they will. They have been very anxious to come, but you have had a very dangerous illness and the doctor forbade them to come anywhere near you.'

Edward knew that before very long Alice would be asking for news of the children at school, and especially the little girl and her mother, whom she had visited, probably to her own peril. He would do his best to divert her attention for a while longer.

Many of the children taught by Alice and Edward, had died that winter. They died from dysentery, tuberculosis and diphtheria. There had indeed been an epidemic of both diphtheria and whooping cough.

Alice asked about the child she had visited. Edward and Lily did not want to tell her that the child had been discovered sleeping next to her mother, not knowing that her mother had died during the night, and would never wake up.

'The child is fine. She is staying with a neighbour,' Alfred hoped that would suffice, until later. Alice was astute enough to understand. This was her incentive to get well again.

Alice resolved to look after the child herself. Her name was Rose.

'How can you possibly look after a child?' Alfred questioned Alice, when she was well enough to discuss things properly.

'She has no relatives that we know of, Alfred. She would have to go to an orphanage. What sort of life would she have there? We can all look after her. Wouldn't you and Fran like a little step-grandchild around the place?'

Alice realised that she might have gone just a little too far, but she persisted.

'I will apply to the magistrates as soon as possible. I will aim to have temporary custody of Rose, until something more permanent might be possible.'

Alfred was an astute character, and his mind was full of the possibilities Alice might be suggesting.

Chapter Fifteen

Nobody came to claim Rose after her mother had died of sheer starvation, and had to be buried by the parish. All of her immediate family had perished one way or another through the war. Efforts were being made to ascertain whether Rose might have some extended family. In the meantime Alice had been granted temporary custody of Rose.

A pretty room had been prepared for her at the Highgate house. Rose was completely overawed, and struggled to find the right words to explain her feelings.

'This used to be my room when I was a little girl,' Alice said.

'It's very pretty, thank you miss. I feel like it's a fairy tale. I've never had a room all to myself before. When will I have to leave miss, and where will I go?'

Alice wasn't sure quite how much she should tell the child, but she decided that she ought to be completely open and honest.

'The children's department are trying to see if you have any other relatives who could care for you. Until then you are very welcome to stay here with me, and Lily will look after both of us.'

'Shall I help Lily in the kitchen miss? I know how to make soup now.'

Alice was very touched.

'I'm sure Lily will enjoy having you around. Perhaps she will show you how to make bread. Would you like that, Rose?'

'Yes miss, I would,' Rose replied.

The first night that Rose came to live in Highgate with Alice was far from easy. There would be many new things for Rose to learn which were alien to her former life.

She had arrived with only the shabby clothes she stood up in, most of which badly needed laundering.

Her black boots had holes in, and her bare feet were covered in blisters where the cardboard covering the holes had rubbed her feet. The heavy black coat was too big for her, having been passed down from her mother. Nevertheless, Rose was at first reluctant to take it off.

'We'll send it to be cleaned,' Alice told her, 'and we will ask the tailor to shorten the sleeves, and the length. Then it will fit you better, won't it?'

'I suppose so, miss,' Rose replied as she gave up the coat. Lily appeared with a pile of soft, new towels.

'Come on, young miss. I've run you a nice warm bath, and Miss Alice has given you some beautiful rose-scented soap.'

'Rose?' she queried.

'Yes, pretty pink soap, smelling of damask roses. Just like you will be.'

'What's damask?' she asked.

'Oh! It's a special kind of rose. A big, beautiful, velvety soft-petalled flower.'

At that explanation, Rose complied and followed Lily upstairs. She was quite willing to climb into the bath, another new experience for her.

'I only wash me hair on Sundays,' she told Lily matter-of-factly, 'for Sunday school.'

'It's *my* hair Rose, not 'me' hair. Can you remember that?'

'I'll try miss.'

'No need to call me miss, I'm just Lily. That's *my* name.' Lily stressed the word *my* so that Rose would remember to speak nicely.

Lily was very patient with Rose.

'I'll tell you what Rose, let's pretend that it's Sunday today, and we'll make you feel very special on your first night living here with us.'

'Will I have to go to Sunday school?'

'No, not today,' Lily laughed. 'It's my guess that Miss Alice will take you to church with her on Sunday. You might even meet Mr and Mrs Richards; that is, Miss Alice's sister and brother-in-law.'

Rose listened intently to Lily without passing any further remarks. She began to feel anxious about meeting more new people.

'Don't you worry. Mr and Mrs Richards are very fine people.'

'Will they like me?'

'I'm sure they will, and especially if you go smelling of roses, and you can show off your shiny, clean hair.'

Rose allowed Lily to wash her hair, but she wanted to dress herself in the new nightclothes which Alice had bought for her.

When it was time to go to bed Alice accompanied Rose to her room and Lily followed on behind.

'Here you are Miss Rose; I've brought you some warm milk. It will help you to sleep. It's always strange trying to get to sleep in a new bed, isn't it?'

Rose thanked Lily for the milk, and she sipped it slowly and appreciatively.

'I must be having some sort of a dream already,' Rose told Alice.

'How so?' Alice replied.

'All the new clothes; this lovely room, the milk and Lily. She's like me... *my* ma used to be, before she got sick.'

'Well, we are both glad that you feel happy and safe here. Finish up your milk, don't forget to say your prayers, and then off to sleep with you. We'll see you bright and early in the morning. Good night Rose. Sleep well.'

'Good night miss, and thank you for everything.'

The war was over, but nobody felt that life could return to normal, as it was before. There were as many problems to deal with, perhaps even more, after the fighting was over. Houses had to be demolished, or repaired wherever possible, and because most of the skilled men had been conscripted to their deaths, in the army and navy, there was a shortage of carpenters, builders and all the other skilled tradespeople needed to restore the city. The East End of London had been particularly hard hit. Alfred was deeply distressed every time he was called out by *The News*, to sketch some of the buildings which would remain as ruins for some time to come.

'It's all beginning to take shape, Alice.' He was trying to explain his ideas. 'You see, there are so many men returning from Europe every day now, some were injured, sick or shell-shocked, many are certainly malnourished, demoralised, especially when they come home to discover that their home has been blown up, and some can't find their families. They might have been killed, or they might be living elsewhere. It is a very daunting task for them.'

'But what will you do to help, then, Alfred?'

'Well, I don't pretend I can cure everything. Certainly, I can't house people, or cure alcoholism, and I can't stop them begging on the streets, but I can provide some with the chance to pick up a skill, so that they could find work. We can nurse them back to health in a way, and give them some self-esteem. My aim is for them to help each other.'

'Alfred, dear brother, I am filled with admiration. Fran must be very proud of you, and Charles would have been too.'

He flinched at the sound of Charles' name, and then pulled himself up straight.

'Your friend Ellice has been a big help, you know. She has badgered the council, and we have permission to go ahead with the workshop and the women's refuge on a daily basis.'

'That's amazing, Alfred. Well done, and I shall thank Ellice too, when I get to see her. She is so busy now that I have hardly seen her for months.'

'She will surface sooner or later,' Alfred laughed.

'Ellice has been magnificent over the school repairs, and getting us supplies of food and fuel. We have some soldiers at school now, trying to repair the kitchens. They have even brought us some trestle tables, so on soup-making days we have room to prepare, and room to serve it.'

'Do you serve soup to the soldiers?'

'Oh, yes! The children love that. The problem on soup days is that our numbers seem to mysteriously increase, and it isn't because of the soldiers.'

'What is it then?'

'I think it's because of the food rationing, Alfred. The mothers can't afford to buy much at all, that is nourishing, and I suspect that they somehow slip their younger children in at lunchtimes, for a bowl of soup. I do notice, but since we are given much of the ingredients, I have chosen to turn a blind eye to it, that is, as long as our schoolchildren get their share.'

'I expect Edward is a help; being vigilant, I mean?'

'Yes, Alfred. He is a big help. I owe him so much.'

Alfred left Alice with a glint in his eye and a skip in his step. If he wasn't very much mistaken, he detected a growing relationship between Alice and Edward, and he was glad.

Alice watched the soldiers at work on their school building, and for some reason it crossed her mind that she had never asked Edward, a single young man, at the start of the war, why he had not been conscripted into the forces.

'I thought I might get called after mother passed on,' he told her nonchalantly, 'but I failed the eyesight test the first time round. I guess they must have thought that I'd be useless with a rifle, eh?'

'Still, you were allowed to join the Home Guard?'

'Yes! I did my bit. I was out every night with the rest of my crew, which is really ironic, since I can hardly see at night.'

'You are being flippant about it now, Edward, but I guess it must have been quite scary, dousing fires from rooftops, and other dangerous places?'

'Well I guess it was better than the muddy fields of Flanders and I haven't been shot at.'

'I'm so glad you weren't, Edward. At least now, I know you are safe. As safe as any of us.'

'Does that mean you care, Alice?'

'Of course I do, Edward. How could I not?' she hesitated. 'How could I, how could we have managed without you? You have been a tower of strength, especially when I thought that I might crumble, under all the stress and anxiety. After losing poor Charles, life seemed very bleak indeed, and then, of course there was diphtheria. You and Lily saved my life.'

'And now? How do you feel now?' He took her cold hands in his, and on this occasion she didn't pull away.

'You have become a good friend and a wonderful support.'

'Only a good friend?' he teased.

'A dear friend, Edward. A very dear, treasured friend.'

He kissed both her hands, very gently, and then her head. Her heart leapt. It was the very first time in forty-one years that any man, except for Alfred, had shown her any tenderness, other than brotherly affection. It was a new, totally unexpected feeling.

The pair were interrupted, and Alice, her face quite flushed, hurried from the room. She chided herself for behaving like a silly schoolgirl. She had been so taken aback by Edward's actions and her own admission to him, that she worked through the remainder of the day in somewhat of a trance. She almost forgot to collect Rose from her reading group. But there was Edward again.

'I have brought this young lady for you. I found her waiting on the cold doorstep.'

'Thank you Edward. I was just coming. I'm a little behind today. I don't know what has happened to me.'

Edward gave her a wide, knowing smile.

'I'll see you both tomorrow then, ladies,' he said, grinning as he raised his hat.

They waved goodbye and gathered up their belongings. Tomorrow would be Friday, Alice thought, the last day of the school week. There would be two more whole days before she would see Edward again. Her mind was in a perplexing whirl. She would have difficulty concentrating on the week ahead.

Lily was waiting for them.

'Here, let me take your coats. Come into the warm, and I will bring you some tea.'

'Thank you, Lily,' Alice smiled. She was sure that Lily would be able to read her face. She would know instinctively that something had happened between her and Edward. She was sure to guess that Edward had kissed her. Lily re-appeared.

'It's fish pie tonight, miss. Is that all right?'

'That will be fine, Lily, Thank you!'

'You seem less tired tonight, miss, you must have had a better day.'

Alice gave Lily an enigmatic smile. *Yes*, she mused to herself, *I've had a much better day*. Alice quickly changed the subject, lest she should give anything away.

'Come, Rose, while Lily is preparing our fish pie, we have some decisions to make.'

'What decisions, miss?'

'We have to choose your clothes for Saturday and Sunday.'

'Won't I wear the same clothes as I wore today?' she asked.

'No, dear. We are going visiting on Saturday. You are to meet my sister Frances, and her husband Alfred. We will have lunch with them both, at their house. Then, on Sunday, they will come here. We will all go to church together, and Lily and Mrs Cole will be here to cook lunch for us.' Rose was slightly confused about who was who.

'Mrs Cole is Lily's mother,' Alice explained.

'She must be very old,' said Rose.

'I am sure she is. Probably sixty-something, I should guess. She is a very kind and thoughtful lady who has looked after Alfred and his parents for many, many years. He is like my big brother.'

Alice thought she would tell Rose that it had been Mrs Cole who chose her new clothes, from the church bazaar.

'What's a bazaar?' Rose wanted to know.

'It's a sale of goods, and lovely things to eat, which very kind people have given to the church. The money raised will go to help poor and sick people.'

Rose reflected upon the clothes that she and her mother used to wear. One day-dress, and another for Sundays and funerals. She had one pair of handed down black boots which had to do for every occasion. She had never had a new coat.

'Look, Rose, what a lovely coat, dark red. Do try it on and we'll see if it fits you.'

Lily picked up the matching wool hat.

'A red beret too. How lovely,' said Alice. 'Put it on, Rose. What a picture you look.'

Rose was thrilled beyond words. She gave Alice and Lily a twirl, right around the room. The whole outfit was nearly perfect, just a few inches too long, but she would soon grow into it.

'So, that is your best new coat and hat, for outings. Now let's find you a couple of dresses too, and some stockings.'

Rose must have tried half a dozen dresses before Alice had to help her decide. Rose had never had to choose anything before. She liked everything!

'I won't be able to pay for these clothes, miss.'

'You certainly won't have to pay for anything, Rose. You are not to worry about anything. If you wish, you can call it an early Christmas gift, from me.'

'Well, young Miss Rose,' Lily enquired, 'which dress is for Saturday visiting, and which is for Sunday church?'

Rose handed her the grey wool dress for Saturday, because it might be chilly outside, and the navy blue tunic dress was for

Sunday, because it looked more serious and grown up, for church.

She had never been to church before, except for funerals, and she had been to quite a few of those in her young life. Rose had enjoyed Sunday school though. An elderly lady used to read stories to them about Jesus, and she made all the children recite the Ten Commandments, and the Lord's Prayer, at least twice. Rose liked the hymn-singing best. Her favourite was *What a friend we have in Jesus*. Rose hummed the tune softly to herself. The new clothes, which she fondled as she sang, and the fact that Alice thought her worthy to join the family at Sunday church, made Rose feel a little more grown up.

Saturday arrived, and Rose was up before anyone else in the house. She took the grey wool dress off the hanger, where Lily had left it, and she carefully laid it out on the bed, so that she could look at it properly. She washed herself carefully, just as Lily had shown her, not forgetting to wash behind her ears, and not forgetting about the elbows. Rose wished that her mother could see how clean and pretty she looked.

Lily knew instinctively what to say when she saw how very carefully Rose had made herself ready for the day's outing.

'Your Ma will be very proud of you,' she said, 'sitting up there in heaven, looking down on you.'

'Can she see me, Lily?'

'She knows you are safe here with us.' That satisfied Rose for now.

After breakfast Alice insisted on yet more hand and face washing, and cleaning of teeth.

'Cleanliness is next to godliness,' she told Rose.

So Rose obliged, and brushed her teeth a second time. They travelled by omnibus to the city, and then for the last mile or so Alice found a carriage to take them right to the front door of the house in Han Street.

Before she rang the bell Alice felt the need to prepare Rose and prompt her, a little.

'My sister is a very quiet lady, and a little nervous. She has been quite ill, so you mustn't mind too much if she doesn't talk to you. She is like that with everyone, even me. But, you may give her the little box of biscuits which you helped Lily to bake. She will like that.'

'Will Mr Alfred speak to me?' she asked.

'I am sure that he will. You must be as quiet and polite as you know how.' Rose nodded. She understood perfectly what was expected of her.

'And will there be any children?'

Alice almost choked with emotion, trying to find an answer for the child. Of course, she would not have known anything about their background, or of Charles being lost at Gallipoli.

Being forced to think of the tragedy caught Alice off guard.

'No, no children. They did have a wonderful son called Charles. He was my nephew. Very sadly, he was lost at sea, in the war. Charles would have been twenty-three by now. Sadly, very sadly, he was lost. We are all sad about it, but my sister, his mother, has been the least able to cope with what happened. Sometimes she believes Charles is coming home. There, young miss, I have told you some very personal things, so that you will understand a little more about us. It would be best if you do not say anything about it, unless they do. Is that all right? Do you understand?'

'Yes, miss. It's just like me, losing Ma and Pa, and my uncle. I feel sad when I think about it, so I try to think about something else, or I sing a song. It doesn't mean that I don't miss them all.'

'I know,' Alice hugged her. 'Go on then, Rose. You ring the bell and Mrs Cole will let us in.'

The door opened, but it wasn't Mrs Cole who greeted them. It was Alfred, with the widest smile on his face.

'Hello, you two! I was watching for you, and you took your time ringing the bell. Who is this young lady then?'

'Alfred, meet our new friend, Rose. She is going to stay with me for a while. I will explain everything later.'

'Come in, come in, it's chilly out there. Come into the parlour, and Mrs Cole will bring us a drink and biscuits.'

Mrs Cole appeared a few minutes later, as if by magic, and brought in some mugs of hot chocolate and shortbread biscuits.

'Let me take your coats,' she said to the visitors. 'My, what a lovely red coat this is,' she smiled at Rose.

'Yes, miss. Er, missus.'

'My name is Mrs Cole. I am Lily's mother.'

Alfred was clever at awkward, shy moments like this. He knew just the right thing to say to make Rose feel better and more at home.

'Yes,' beamed Alfred, 'you look really splendid. I think I shall call you Rose Red.' Rose gave a little giggle.

'That's better,' he said, with a twinkle in his eye.

'That's a German fairy tale, sir,' Mrs Cole reminded him, with a deep frown of annoyance on her face.

'Never mind that now, Mrs Cole.' He ushered her away.

'The brothers Grimm would turn in their graves if they knew about the terrible war,' she muttered under her breath.

Alfred apologised to Alice, a little tearfully.

'I am sorry about Frances. She will come down by lunchtime. She seems to spend more and more time sitting up there, looking out of the window, wrapped in her thoughts. She is all right once she decides to come down. She is quite capable of putting on a show, if you gather my meaning.'

'Of course I understand, Alfred. I pray that one day we shall have the old Frances back again.'

'Here, Rose Red,' Alfred beckoned Rose to come to his bookcase. 'Do you like to read poetry?'

'I think I do, sir,' she said shyly.

'Well here is one of my favourite books. It's called *A Child's Garden of Verses*. It's by a Scottish writer called Robert Louis Stevenson. Mrs Richards and I went to see his house in Scotland, a long time ago, now. See, there are the most beautiful pictures in here, to go with each poem. The lady artist is called Jessie Willcox Smith. Do you like the pictures?'

'They are very nice, sir. I wish I could paint pictures like that.'

'Well, if you are a very good girl for Alice, we will see if we can find you some paints, and I will show you how to begin.'

Her eyes lit up as she thanked Alfred.

'Thank you very much, sir.'

Alice joined them to look at the poetry book.

'Rose is a good little reader, for her age.' Alice gave her the book of poems so that she could sit by the window and read, while she and Alfred could talk by themselves. Rose glanced at the garden, but was soon absorbed by the lovely poems and the very magical pictures.

Alice explained the tragedy of Rose and her mother, before Frances came downstairs. She didn't want to cause any more disquiet.

'It's all very admirable, Alice, taking the child in like that, though she is a delightful little girl. Surely you won't be allowed to keep her?'

'Why not? If nobody claims her, where else can she go but to an orphanage? I can't let that happen. She is a good and decent girl. She is good-natured, intelligent, and all she wants is to love and be loved.'

'Don't we all,' Alfred said quietly.

He pressed her again for explanations. He wanted to be sure that Alice had really thought it through properly.

'Lily will help. They like each other already. It will be good for Lily too, you know. After losing poor Artie, and who knows if Jimmy is alive or dead? It will occupy Lily's thoughts, as you and Frances have helped Mrs Cole to cope each day.'

Alfred shivered.

'Don't let's talk about it anymore, just now. It's all still too awful. I just wish I could get Frances right again.'

'I know,' said Alice, 'and I may be able to help in that direction, but you will have to be patient just a little longer. I do have some ideas. Trust me, Alfred.'

Frances appeared, as Alfred had predicted, just before lunch. She greeted Alice with a smile and a hug, and she gave Rose a cursory nod. Rose put down her book and stood by Alice's side.

'Frances, I'd like you to meet our new little friend, Rose.' Rose gave a short bob, as Alice had taught her to do.

'Good morning, Mrs Richards,' Rose said confidently, and took the pretty biscuit box from the table to present to Frances.

'Rose helped Mrs Cole to make these for you,' Alice said.

'No, it was Lily,' corrected Rose.

'I beg your pardon, yes it was Lily.'

Frances thanked her for the biscuits and admired the box. She seemed very confused, and kept muttering Rose's name, and that of Alfred's mother, Rose Maud. Alfred trembled to hear his mother's name like that, but then he thought it might be a good sign. Frances was trying, in her way, to connect with reality on some level.

'No, my darling Fran. This is Rose. I am going to call her Rose Red, after her lovely red hat. She doesn't mind a bit, do you, Rose Red?'

'It's a lovely name, Mr Alfred, sir.'

Alfred and Alice engineered polite conversation during their lunch, although most of it seemed to float above Frances, quite out of reach. She smiled now and then, and was much more at ease as she watched Rose eating her meal, displaying impeccable manners. She was an unusual and engaging child, and brave too. She was open and willing to join in things when she was invited, but sensitive enough to know when to withdraw and be quiet. She remembered her mother teaching her about "p"s and "q"s.

CHAPTER SIXTEEN

Rose had endeared herself to everyone, even Frances, with her calm and even nature, and by her unfailing willingness to be a helpful girl. As it became clear that Rose had no relatives who might have claimed her, Alice decided to take legal advice. She was very unsure of whether she, a single woman, would be allowed to formally adopt Rose. She sent for Peter Lawrence, and together with Alfred, they asked for his advice.

'We can certainly draw up Deeds of Guardianship,' he said. 'The court could not object, in the circumstances, though you may need to give Alfred's name as a guarantor.'

Alice bristled at this.

'Goodness gracious, Peter. I am well over thirty years of age now. With luck I will be able to vote in the next election, for the first time. That will make me Alfred's equal, won't it?'

'Well, not quite,' the lawyer prevaricated, and tried his best to change the direction of the discussion.

Alice was not going to be deflected. She could feel herself becoming very angry with him.

'Excuse me, Mr Lawrence,' Alice pressed him, 'and what pray would happen if I marry? What then?'

Alice, in her annoyance, had accidentally let slip her secret.

'Marry? Are you considering marriage? It's the first I've heard of it, or are you asking me a hypothetical question?' As usual, Peter

Lawrence had the loudest voice, and it reverberated throughout the house. Alfred came running. Frances and Mrs Cole were close behind.

'Did my ears deceive me, Alice?'

'Alfred, I do apologise. You were not meant to hear the news like that, and certainly not in front of Peter Lawrence. Peter has provoked me, far more than I could cope with, and it just slipped out.'

'But is it true, sweet girl?' She nodded, and he hugged her.

'We will do this properly, Alfred, Fran, Mrs Cole, Edward will have lunch with us next Sunday, at Highgate, and you will all be there, won't you? We will invite Ellice too. Edward will have a private talk with you first, Alfred, as though you were my real father. I know that nowadays, and considering our ages, we could just dispense with all that formality now. We could just take ourselves off somewhere, and have a quiet wedding, but I wanted to give you all something to look forward to, to make you happy.'

Mrs Cole had need of her handkerchief again, and Alfred grasped his sister-in-law's hands.

'We have all had such an unhappy few years; it will be so wonderful for us to have something to celebrate. I will be overjoyed, at long last, to be your stand-in-father.'

Frances nodded her agreement, and she too gave Alice a hug.

'You deserve to be happy, Miss Alice,' Mrs Cole joined in. She scurried off to the kitchen to see if there was the tiniest bit of sherry, enough for the three of them. Peter Lawrence had made a dignified exit. He wasn't going to argue with any of the family on such an occasion.

Young Rose was listening, taking it all in. She had made a promise that she wouldn't breathe a word to anyone, until after next Sunday. It was the hardest secret she had ever had to keep.

The next Sunday arrived, and everyone, except for Ellice, had dressed for church. Although it was July, the air was quite cool, and the sky was ominously overcast.

'I hope we get there and back without getting wet,' said Alice, 'we'd better take umbrellas.'

'Good morning, ladies, Alfred,' Edward greeted them at the church. He was planning to sit beside Alice, but Rose had other ideas, and managed to wriggle herself a place between them both.

'Perhaps it's best,' he whispered, 'after all, the banns have not yet been called.'

Alice couldn't help herself, and she beamed throughout the service, leaving no doubt in anyone's mind that she and Edward were most definitely a couple with intentions.

Edward, possessed of a fine tenor voice, sang even more lustily than the aged Miss Bell, whose eyes seemed to be as bright as ever, as she surveyed the family group.

'It is very good to see you and Mrs Richards here again,' the vicar remarked pointedly to Alfred.

Alfred felt slightly embarrassed that he had often used Frances and her depression as an excuse for his lengthy absence from church. Although it was true that he was reluctant to leave Frances by herself, if at all possible, he had truly felt that the church had nothing to offer him. He still felt that way, but he had noticed a huge uplifting of Frances, since Alice had made public the news of her engagement. Anything which would build on that was surely a good thing to do. So, for now at least, he was happy to accompany his ladies, including Rose Red, to church on this special day.

Before the final blessing, the vicar took the unusual step of announcing that because of the government food rationing being severely cut, yet again, he would welcome ideas from the good people of Highgate parish as to how poor families might eat healthy meals on the reduced rations.

'At the same time,' continued the vicar, 'we must not forget that since the Russian royal family were murdered, there are many thousands of poor people there who are starving to death.'

The vicar gave his final blessing, but Alfred hardly heard the words. His thoughts were never far away from Charles.

The vicar had reminded him of the war, and now he thought of all the lost men and boys, lost forever. The war and its repercussions meant a waste of much of the younger generation of men, and for what? Alfred felt suddenly that he had spent too long grieving, and he now realised that he must use that energy to try and improve things where he could, in his own corner of the world. He used to have a fund of ideas and projects. *Where had all that optimism and productivity disappeared to?* he asked himself.

Frances too had been very moved by what the vicar had chosen to say, but surprisingly, it was eventually the non-religious, bohemian, practical suffragette, Ellice, who managed to galvanise people, and especially to spur Frances into action.

Ellice joined the family for their special lunch.

'My, it seems a long time since I shared this house with Alice. It has hardly changed. Still calm and pretty.' Alice welcomed her friend, and introduced Rose.

'Do you remember our new addition, Ellice? This is Rose.'

'Gosh! Golly! Aren't you looking grown up now? You used to be so tiny, and always had a cough, as I remember.'

Ellice, straightforward and to the point, had no idea that her comments were upsetting to Rose, who didn't need reminding of how ill she had looked. Alice rescued the situation.

'Well, she is fit and healthy now. Rose loves her school work, and she is a very good reader,' Alice announced.

'What do you like to read then, Rose? Do you have a favourite storybook?' Ellice prompted Rose to speak.

'I like the poem book that Mr Alfred gave me. It's by Robert Louis Stevenson. Mr Alfred and Mrs Richards have seen his house in Scotland.'

'Fantastic! I like poetry too,' Ellice encouraged her.

Ellice handed a packet of magazines and leaflets to Alice, for her perusal later. Alice frowned at her.

'I hope these aren't your Labour Party leaflets, Ellice. I can't go out canvassing for you. I'm sorry. I really can't.'

'No my dear Al, not at all. I know you have your hands very full, perhaps even more so now that you are about to cave in and become a married woman!'

'Ellice, really! I had hoped that you would be glad for me, and Edward.'

'Of course I'm glad. I'm only kidding. This pile is the government list of the rationing foods allowed. It's very sparse, isn't it? What I am attempting to do is to find a few, good, educated people who would be willing to set up some classes, to show people how best to use their rations, to make them go further, whilst giving the children enough to eat.' Mrs Cole and Frances had been listening carefully to the conversation between Alice and her councillor friend.

'What an excellent idea,' Mrs Cole intervened, 'I would be more than happy to lend a hand on my days off. Where will the classes be held?'

'Anywhere that we can find rooms with clean kitchens. Schools, church halls, the Temperance Hotels; we're open to suggestions.'

'And what are these magazines for?' asked Alice.

'Yes, well this is the suffrage paper for women, and I know you don't want to get involved, but perhaps you wouldn't mind just reading the small ads. You will see how ordinary women can help each other. Look out for the jumble sales. Perhaps you and Frances might be able to send some clothes, books, anything you can spare. All the money is to go to families without fathers.'

Rose was sitting quietly, listening to every word, taking it all in. She cast a glance in Alice's direction. Alice smiled at her.

Ellice was quite undaunted. If she had a point to get across then she would pursue it to the bitter end.

'You know, Al, many hundreds of women are having to do the men's jobs, in the fields, factories, in the post offices, yet they receive only half the wages that men do. It's shameful. You must surely agree?'

Alice did agree, but she was relieved at that point in the

conversation to see that Edward and Alfred had emerged from their private talk in the lounge.

'Come on ladies, let us eat.'

Alfred was in jovial mood, and looking more like his old self. Edward couldn't stop smiling across the table, to Alice.

In spite of the meat rationing that week, Mrs Cole had still managed to provide a special enough meal. She saved the meat for another day when there would be fewer mouths to feed. She had scoured several fishmongers' shops in order to find sufficient for a very sumptuous fish pie. For dessert she had made a sponge pudding with syrup sauce. Goodness knows, Mrs Cole wondered, how much longer they would be able to find eggs enough to make sponge puddings.

Rose had become very appreciative of Mrs Cole's cooking, and Lily's too. She still had many moments of insecurity, and wondered whether this new life, which had been so generously given to her, would last. Every day she thought it might be the last day, with Alice, and her new family.

When the meal was almost over, Mrs Cole, ably assisted by Rose, brought a tray of glasses and a bottle. Rose very carefully arranged the glasses before the guests, and Mrs Cole apologised to them all.

'I'm sorry, it's only elderberry wine.'

Alfred stood up, now in semi-formal mode. He cleared his throat, ready to make a speech, and straightened his tie.

'I am sure that we would all like to thank Mrs Cole and Lily for a really delicious meal and I, for one, am looking forward to drinking the elderberry wine. Mrs Cole, please stay for a moment and have a glass yourself. We have a very important announcement to make.'

'Thank you, Mr Alfred,' she responded, 'I will just stay here, by Rose.' She was, of course, fully au fait with what was about to happen next. Alice had been quite unable to keep the secret from her.

Alfred cleared his throat again.

'Ladies and gentlemen,' everyone laughed.

'There's only one gentleman here,' Rose offered.

'Quite right. Let me begin again.' He tweaked Rose's ear.

'Ladies, young lady Rose and Edward. It is with the greatest happiness that I announce the engagement of our dear Alice and Edward. In these very sad and difficult times it is truly heart-warming to have something to look forward to. I think we have all come to learn that we need to take hold of life, while we can. Our love and congratulations to you both. Everyone, please raise your glasses, to Alice and Edward.'

'To Alice and Edward,' everyone repeated enthusiastically. Edward, unaccustomed to any kind of solo public speaking, stood up, and attempted to respond to Alfred's words. He stammered and struggled to find his words.

'Come on Ed,' chided Ellice, 'you've been on a stage hundreds of times, in front of audiences.'

He grinned and nodded, nervously.

'Yes, I know, but that was mostly singing. Speaking is different, especially today, when it is a momentous occasion. I need to get it just right, don't I?'

Eventually Edward managed to control his nerves. He did as Alfred had done, cleared his throat, and straightened his tie, and then spoke, calmly and carefully.

'I would like to thank Frances and Alfred, as Alice's only family, for making me feel so welcome, and for allowing me to become a part of it. I am deeply thankful to Alice for agreeing to become my wife. We have both waited far too long in our lives to find someone to love and care for, and, as Alfred intimated earlier, we intend to grasp hold of life, now that we have found each other, and we will try to make the best of what we have in these difficult times.'

There was a ripple of applause. Then it was Alice's turn.

'I wish to thank Mrs Cole for her unstinting help over many

years, through good times and bad. I thank Alfred and Frances for their patience, and for accepting Rose so happily as part of our family, and lastly, I thank Ellice for her unfailing support and her common-sense advice, although I haven't always taken it kindly! Oh! And I almost forgot to thank Edward for daring to risk marrying me. I think we will fare well together, and God willing, we shall together enjoy having Rose in our family permanently.'

'Does that mean forever?' asked Rose.

'Forever,' they answered. 'Together, forever.'

'Edward and I are to be allowed to become your legal guardians after we marry. You may have to come with us to see the judge. He will ask you if you wish to stay with us, and you must tell him exactly what you feel about it.'

Rose gave Alice a hug. She wasn't sure about hugging Edward, but Alfred, delighted by the news, whisked Rose off her feet, and danced around the room with her.

'Will you have me as your honorary uncle, then?'

'Yes please, Mr Alfred. Do I still have to call you "Mr" — and what should I call Mrs Richards?'

Ellice interrupted them. All the talk of families made her feel a bit edgy and uncomfortable.

'Perhaps Rose has had enough excitement, for now. I'm sure you will sort out names eventually. Whatever feels right, will be right, in time. Would you like to show me the garden, Rose, while we still have a bit of sunshine?'

Alice squeezed Alfred's hand.

'It was really nice of you to speak with Rose that way.' Frances smiled, and nodded her agreement. She was beginning to show signs of her old self, and willing to at least appear to be listening to conversations, if not actually joining in. Alfred was sensing a much better mood.

'Rose is a delightful child,' he said, 'it is so nice to have a youngster about the place. She is as welcome in our home as you have obviously welcomed her here. Frances and I have both agreed that whenever you and Edward want to have time by yourselves, Rose will be more than welcome to come and stay with us, if she would like that.'

Alice thanked them both again, and since Edward had excused himself, in order to share the garden with Rose and Ellice, she broached the subject of children.

'You do both realise that I have turned forty now. It is highly unlikely that Edward and I will be able to have our own children.'

This brought a few tears from Frances, since thinking about it more deeply reminded her that she and Alfred would not have any grandchildren either. But, with that realisation, it did signify that Frances had at least, in part, accepted that Charles would not be coming home for Christmas. She was certain that he would be with them in spirit.

Chapter Seventeen

Everyone's imagination had been captured by the excitement and anticipation of Alice and Edward's wedding, especially Frances.

'It seems as though she has emerged from her cocoon,' Alfred explained his wife's steady recovery to Alice.

'Yes, I've noticed that she is becoming more interested in daily life, not just the wedding preparations.'

'It's such a relief,' Alfred confided, 'I began to think that Fran would never recover. Now I feel there is a chance for all of us to go forward.'

'We mustn't forget little Rose's presence in all this,' Alice reminded him.

'Of course we mustn't forget that. She is a special little girl, and Frances loves her, as do I. She has rejuvenated us both. But, dear Alice, I haven't forgotten that if it hadn't been for your generosity of spirit in looking after her, after the sadness of her mother's tragic death, we would not have her at all?'

'I fear that there will be many such children in the next few months, Alfred. The Spanish flu has emerged in London, and it is thought to be very serious.'

Alfred shuddered as he reminded Alice how desperately ill she had been herself, during the diphtheria epidemic.

'You must be doubly careful now,' he warned her, 'no more visiting homes of sick parents. Leave it to the families and the doctors.'

Alice had to change the subject.

'Did I hear Ellice say that she would help you get the workshops opened again, Alfred?'

'Yes, she will. Do you know, Alice, I have misjudged Ellice. She used to appear quite scatter-brained, and too forthright for her own good.'

'And now?'

'Now I see that she cares deeply about social problems, and she strives for a more fair and equal society. I think it's what we should all want. It's just that people have different ways of putting their views forward, and I suppose the fact that women are becoming more forceful, and in some cases, even militant, frightens those who are afraid of change.'

'Are you one of those people, Alfred?'

'I don't think I am, Alice. It's the reckless speed at which things seem to be happening which perturbs me. The war has just exacerbated problems in society, and quick fix solutions are not going to be permanent ones, are they?'

'My, we are getting very serious now. Does your change of heart mean that you will accept Ellice's help?'

'Yes and gladly. We have re-opened the workshops. I have a team of volunteers, and we are going to try to help soldiers and sailors, returned from the war. Many are recovering from injuries. Some have lost limbs, or their eyesight, through the mustard gas, and others have become deaf because of the constant shelling in their field of battle. Mostly these men have lost homes, families, jobs and their possessions. They have nothing.'

'And you are going to find practical help for them?'

'I'm going to try my best, Alice.'

Alfred was astonished and amazed by the men's courage and determination. He remembered Jim Cole, and how bravely he had tried his utmost to continue working in spite of his injured leg. He had shown immense patience with his young grandson, Artie. He looked upon the making of beautiful things as his way of making the world a better place.

'I'm going to seek out that carpenter friend of Jim's. I'm sure he would give us a few hours. There is quite a lot of timber left. He would know what to do with it.'

The soldiers and sailors arrived daily. Word was quickly circulated amongst comrades who couldn't find work. Some had come home to find their houses had been bombed, damaged or destroyed. Families had dispersed, or died. It was a sad and difficult home coming for many of them. Before long there was yet another young soldier, who had lost his lower leg, requesting Alfred's help.

'Welcome,' Alfred welcomed the young corporal, who was still wearing his dirty, tattered uniform.

'I'm sorry, sir, I don't have any other clothes to wear.'

'Never mind that just now. I'm sure we can find you something to wear which will be more comfortable, for the time being.'

The vicar, amongst others, had been collecting clothes for just this occasion. Mrs Cole and Lily had taken turns at cleaning and repairing the donated goods. Frances didn't like darning, but her tiny fingers were adept at sewing on new buttons.

'My mate said that you might be able to help me with a job, sir,' the corporal explained. 'I'm George, sir, George Farmer.'

Alfred helped the corporal into the workshop.

'As you can see, Corporal–'

The soldier interrupted him, 'It's George now, sir!'

'I beg your pardon, George.'

Alfred found a quiet corner and took the young man away from the group of other servicemen, who were curious about him, as they had been of each new arrival.

'We are just about full to capacity, but I think we can squeeze you in somewhere. Let me tell you what we are doing here.' Alfred explained that he had created a daily refuge for returning soldiers and sailors, who had been unable to find any work.

'I can't actually give you a paid job, but you might be able to pick up new skills, to improve your prospects. We have a team of volunteers, carpenter, blacksmith, mechanic and painter-decorator. What did you do in the army, George?'

'I was a cook, sir.'

'Were you a good cook, George?' Alfred asked.

'I can't pretend to be a high-class chef, sir. I only had basic army training, but I can tell you that I have cooked for hundreds of men, in all kinds of situations, and nobody died of food poisoning, or hunger!'

'That's more than good enough for me,' Alfred shook his hand. 'Would you be interested in helping in the Food Economy Kitchen, George?'

He showed George into the new kitchen area, where they had hastily organised a demonstration corner.

'This is the leaflet the government have issued about the rationing of food. They are urging people to have two meatless days each week. So you can see the challenge. We hope to devise meal plans, so that people can make the most of their rations.'

George perused the leaflet:

THE WEEKLY CONSUMPTION BY EACH FAMILY OF THE THREE STAPLE FOODS SHOULD NOT EXCEED PER HEAD:- FOUR POUNDS OF BREAD OR THREE POUNDS OF FLOUR. MEAT — TWO AND A HALF POUNDS. SUGAR — A QUARTER OF A POUND

'We plan to hold groups of demonstration classes. My wife will help, and Mrs Cole and Lily, our housekeeper and her daughter, will demonstrate the dishes. The class will be able to take home a written recipe, with instructions.'

The newly recruited cook, George Farmer, assured Alfred that he would certainly enjoy lending a hand with that.

'In the field we hardly ever got fresh meat. We had to improvise every day, with whatever ingredients we happened to have. Sometimes we only had potatoes,' he told Alfred.

'What did you do with potatoes?'

'Soup mostly,' George said, 'but now and then, if we were lucky, we would come across wild rabbits, or a friendly farmer who would give us a few chickens, or a goose. Goose was good because we could render the fat and fry the potatoes instead of having soup all the time. It was a bit more filling.'

Alfred was amazed and fascinated listening to George's experiences in Europe. It made him feel very humble.

'You will be an enormous asset here,' he told George, 'do you think that you could put pen to paper and write down some very basic ideas for meals, and the method of preparing them?'

'I don't think that would be a big problem, sir, though I think I had better practice my handwriting so that it is legible. I am a bit out of practice.'

Alfred thanked him.

'We are getting a small printing machine tomorrow, so we will be able to print out recipe sheets, and details of the classes.'

'I'm not much of a writer, sir, but I'll do my best.'

'Good chap, many thanks. I am sorry that we can't pay you for your work, but you will be fed at least, and we will find you all the clothes and boots that you need.'

'Thank you very much, sir, I am grateful.'

Alfred gave George a writing pad and a box of pencils; that was something Alfred was never short of. He found a table for George, near to where the printing machine would be. He took to George. Here was a man who had suffered a terrible injury, cared for his comrades amidst dangerous warfare, and now prepared to turn his hand, willingly, to any kind of menial task put before him.

'I must help him, Mrs Cole!' he confided in her. 'I want to do something about his leg, when the time is right. I'm going to ask Tom, Jim's carpenter friend. Do you remember him, Mrs C?'

'Yes, I do remember him. He was a very good friend to Jim, before we lost him.'

Talking about Jim like that, reminded Alfred of all the

wonderful things that Jim had made. It reminded him too that his own creative work had been almost non-existent for months. His work for the *Illustrated London News* had become very depressing. He had found little joy in sketching bombed outbuildings, or the many injured and exhausted troops returning home from the war.

He found it painful, sketching the poor farmers, who were trying so desperately to salvage their crops during bad weather, and with fewer strong male workers.

'Perhaps Mrs C, when the world is more tranquil, I might find more peace of mind, and the energy to draw beautiful things once more.'

'I am sure you will, Mr Alfred.'

The printing machine, donated by *The News*, caused great interest and curiosity. A group of men were formed into two teams, in regimental fashion. It was how they knew to do things. The men took it in turns to dismantle and clean it, then to re-assemble it, spotless and gleaming, and in full working order.

'That's the best way to learn about machinery,' George said.

He prepared some practice papers for the men to work on.

'They look really good. This is a great idea!' he approved.

'We may have a problem, longer term,' he told Alfred.

'What sort of problem?' he asked.

'Ink, sir. If we are going to be printing a lot of papers, we will need much more ink than we have at present.'

'Of course, fancy me forgetting that. Leave it with me, and I will see if I can obtain more supplies.'

George busied himself writing recipes, and lesson sheets, and the team of novice printers spent time learning how to set type. After a few mistakes and minor errors, the former soldiers and sailors had mastered a completely new skill. Some had been engineers, so the machinery element came much easier to them.

Frances, Lily and Mrs Cole were enlisted to read through the recipe sheets, checking for accuracy of spelling, and of course making sure that the method of cooking required, was feasible.

'I don't want to seem as though we don't trust George's work, but it might be more diplomatic if you ladies just give it the once over,' Alfred urged.

Violet Cole was very impressed with George's recipes, and the way that he had written everything down.

'Very good. Clear and concise,' was her verdict. 'He's even written on both sides of the paper, so as not to make waste.'

	CLASS SUBJECTS
MONDAY	FLOUR AND BREAD RATIONS ALLOWED. FLOUR SUBSTITUTES
TUESDAY	MEAT RATION EXPLAINED. POT ROAST STEWING AND MEATLESS DAYS
WEDNESDAY	CEREALS AND PULSES
THURSDAY	PUDDINGS WITHOUT FLOUR
FRIDAY	SOUP. VEGETABLES. POTATO SUBSTITUTES
	DEMONSTRATION MEALS
MONDAY	RICE. BREAD. ROLLS. PORRIDGE. BARLEY CAKES.MAIZE
TUESDAY	BROWN STEW. STUFFED MUTTON BREAST. SEA PIE
WEDNESDAY	BAKED BEANS AND CHEESE. VEGETABLE AND LENTIL PIE
THURSDAY	GOLDEN PUDDING. SAGO. RICE PUDDING
FRIDAY	LENTIL AND TOMATO SOUP. BARLEY BROTH. OATMEAL PUDDING

These were George's meal ideas, but he explained to Frances and Mrs Cole that he was quite happy if they wished to add some ideas of their own.

'I wouldn't want you to think that the troops ate these meals,' he told them. 'It was usually anything we could throw into the pot.'

They both continued to be impressed.

'Thank you, George. This will be very useful. We'll see how these ideas go down, then perhaps we might add one or two changes to give them a bit of variety.'

'Anyway, George' quizzed Mrs Cole, 'how come you know so much about food and cooking things that you didn't use in the army?'

He was reticent to talk about himself at all, if he could avoid it, but he warmed to Mrs Cole.

'I'm afraid before I was conscripted I had to look after my mother. She was bedridden with crippling arthritis, for as long as I can remember. She taught me how to cook. She would read things out to me, from her bed. She died of pneumonia, the year I was sent to France.'

'I am so very sorry to hear that,' she sympathised. 'How very sad for you.'

'I'm glad she can't see me like this, only one leg, no job, and no home to go to.'

'Where are you living then, George?'

'I'm sharing a room with two other sappers. We're in an army hostel. It'll do for now, but if I could find a proper job, even part-time, I'd be on my way up again. I'll do it one day.'

George was a very positive person, and that was a good thing. Mrs Cole was afraid that however positive he was, he might have difficulty holding a job, while ever he had to rely on the crutch.

She was remembering how her Jim had struggled.

Word soon spread about the food economy classes. Women enrolled in their dozens. Classes had to be arranged morning, noon and night. People were keen to hear of anything which might help improve their lives. Many offered to volunteer their help, especially if there was something to eat at the end of the day.

Ellice Bell, stalwart friend of Alice Combe and Edward, proved to be one of the most valued volunteers, and also one of the printing section's most valued paying customers. She had her eyes on the printing machine, from the moment it was installed.

'I'll pay the going rate for you to produce some of my party leaflets, Alfred. Could your team manage that?'

'Would that be your Labour Party canvassing leaflets, or the suffragist "Votes for Women" pamphlets?'

'Don't worry, Alfred, the suffragist paper is published for us in Fleet Street. Huge circulation now, you know. No, these would be administrative things. Dates of meetings, agenda sheets, lists of names and addresses, that sort of thing. It will save me having to pay for an office, just at the moment.'

'Won't you need an office eventually?' he asked.

'Alfred, I do believe that's the nearest thing you have said to me by way of encouragement,' Ellice teased him.

'Well, I may not entirely agree with everything you stand for, I must say you work damned hard, and to be one of only seventeen women standing for Parliament, for the very first time, must count as a great achievement. Well done, Ellice, of course we will attempt your printing requirements.'

Alfred had always felt slightly uneasy with Ellice. She did have a good heart, and admirable intentions. She only wanted what was fair and right, for women and children particularly. The trouble was that she had an unfortunate knack of antagonising and upsetting people, and sometimes her efforts were counterproductive.

Ellice sat in on one of the food classes and congratulated George on his presentation that morning.

'You are obviously a great hit with the ladies, George, and the numbers seem to be growing daily.'

He just smiled in acknowledgement. He too felt a bit wary of Ellice, but there was something beguiling about her. He couldn't quite find the words to describe her. She was different to any other woman he had ever encountered, except perhaps, in part, just a slight resemblance to his mother. He turned his attention to the ladies in his class.

'I know that many of you ladies just put things into a pot, or basin, without measuring anything. You keep tasting to see if it needs more of this, or a little more of that; is that right, ladies?'

There were nods and smiles all round, and the rise in banter back and forth.

'If you follow my recipes to the letter, your meal will be absolutely perfect. You will save ingredients, and money. So, no more guess work then, at least while we have to work with strict rationing.'

There were cheers of approval all round, and Ellice, before she excused herself said loudly, 'You ought to be in politics!'

George did the talking and explaining of the rations in the first half of the session, then either Mrs Cole, Lily or Frances would alternate, each with a dish of their own to demonstrate.

On the days when brown stew was on the menu, the gorgeous aroma of onions frying wafted throughout the whole building, and even along the road outside, much to the annoyance of close neighbours, in this very upper middle-class street.

Some of the wealthier neighbours disapproved of Alfred turning the beautiful house into a day centre "for all and sundry", so completely misunderstanding his aims. Housing an art gallery was one thing, but this was something else.

Alice and Edward did their stints working in the evenings, to give the other volunteers a rest. Alfred kept his eye on Alice since she had been so ill with diphtheria.

'You have to take care, Alice. Don't become overtired. You have Rose to think of now, and the wedding, very soon.'

'I am aware of that Alfred, but I am also worried about the

school children. We have a growing number with tuberculosis, and I had to send several children home because of the influenza. It's being called the Spanish "flu".'

Edward assured Alfred that they were taking the most precautions possible.

'We are walking around school with face-masks on, and we have disinfectant sprays in every room. We are regularly spraying all the classrooms and public areas. We just have to be very vigilant.'

On one of the better, sunnier days, Alice took Rose to look around the London stores for wedding clothes, or for suitable fabric. They even scoured Camden market, and took several samples to show recommended dressmakers, for their approval.

One rather haughty dressmaker, on the King's Road, ran her fingers over Alice's silk samples.

'Yes. This group would suit a lady of mature years,' she said, 'but I suggest you steer clear of white. It's so unforgiving a colour! So is the cream. Why not try the pale grey?'

Alice disliked the woman, and she couldn't leave the shop fast enough.

'Horrid, little woman!' she shouted, when they were outside.

Rose was laughing hysterically. She had never heard Alice talk like that before. Alice took Rose by the hand.

'Come on, Rose. We'll go back to that nice lady in the Tottenham Court Road. We'll see if we can persuade her to do it.'

'I'll do my very best, dear,' the dressmaker said.

'I've decided on the cream silk,' Alice said, almost defiantly.

'That will look lovely on you, dear.'

Alice and Rose returned to Highgate, tired, but pleased. No! Pleased wasn't the right word. Alice felt triumphant but she was trying not to get too excited, too soon. She was only too aware that she and Edward were surrounded daily by children whose families were suffering real hardships. She felt it was a bit too frivolous to be buying anything new at all. She did her best to be practical, and as thrifty as she could. She and Edward had decided that they would have a very small wedding, with only a few close friends and family at the church, and a very small lunch party afterwards. They would live quietly at Highgate, with Rose, and perhaps one day, when the world was a more settled place, they might manage to take a short holiday, a honeymoon, in the sun somewhere. Edward had missed his summers in France. Perhaps they would go there.

She stopped dreaming.

CHAPTER EIGHTEEN

Alfred Richards could never have envisaged that his small idea of a craft workshop, and then, as a result of food rationing, the need for the food classes, would have blossomed as they did.

He was written about in the newspapers as a pioneer in social care and a generous philanthropist, much to his genuine feeling of embarrassment.

'I am pleased, of course,' he told Fran, ' but I am not the only person trying to make a contribution to society. We set the ball rolling, and now there are several other groups like ours.'

Frances agreed, and she pointed out that there was now a lot more help for soldiers and sailors who were returning home in ever-increasing numbers.

'Do you know Fran,' Alfred confessed, 'I feel better now, and less guilty, for owning such a large, fine house. We are making very good use of it, and when we no longer need to provide for the troops, and the poor of this part of London, we will have our gallery back again, and I will draw better pictures.'

The printing team had acquired a constant stream of work, and some of the men felt confident enough to seek proper work in the newspaper industry.

Former sappers (engineers) had helped Alfred to find other small machines, all donated by charitable foundations, or the many businessmen who admired the work they had begun. It now gathered a momentum all of its own.

Tom, the carpenter friend of Jim Cole arrived. He was very pleased to give his spare time to teach men how to build, and to restore furniture. Of their own volition, the men had decided to use spare off-cuts of wood, just as Jim had done.

They made toys for sick children in the hospitals, and children who were forced to live in orphanages. There were alphabet blocks, and blocks with numbers on, small wooden animals, and tiny trains and dolls. None of the men wanted to make toy soldiers.

Alfred thanked Tom for his efforts.

'I am deeply grateful to you, Tom, for giving your precious time, and especially for the way you are helping George to get used to the new leg you have made for him.'

'It's given me my life back again,' George told him later.

'You deserve it,' Tom said.

'You never know, Tom, I might even find myself a wife.'

This half joking remark came from George's lips just as he had spotted Ellice and Frances. They were collecting some of the toys, and were planning to take them all to the nearest hospital. Frances seemed in her element, helping Ellice, so while she was in such an amenable frame of mind, Ellice thought she should try and build on Fran's new found confidence. Try as she might, it was rather an uphill struggle to get Frances talking.

'Will you be going to the court hearing with Alice and Edward?' Ellice asked innocently. She did already know the answer, but she feigned ignorance. She tried to encourage Frances to talk about Rose and the question of guardianship, but Frances continued her nods and smiles.

The morning of the hearing arrived, and Alfred and Frances joined Alice and Edward, and little Rose, as the honorary aunt and uncle. Rose was wearing her lovely red coat and beret. She clutched Alice's hand tight as they climbed the steps into the court office.

'Will I have to see the judge by myself?' Rose asked.

'I am not quite sure how these things are done, Rose, but you have nothing to feel nervous about. Remember to smile, and speak nicely if the judge addresses you directly, won't you?'

Edward encouraged Rose too.

'Rose, it will all be over in a very few minutes. We all have excited butterflies in our tummies, don't we?'

The others laughed at this description of how they were all feeling.

'My tummy is rumbling,' Rose added.

'That's because you refused breakfast, silly,' said Alice.

'I'll tell you what,' offered Alfred, 'when it is all over, how would you all like to go for a cup of tea and toasted teacakes?'

'Ooh! Yes!' cried Rose.

'That would be very nice Alfred, but you spoil her.'

'Not at all. We are all a bit hungry, I suspect, and we will feel like a little celebration afterwards, won't we?'

'Yes!' shouted Rose and Edward in unison.

The court building was quite dark inside, through lack of fuel for the lamps. The single light burning in the corridor threw shadows on the walls. Edward joked that the shadows of all their hats appeared to be dancing, as they moved about. His jocularity helped to keep Rose relaxed.

They were shown into the courtroom, and ushered to their seats on the front bench, facing the judge. Peter Lawrence, Alfred's lawyer, had employed his senior solicitor to act on the family's behalf. It was clear that all the necessary paperwork had been completed. The solicitor, dressed in his wig and gown, hurried into court, carrying his file of notes. He bade the family good morning. Then Rose gave a little giggle, when the solicitor, forgetting that he was wearing his legal clothes, went to raise his hat, as he would have done outside. In his absent-mindedness his wig fell off and onto the floor.

'So sorry, M'lud. Mr Richards.'

'Shall we begin, now?' the judge implored impatiently, 'We have a lot to get through this morning.'

'Yes, M'lud. So sorry.'

The judge took his time to look carefully through his papers, then, peering over his spectacles, and towards the family group, he spoke kindly, and directly, to Rose.

'Young lady, Rose.'

'Yes, sir,' Rose answered politely, as she stood up.

'I have read about the demise of your poor mother, and firstly I want to tell you how very sorry I am that she is no longer with you. However, these kind people, the Richards family, and Miss Combe and her fiancé, Mr Edward Gardner, have agreed to look after you now.'

The judge paused, and looked to Rose, for her reaction.

'Are you happy with the arrangement, child?'

'Yes, sir, I am very happy. The most happy I have ever been.'

'Then, I shall grant temporary full guardianship to Mr Alfred Richards, until the day of the marriage between Miss Combe and Mr Gardner, who will then become your permanent guardians.'

The judge made a loud noise stamping the papers, for effect. He handed the papers to the clerk of the court, then climbed down from his high bench, and came towards the family. He shook everyone's hand in turn.

'Congratulations, and good luck to you all,' he said to the grown-ups. Then bending down to Rose, he took her by the hand, and whispered softly. 'You must be a very good girl. Be helpful in your new home, say your prayers every night, and include your new family in your prayers. Will you do that?'

'Yes, sir, I truly will. Thank you, sir.'

Before the judge straightened himself, he brought out a small leather bound bible and gave it to Rose.

'This is a momentous day in your life, young lady. Write today's date in the front page of your bible, so that you remember it always.'

Peter Lawrence's man disappeared with his papers. Alfred expected to receive copies, in due course. He was a little

254

disappointed that Peter Lawrence had not seen fit to be present himself.

It was a very happy Rose who skipped down the steps from the courthouse. She started singing as they followed the pavement round to the nearest tea room. Hot buttered toast and scones, and a mug of tea proved to be "the bestest breakfast", according to Rose.

After the excitement had subsided, and the "bestest" breakfast had been consumed, Rose had a few questions for Alice. Now that she felt more secure, and her tummy butterflies had gone away, she quizzed anyone who would answer her.

'Why is Mr Alfred my guardian, until December?'

'It's the law, dear Rose,' replied Alfred, 'Alice isn't allowed to adopt you because at the moment she is an unmarried lady.'

Alice tried to explain matters further.

'You see, it would be illegal for a single lady to adopt you. So when Edward and I are married, we can both be your legal guardians.'

Rose was still very confused.

'I don't understand why unmarried ladies are unlawful!' Alice and Edward laughed openly. The thoughts of Alice being unlawful was just too funny. Alice calmed down, and had another attempt to explain it to Rose.

'I know it must seem strange to you, but I am quite certain that when you are a little older Ellice will tell you all about the rights of women. She and other ladies called suffragettes are trying to persuade the government to change the law, so that women and men will have equal rights.'

Edward tried to help Alice.

'You see, Rose. By the time you are grown up, women will be able to do lots of things that they aren't allowed to do now. For one thing, you will be allowed to vote for a member of parliament, that means a member of the government. They make the laws that we all have to live by.'

'Is Ellice a member of parliament?'

'No dear, not yet. She is a candidate, and people will be able to vote for her when it is the big general election. If she gets enough votes, then she could well be a member of the parliament.'

'Then I shall vote for Ellice,' announced Rose, without really understanding much about it. She was just glad to be part of the grown-ups' discussion. Rose decided that one day, when she and Ellice were alone, she would ask her about the suffragettes. She sensed that her honorary aunt and uncle didn't care too much for Ellice's work with the Labour Party, or the suffragettes.

Before the family left the tea room, Alice and Edward had saved one more surprise for Rose.

'How would you like to be my very special bridesmaid, Rose?' Rose was speechless, and her eyes as wide as saucers, but the huge grin which spread across her face said it all.

'We will measure you up, and then we will choose some nice material, so that you will have a dress every bit as pretty as mine.'

Rose was very excited; all her nerves about meeting the judge were forgotten.

'I can't wait for the wedding to happen,' she cried, 'what colour will my dress be?'

'I don't know yet, but we will go out one day and look at everything in the shops, and then we will see what suits you best.' They had all grown close to Rose. There was nothing to find fault with in her character at all. Now the realisation dawned on them that as Rose was to become a permanent member of the family, they would have to decide on names.

'Rose can't go on calling you "Miss", after you've married,' said Alfred. 'Mrs Gardner wouldn't be right either.'

'Well, she can't call me "Mother", either.'

'And you aren't really cousins,' Edward offered. Rose didn't know what all the fuss was about.

'Why don't I call you all my honorary aunts and uncles?'

Rose liked that. So did Alice and Frances. It didn't sound rude or discourteous. It was affectionate, but not too personal.

'Aunt Alice and Uncle Edward and Aunt Frances and Uncle Alfred. What's wrong with that,' Rose asked.

It sounded good. So that was happily agreed, and they all practised reciting their names and new titles, just for Rose.

CHAPTER NINETEEN

'Who do you think will win, Ellice?' George asked.

'Difficult to say George, a close call I'd say. I suspect that we will end up with a coalition government, when the votes have been properly counted in two weeks' time.'

'And what about your own chances?'

Ellice was quite open and forthright about her own position as a female candidate. She was touched that George had enquired.

'I am quite realistic, you know. I was lucky to be one of only seventeen women. I will have gathered a few hundred votes, I'm sure of that, but I won't win, not this time, anyway. It feels like a momentous first step on the ladder. We can all go forward now.'

It seemed like the whole of London was caught up in a great frenzy of excitement, and in some constituencies, mostly in the middle class areas, there were impressive lines of women who had banded together, to vote all together. They made a very colourful scene, especially the ones who decided to go to the polls wearing their purple and green colours of the Women's Movement, and the suffragettes.

'Votes for all women! Votes for all women!' The cries could be heard all over London streets.

It was clear that the women's organisations were not going to stop demonstrating until women had equal treatment, everywhere, and were able to do everything that men did.

'It will be interesting to see how Mr Lloyd George will go about making this a country fit for heroes, as he promised.'

'We shall see,' said Ellice. She thanked George for helping her put more papers into brown envelopes.

'You are still canvassing then?' he asked

'No, George. These are thank you letters to all the people who have helped me to canvass. I have to keep all my supporters on side if we are to continue building.'

'I do admire you, tremendously,' declared George. He had been longing to say that to Ellice for a long time, but couldn't seem to find the right words, without it sounding too forward.

'Well, thank you George. I admire you too. You've had a great deal to contend with, and showed enormous courage.'

'No more than many other soldiers and sailors. We just did what was expected of us. I don't think any of us had a single idea of how the war would be, and how difficult it would prove to be afterwards, when we came home, that is, if we came home.'

The friendship which had grown between Ellice and George had blossomed slowly over many months. There were no moments of passion, or sentimentality, but better, thought Ellice, a strong bond of mutual understanding and respect. George had found his voice, and without a lot of anxious striving, as he anticipated that he might. Their relationship had developed naturally, with neither of them expecting anything else to cloud the ease of friendship.

'I've been thinking about all this work you do for the party, Ellice, not to mention your other work on the education board, and so on. How would it be if I were to act as your office assistant? I don't know what you would call it? Clerk, secretary, agent?'

'What a brilliant idea, George. It's true, sometimes I have to work all day and evenings too, but I'm afraid I couldn't pay you very much.'

'We can talk about that later. I might be able to get a proper job very soon. Mr Richards won't need to keep this centre going forever will he?'

'One hopes not, George. But I fear there will always be a need for a rehabilitation place like this, for some time to come.'

It was growing dusk, and George and Ellice prepared to lock up the workshop, when the door opened quietly, and a young sailor, still in his uniform, came slowly through the door.

'Hello, I saw a light on, and wondered if my mother was here?'

'My, goodness!' shouted Ellice, 'It's Jim Cole, isn't it?'

'Yes miss, I'm Jim Cole.'

'Well, Jim Cole. Do come in. I can't tell you how pleased I am to see you, and what a shock your mother and sister are going to have when they see you.'

'Yes, I know that, but I wasn't able to write and let them know that I was coming home.'

'I'm Ellice Bell, friend of Alice Combe. Do you remember me?'

'Yes, I do remember you, miss. I remember seeing you at my grandfather's funeral.'

'That was very, very sad. He was a fine man.'

Ellice took off her coat and hat again, and laid them down on a table, with her bag.

'I will make you a cup of tea,' she said, 'I expect you could do with one?'

'That would be great, if you don't mind, miss.'

'Let me do that,' said George, 'you just have a chat and I will bring it in a few moments.'

'Thank you, sir,' said Jim.

'No need to call me sir. I'm just George.'

Ellice took Jim's bag and cap and ushered him to a comfy chair.

'Here, sit down, and tell me all about yourself.'

'I don't know rightly where to begin, miss. My story isn't very interesting, but I do need to see my ma and Lily, and Mr Richards, as soon as I can. I have something for them.'

'All in good time. I will take you myself. They are all at the Highgate House. We have good news, at last. Alice is being married, tomorrow, to Edward Gardner, a school teacher,' she told him.

Ellice thought that Jim was looking very weary, and was a little reluctant to talk. Perhaps he would relax, and open up to her and George after he had drunk his mug of tea. She told Jim about the Kensington house and how Alfred had turned it into a craft workshop and social centre for the time being, to help returning soldiers and their families.

'Everyone has done their bit,' Ellice explained, 'even your mother and Lily have helped with the cookery classes. George, here, came to us in a very poor state. He won't mind talking about it, will you, George?'

'No, of course not,' he said, 'this place has really given me my life back again. I lost a leg in the war, but Tom, your grandfather's pal, has made me a new leg, and I can walk very well.'

'Just like my grandfather.'

Jim was remembering the awful time his grandfather had suffered his accident, and he told Ellice that he had felt more than a little guilty for running away to sea.

'I thought it would be one less thing for my mother to have to worry about,' he revealed.

'Well,' said Ellice, 'that was a long time ago, and I know that your mother has forgiven you for that.' What Ellice didn't know, and she was hoping that Jim would tell her, was whether he knew about Artie.

He could tell that Ellice was waiting for him to talk about Arthur, and Charles. He finished his tea, even though it had gone cold, while they were talking. When he tried to speak, his eyes were filling up, but he swallowed the tears, and took a deep breath.

'I do know about Arthur and Charles. Do you want me to talk about it?'

'Only if you want to, Jim.'

'Yes, well, Charles started out as a writer, on the shore base at Devonport, and he liked it there. He didn't really have much of a choice when they drafted him on to a ship, *The Goliath*, at the same time as Arthur. That was at Chatham. The ship had been in for a re-fit. So had mine. I went on the *Halcyon*. It was a minesweeper, bound for the North Atlantic. I didn't know where *Goliath* was bound for, but we did get a quick meeting together before we sailed.'

'Jim, don't go on if it's upsetting you too much.'

'It's all right, miss. Now I've started I don't feel so bad. I haven't really talked about it with anyone, till now.'

'Go on then, Jim. If you want to.'

'As I said before, we had a few minutes to talk before we had to board ships. Charlie, sorry, Charles, was joking that they had a major re-fit, almost new, and my ship had a lick of paint, a spring-clean, he laughed. He promised to look out for Arthur.'

'Were they based near to each other on the ship?' George asked.

'I'm not exactly sure where they were on the ship, but what Charles did tell me was that if they were hit, the enemy would go for the turrets, and the guns. They'd most likely go for the middle of the ship, to sink it.'

'He seemed to be very informed,' said George.

'He was very clever, sir, and could understand much more than Arthur. In a way that was a blessing, in disguise.'

'How, so?' said Ellice.

'Charles took me on one side, away from Arthur. He said that if they were hit, he and Arthur would be unlikely to be blown to pieces, like the midshipmen. They might be in the water, with at least some chance of swimming.'

All three of them remained silent, contemplating.

Jim, Ellice and George sat in the room together, quiet, and in the semi-darkness. It was dusk outside, and there was only one lamp lit.

'We should make a move,' said Ellice, thoughtfully, 'I am just wondering what is the best thing for us to do for Jim, now?'

'I'm afraid I can't take him to my hostel. It's full up.'

'Don't worry, George. We will fathom something out. It's just that all the family, and Mrs Cole and Lily, are all at the Highgate House, preparing for the wedding tomorrow.'

Jim could see that he had arrived at a really awkward time.

'I can't go to my mother's house, I do not have a key.'

'Could we make a bed for him here, in the workshop?'

'No,' said Ellice, 'it would be very cold for him, and besides, we have a night watchman checking the building. He might find Jim, and think he is a burglar.'

'I've decided,' Ellice said, 'Jim will come home to my place. I'm afraid you will have to sleep on the settee, but at least you'll be warm, and then I can take you to Highgate tomorrow.'

'I thought you weren't going to the wedding,' said George.

'I'm not going to the church, but I'm not missing the party, afterwards,' she joked, 'that might be better anyway, we don't want Jim's appearance to cause anyone upset, before the wedding, do we?'

'You are quite right, Ellice,' Jim concluded, 'if I had known about the wedding I would have come a day later. Can't be helped. I will do whatever you feel is best. I must tell you though, that I have a most precious gift with me, and I am in a great quandary as to who should have it.'

'That sounds intriguing, Jim. Do tell.'

Jim reached for his bag. He took out a package and carefully unwrapped it.

'Charles gave it to me, for safe keeping,' he said. 'If I were to get home, and he didn't, I was to give it to his Aunt Alice. She would know what to do with it.'

Jim handed the small blue book to Ellice. She opened the pages one by one. She read Charles's perfect handwriting, describing all his daily commitments at Devonport, since he had been there. Other pages told of important naval events, and visitors, and about the fun he had with friends when they were off-duty. Football matches at Plymouth Argyle, concerts at the Guildhall, even songs that he had taken down in tonic sol-fa. There were photographs of his new friends, including some of young ladies, whom they didn't know.

Ellice was completely overwhelmed, tears streaming down her cheeks. She didn't know if they were tears of sadness, or joy, or both at the same time. This usually very earnest, serious, and for the most part unemotional woman, was unused to displays such as this. George put his arms round her, and she didn't stop him. The sadness was for all they had lost, and not least that Charles would not be at Highgate for Alice's wedding. But, the feelings of joy were for the miraculous return of Jim Cole, and for the very beautiful and precious book; a part of Charles, for his family to keep and treasure forever.

Ellice pulled herself together, and once more adopted her usual calm and practical self.

'I know why Charles wanted his aunt to see the book first,' she told Jim, 'it's because Frances, his mother, has suffered a really bad depression, and although she is much recovered, she will never be her old self again. We have to look after her fragile state. We will take Alice's advice after the wedding, and after the lunch party.'

Jim agreed, and said he would keep the little book secret, until later.

'I will take you to Highgate to surprise everyone with your presence, Jim.'

'What a surprise this is going to be for your mother, and your grandmother, Jim.'

'Yes, I am beginning to feel better now. Safe and more relaxed. Thank you both.'

'Will you be returning to the navy, Jim?' George asked him.

'No, I am not. I've done enough of that now. Got it out of my system. The war has done for me. I want a quieter life, maybe a wife and family. But I need to find a job first. The rest will come in time.'

'What did you do in the navy?' Ellice asked.

'A bit of all sorts really. I'm not very good at the machine stuff. I'm no engineer. Mostly I ended up in the galley, cooking.'

'What about that for a coincidence,' George laughed, 'I'm a cook, too!'

'Perhaps you could work together, open a shop, or an eating house,' Ellice suggested flippantly, 'you could do much worse.'

Jim's homecoming hadn't been exactly how he had imagined it, but he was glad that he had met Ellice and George like that. It was good that he had been prepared about everyone, before he would shock them all with his appearance. He went home happily, with Ellice. She wasn't at all like he remembered her, but then a lot of years had passed, and he was remembering her as he did when he was a boy. He thought she was still a touch bossy, but well-meaning, rather like a mother hen.

Ellice found Jim a decent change of clothes, from their donated "good box" – but she was diplomatic enough to suggest that it was his choice whether he went to Highgate in his clean, but rather worn uniform, or the new donated clothes. He said he would sleep on it, and tell her in the morning.

Jim Cole didn't really sleep much at all that night. He was far too excited about seeing his mother and grandmother again. He had washed and dressed in his new clothes, which fitted him perfectly. Ellice was always up early. Jim felt a little awkward, sitting down with Ellice in her small kitchen, but he needn't have felt embarrassed. Ellice didn't.

'Poached eggs on toast all right for you, Jim?'

'Thank you, that would be fine, Miss Ellice.'

'I see that you decided on the new clothes,' she said, 'stand up again. Let me see how you look?'

Jim stood up and stepped away from the table. He didn't know what to do with the buttons. He fumbled to do them up properly.

'You look very smart. Everything fits you perfectly.'

'Thank you, very much indeed, miss. I thought it might upset people if I turned up in my uniform. This way I shouldn't cause any offence.' He undid the buttons again, and tugged at the tie. 'I'm not used to wearing ties, but I will get used to it.'

'Here, take this napkin, to cover your front. We don't want you to spill eggs down your new shirt, especially today, do we?'

Jim's laughter certainly broke the ice, not that his feeling awkward was anything at all to do with Ellice.

'You remind me of my mother,' he told her.

'Well, that's good. It means you feel at home here, and I will tell you, Jim, that had I married and had children, I would be very proud to have had a son like you.'

'Now you are embarrassing me,' he said.

They finished breakfast, and Ellice left Jim reading the newspaper.

'I have a few telephone calls to make,' she said. 'I won't be too long. Perhaps you could scour the pages. See if there's much about the polling stations. I doubt there'll be any photographs yet.'

Ellice had been considering Jim's position carefully, and because it was to be an exceptional day, his arrival would stun everyone, not just his mother. She hadn't wanted to pre-empt Jim's big moment, arriving at Highgate, amongst all the wedding guests, so she decided the best thing to do would be to speak with Alfred first. He would still be at Kensington, preparing himself for his momentous day, as Alice's stand-in father. Mrs Cole would be there, at Kensington, helping him. Lily, Jim's mother, would be at the Highgate house, helping Alice. What a dilemma! What would be the best plan of action? She mustn't dither. She had to speak with Alfred, and soon. Ellice hoped that he hadn't left already.

'Alfred, thank goodness I have managed to speak with you.'

'Ellice, I hope this call is important. I don't have much time before the carriage comes for me. Please don't start on about the election. That will have to wait.'

'No, listen carefully, Alfred. I know that I am the last person you want to speak with right now, but I have some really wonderful news. You will certainly want to hear this.'

Ellice told him the news about Jim, and how he had arrived in his uniform, with a very special gift, for him and Frances.

266

'Jim has carried it with him for three years, Alfred, unable to get home, until now. What would you like me to do?'

Alfred was silent for a few moments, trying to assimilate the news from Ellice.

'Are you there still, Alfred? Speak, please.'

'Yes Ellice. Listen, my carriage will come close to your house. Stay there, with Jim. I will bring Mrs Cole in to see Jim. Then we will all go up to Highgate together. There will be room.'

'That's very good of you, Alfred. I will prepare Jim. What a day this is going to be.'

'I have spoken with Alfred. He will come here, with your grandmother. They will be here very soon.'

Jim's eyes welled up with emotion, but Ellice, being Ellice, didn't allow him to become too sentimental.

'Come on now, Jim. Stiff upper lip is called for. Your grandmother will have enough tears for all of us. We will wait by the door; to see them arrive then we will have to leave for Highgate. I told Alfred that you have something special, but I didn't tell him what it was. I hope you approve of my doing that?'

'Yes, thank you, Miss Ellice. I have been worrying about how I should do this. Perhaps I should do it on another day?'

'No not at all, Jim. This is the most perfect day of all. We just have to choose the right moment. Alfred thinks you should do exactly as Charles asked you to do. I will be there with you, after all the greetings, the tears, and the wedding, of course. Alfred will give me a signal, when the time is right, then I will give you the signal. Will that be all right with you?'

'Yes, thank you,' he said.

They both stood outside, by the pavement's edge, waiting for the carriage to draw up. Jim couldn't stand still, and Ellice kept looking anxiously at her watch. They mustn't be late.

'There they are,' shouted Jim, 'I see them!'

The carriage pulled up, and Alfred helped Violet Cole out on to the pavement. She stood for a few moments, looking at her grandson, hardly believing that it really was him. She held her arms open to him.

'Grandma! Grandma! It's so good to see you.'

She hugged him tight. She didn't want to let him go. She could hardly speak for the tears and the laughing together.

Ellice ushered them back into the carriage. Alfred grasped Jim's hands, trying hard to maintain his own composure.

'I'm so happy to see you, Jim. We'll have time to talk later, after the wedding. You will join the family, won't you? Your mother doesn't know that you are here, yet.'

'She's in for the surprise of her life,' laughed Jim. Ellice's friend George, the soldier cook, had been helping Lily put the last-minute touches to the table, and the flowers. The food was ready and waiting for the guests who would come after the wedding. Lily began to tidy herself when the front door opened. She saw Ellice first, then her mother, Violet. Mr Alfred followed on behind. Lily hadn't noticed that his body was hiding that of Jim's.

'Good morning, Miss Ellice, Mr Alfred, Mother. Miss Alice is upstairs with young Rose, and Mrs Richards. They must be ready by now. I'll give them a call, shall I?'

'Not yet, Lily,' Ellice said, 'you aren't quite ready yourself!' Ellice moved towards her, and playfully removed Lily's apron.

'Here is a young man who wishes to escort you to church.'

Alfred stepped aside, to reveal the slightly nervous Jim, who was standing behind him.

'Hello, Ma!'

Lily stared in amazement. She could hardly catch her breath.

'Jimmy! My Jimmy!' Lily cried, 'Am I dreaming?'

'No, Ma, you aren't dreaming. It's me, all right.' George went to find Lily's coat and hat.

'You'd better hurry, all of you,' said George, 'if you want to be in church by the time the bride arrives.'

'But,' Lily said urgently, 'I'm supposed to see to the food.'

'We will take care of that, until you return. Off you go!' Ellice and George waved the four of them off.

'Did you really not want to be in the church, Ell?'

'No, George. Alice understands. We've talked about it. I will welcome them back later, and we'll get a sneaky look at their clothes, before the congregation does.'

It was just a short ride to the church. Alfred accompanied Jim, his mother and grandmother to Highgate Church, and made sure they had seats of honour, then he took the carriage back to the house to accompany the bride, the little bridesmaid, and Frances, his wife, to one of the happiest days of all their lives.

Alice, in her fashionable, ankle length, slim, cream satin dress, looked for all the world like a young twenty-year-old bride. She was holding a small bouquet of green myrtle leaves, with three dark red roses. The roses were chosen to match Rose, who was thrilled beyond measure, to wear her new red velvet dress.

'Here, Rose,' beamed Ellice, 'don't forget to wear your little fur cape. It will be cold in the church, and it is so pretty.'

'Ellice, do I detect a slight tear in your eye?' greeted her friend, Alice.'

'Not at all,' she joked, 'it's the cold. You look stunning, Al. I do wish you all the luck in the world.'

'You can still come to the church, Ell. The carriage will take Fran and Rose, ahead of me. You can join them, you and George.' The decision had to be made in a split second.

'All right, we'll come for Rose and Fran. But I won't be singing. You know I can't.'

'At last, I have you alone for a few moments, before the carriage comes for us. Do you realise, sweet Alice, that I actually feel more like your father than your brother-in-law. It's a nice feeling.'

'Thank you Alfred. You've been so good to me that I almost feel like your daughter.'

'There is just one more thing I must tell you. I don't know whether this is the right time or not, but I'm going to risk it.'

'You aren't going to spring the supposed surprise about my schoolchildren are you?'

'Schoolchildren? I don't know anything about that. No. This is something truly miraculous and wonderful, but I need to tell you before Frances knows about it. I don't know how she will take it. Young Jim Cole has carried something of Charles with him for over three years now. Charles gave it to him, with the express instruction to give it to you.'

'Oh, Alfred! How amazing! And today of all days. I wonder what it could be?'

'We will find out later, if you are sure you won't be upset about it.'

'I will be overjoyed, and I expect Frances will be too.'

'Let us go, then sweet Alice. Your bridegroom is waiting.' The short, leisurely ride to the church gave Alice just enough time to mention Jim Cole.

'Isn't it marvellous, for Lily and Mrs Cole to have their boy back, when they feared he was lost forever?'

'Yes, it is. A momentous day for all of us. Look, Alice, there is the tall steeple. We're almost there.'

They paused in the church doorway, the vicar gave the wave to the organist, and as the glorious sound of the *Trumpet Voluntary* began, Alfred walked Alice slowly down the aisle, towards her Edward. The service was short and simple, and suited them both. Alice had chosen the *Trumpet Voluntary*, because it was so happy a tune, and she wasn't fond of the traditional wedding marches.

Edward asked if he could surprise her with the exit music, after they had signed the registers. Alice agreed, though she had an inkling that it might be her schoolchildren singing a Christmas carol. But she was mistaken.

The children were there in the choir stalls, dressed in their Sunday-best clothes, and they sang softly, perfectly in tune and without any accompaniment, except for the very first note.

'*My love is like a red, red, rose...*'

270

'Edward, how very beautiful. Thank you. I am glad that I have married a musician. How clever of you.'

'How clever of the children to sing in tune, and look, look behind you. They haven't finished yet.'

The children continued singing, and followed Alice and Edward to the door of the church, and once outside, they threw paper roses, which they had made in school, in secret, for them both.

'How did you manage the rose petals, in school?'

'I didn't. It was Ellice's idea. She came into school one evening, after you had gone home. The children came back to make them. '

'And I helped too,' chirped Rose.

'You are such a clever girl, and you are so pretty'

'Ellice does have a soft spot, after all,' said Alice.

'Can I ride back with you now, Aunt Alice, and Uncle Edward?' Rose asked. 'We're lawful now, aren't we?'

So Rose climbed up into the carriage, with the bride and groom. Some of the school children had fun picking up the paper rose petals, and threw them again, over each other, and over some of the remaining guests. Even Jim Cole found a few petals round his neck.

Ellice and George felt a warm glow, and it wasn't just that they had done their duty for the day.

'It was such a good idea of Lily's to make us a buffet Lunch,' said Alfred. 'People can sit or stand, as they choose, it's much more fun to be informal, isn't it? But we mustn't forget to be a bit formal. Mrs Cole has made a most magnificent cake.'

The afternoon wore on, guests mingled and chatted, everyone trying to kiss the happy couple, and of course, admiring Rose, in her beautiful velvet dress.

The formal time arrived, and the cake was in pride of place. Mrs Cole and Lily handed glasses of sherry to the guests.

'I hope we shall have enough to go round,' said Alfred,

'I've been saving these few bottles, for just this occasion.' Peter

Lawrence, as Edward's supporter, gave a short speech of thanks, and as Alfred had insisted, he made a special mention of thanking Mrs Cole and Lily for their very hard work.

He didn't dwell on the awful time of the past two or three years, nor of Alice's terrible illness with diphtheria.

'Ladies and gentlemen, please raise your glasses, to the happy couple!'

'To the happy couple,' everyone chimed.

The guests enjoyed their wedding cake, or they took a small piece home with them. That was the signal for people to leave, and the signal from Alfred to let Ellice know that Alice would be very glad to sit down with Jim, for a few moments.

Peter Lawrence took Edward off somewhere, for a second glass of anything that happened to be left.

'No more cycling trips round France, Edward?'

'I don't know, Peter. We will have to see. One thing at a time. Perhaps I can persuade Alice to go with me.'

'Of course, you have little Rose to think about now.'

'Yes, and we are looking forward to doing things with her too.'

Peter wasn't too happy making small talk, and as soon as he could respectfully make his exit from the celebrations, he did so.

Edward could see that Frances was wilting a little. He asked Lily if she would bring cups of tea.

'Yes, sir, that's a good idea. I'll bring it to the parlour for you; it'll be much quieter in there.'

Alfred managed to find a quiet corner in the dining room, so that Alice and Jim could at last talk together, without being interrupted.

'Edward and Rose are keeping Frances entertained, and George and Ellice are helping in the kitchen,' Alfred said, 'I'm sure everyone else has gone. I'll be back in a few minutes.'

Jim gave Alice the small parcel. He handled it as though it were some priceless gold treasure.

'You should have this now,' he said, softly.

Alice unwrapped the smaller of the two treasures. It was the silver pen that she had given to Charles, before he enlisted at Devonport. It was wrapped in a piece of paper, on which Charles had written her a message:

Dear Aunt Alice,
I hope you like what I have written.
Forever, your Charles.

She unwrapped the second treasure, and found the personal diary that he had begun to write in each day. She was overcome, not able yet to read all the words, but she turned every page to feel his writing, admire the small photographs and even to hum one of the tonic sol-fa songs.

'I don't know how I can ever thank you, Jim. I find it quite miraculous that you have looked after this for such a long time, and that you have been able to bring it to us.'

'I cared for him too, you know, and it's thanks enough that I was able to keep my promise to him, miss.'

'I'm a "Mrs" now Jim, fancy that!'

Alice dried her eyes, and went in search of Alfred and Frances. Rose, completely exhausted after such an exciting day, had been taken up to bed, where Lily listened to her and Rose listened to Lily until Rose fell asleep.

Alice and Edward, Alfred and Frances, sat up for many more hours, talking with Jim about Charles and about Artie, his brother. They read the little blue diary, sometimes over and over the same bits again. They pored over the photographs, and Jim answered all their questions as truthfully as he could.

'Do you think we should have invited your mother and your grandmother here, with us?'

'No, that's all right, Mr Alfred, I will go home with them now. We will do it in our own way. They've got to get used to me again, now.'

Jim went in search of his family.

The Richards family had experienced the most remarkable, wonderful, miraculous day.

'I feel that he has come home to us,' said Frances.